CW00865730

Thalia - The New Generation

Thalia - The New Generation

Chronicles of the Maca VII

Mari Collier

Published 2020 by Beyond Time – A Next Chapter Imprint
Edited by Elizabeth N. Love
Cover art by Cover Mint

http://www.maricollier.com/

Contents

Prologue viii

1 The New Maca of Ishner 1

2 The Maca's Home 7

3 The Warehouse At Port Issac 15

4 Another Meeting 20

5 Manufacturers and Schools 26

6 Casters and Accounts 33

7 Surprises 39

8 Thalian Accounts 48

9 Crystals For Ayran 56

10 Conference At Ayran 63

11 The Maca of Medicine 69

12 Logan, Lad of Don 76

13	Radan, Maca of Rurhran	80
14	A Quick Conference	86
15	Romance On Thalia	89
16	Time To Walk The Circle	96
17	Dissention	103
18	The Crystals	110
19	The Council of the Realm Meeting	117
20	The Courtship Continues	121
21	Wrongs Revealed	130
22	Wrongs Righted	134
23	Ma	137
24	Discovery	144
25	Changes	150
26	Tour of Medicine	156
27	Another Challenge	163
28	The Council Inspects	171
29	A Secret Revealed	181
30	Marita Considers	186
31	Marta Before The Council	193

32	Marianne's Revenge	198
33	Aftermath	203
34	The Lab	211
35	Marta, The Lady of Medicine	216
36	Refuge For A Murderer	221
37	Timor's Burial And The Search	228
38	Beltayne	232
39	Marta, Lady of Medicine	240
40	Camp of the Abs	245
41	Council Of The Realm	250
42	Resolutions	259
43	Purifying Medicine	266
44	A Legacy	270
Epilogue		275
About the Author		279
Other Works		280

Prologue

Ishmael, Lad of Ishner, left the Laird of Don dissatisfied with his answer. Daniel, the Laird's laddie, had killed a wild elbenor with his knife two days ago. All Thalia kenned it was the time-honored way of proclaiming to Thalia that the slayer was a true Maca. The Maca of Don, Daniel's elder fither, had hung the elbenor's skin in his Maca's Tower office. It was obvious he was nay worried about a Challenge to the Death from his younger.

Ishmael's dark eyes were puzzled as he entered his fliv and went towards the home of his friend, Lorenz, Laird of Don. The visit was nay productive. Lorenz didn't think Daniel would challenge anyone, but the Laird was Earth/Justine by birth and Thalian by Claiming. He often ignored Thalian ways. Ishmael had kenned Daniel was the Maca of Ishner since Daniel was a laddie. He knew which Maca Daniel should challenge. He just did nay ken when.

It was nearing the hour for sustenance when Ismael touched the buzzer at Daniel's home. He prayed Daniel would be alone. The rumors were Daniel was leaving with a crew from the House of Flight for the stars, and other rumors claimed Daniel would Challenge to the Death one of the Macas. Which one was true?

Daniel opened the door and pulled Ishmael inside. Daniel was six-foot-ten and almost a foot taller. "Why are ye here?" kis voice rumbled out.

"Ishner needs ye, my Maca."

"I am too young and nay ready. The Stars are my calling." The man's lips were in a straight line and the light brown eyes hard. "Ye are to tell nay!"

Despair over the Maca's decision filled Ishmael with dread for his beloved continent of Ishner for many years. That lasted until the night Daniel stopped a rioting mob in Port Issac while roaring out his Maca Challenge to the Death. Nay had dared to oppose him.

Chapter 1

The New Maca of Ishner

"Have ye called in the ones who do the maintenance here?" Daniel asked Ishmael, his newly appointed Counselor of Ishner.

"Aye, Maca, but they refused," replied Ishmael.

Daniel seemed to expand beyond his nearly seven-foot height. "Did they refuse because I am male?"

Ishmael flinched. "Aye, all those appointed by the Sisterhood are still in place."

It was the morning after the Council of the Realm had sentenced the false Maca of Ishner, Ilyan, to a life of being an Ab. The Council then had her parents stripped of power in Ishner. Daniel had challenged all to deny him the title of Maca at the riots in Port Issac of Ishner. None had dared to take up the Challenge or deny that he was the Maca of Ishner. None of the Council of the Realm had challenged him either. Daniel wondered if those members of the Ishner Sisterhood left free after the riots had regained their courage.

"Tis there nay else to call to do the painting here and at the Maca's home?"

"The Director of the City of Iconda tis Ilvina. She may ken who to call." Ishmael's voice sounded doubtful.

"Tis there nay a crew to maintain the city's buildings?" Daniel hadn't had time to check Ishner's finances, but had a hunch they were in disarray. He was dressed in his Warrior's suit of black as there were no teal clothing for someone his size on Ishner. Ishnerites tended to be slighter and shorter than the rest of the Thalians. They were normally around six-foot or an inch or two taller or less.

"Tis she also part of the Sisterhood?" Daniel asked.

"Well, aye, like all others in power, she tis female and probably one of those that agrees with the Sisterhood, to have been appointed to such a position."

"If all in power are the Sisterhood, why did the Troopers leave them when they did their sweep of Ishner?"

Ishmael shrugged. "Maca, Ishner tis like Medicine. The Justine War left the Sisterhood entrenched in both Houses. Some say Rurhran tis just as bad."

Daniel's face became grim. "Very well, rescind the right of the entire Maintenance crew to the homes where they live and the rights to their flivs. Then make up a list of those that might be willing and competent to accept the employment. I shall contact Ilvina. If she tis the same way, have a list ready for those that would serve as Director of Iconda and the other two cities."

He touched the screen and brought up the listing for city directors. "Either way, there will be a meeting this afternoon with all the city directors, whoever they might be." He touched the face of the one called Ilvina.

The screen showed the broad face of a female Thalian that looked to be nearing three hundred years as there were slight wrinkles around the mouth and dark eyes. She appeared puzzled as she recognized Daniel.

Daniel's voice rumbled out as though he were addressing his space crew. "I have just fired the maintenance crew for the Maca's Tower and stripped them of their homes and flivs. I still need painters here and at the Maca's home. My counselor to be, JoAnne, Lass of Ayran, will attend them at the Maca's home and instruct them as to what we will expect. If they refuse, ye are to strip them of their right to the homes they have for dwelling and the right to drive the flivs they have been issued. Ye would then select someone else to take their place. Now hold for a moment while I contact the other city directors. Stay on yere com when I finish with my message to all."

Daniel's finger touched two circles, and two more female faces appeared. As soon as they had, Daniel continued. "There tis a meeting of all of Ishner's city directors, their keepers. Also, the directors and keepers of all the cities's centers are to be here. The meeting tis this afternoon at two o'clock. All of ye, plus yere keepers need to be here. Ye are to have a list of what needs to be done in yere city and how to create a decent place for all Ishnerites to dwell. If there tis a problem anywhere, it should be noted and what resources are needed to address the problem. Since I have nay idea of Ishner's finances, I am assuming it will take time to accomplish all that tis necessary. Also, if any refuse, I will have someone ready to step in as the new Director of any city or any city center. I shall see ye all there." He disconnected all but Ilvina, and he addressed his question to her.

"Now, what about the painters?"

Ilvina's face had gone from angry, to stunned, and to bland while Daniel had spoken to all. "Of course, I'll see what I can do about the painting. I do suggest the meeting of city directors should be tomorrow morning, though, so that all will be ready to respond."

"Ye dinna ken what tis wrong with Iconda?"

"Tis nay that. It might take some time to arrange for painters. I shall need to go to the Maintenance Hall."

"Hall? All are at the Hall? Are nay of them working? Why would ye need to go there? That tis what coms are for: to contact others."

Ilvina wanted to shout at him, but realized it would be a good way to be kicked out of her home and lose her fliv. As long as Ishmael, Lad of Ishner, was supporting this creature from Don, she kenned anything at Ops could be changed. She did nay trust Issing, Lass of Ishner, either. Issing was Ishmael's sib and would be in the Ops Room.

"I believe that tis where I will find their director. She has her office there. She would be able to direct the actual painters to the Maca's home."

"Make certain ye stress they are to be there at eleven o'clock when my counselor-to-be tis there. If any refuse, strip them of their rights to homes and flivs."

"I dinna believe I have such rights." Ilvina was wondering how long she could avoid calling this interloper Maca.

"Then ye are to notify Ishmael, my Counselor of Ishner, immediately." He smiled, but his eyes were hard. "I have also kenned that ye have refused to call me Maca. Dinna make that error this afternoon." He cut off the communication, took a deep breath and exhaled before turning to Ishmael.

"Will ye have a list of names for me by this afternoon? I will need names for replacing any or all of the directors and keepers of any city and any city center. Make sure there are males on that list. I also want them here and available this afternoon."

"In the same room?" Ishmael was grinning. He had avoided participating in the politics of Ishner under Iylan by remaining Captain of a fishing troller and living with his counselor and family in Medicine when necessary while his troller was in port for maintenance. The House of Medicine also harbored the Sisterhood, but they did nay rule there. The new Maca of Medicine, Marita, wore the purple of Medicine, nay the dull black of the Sisterhood.

Daniel considered, and innocence filled his eyes. "Tis there nay a conference room here that large?"

Ishmael was puzzled by the question. All the Maca Towers were alike. "Of course, there tis on the second floor just like at the Tower of Don. Ye really need to tour the rooms here."

"I shall inspect them later, but, aye, they will all be in the same room then." He smiled and continued.

"Since the Director and Keeper of Port Issac were arrested by Thalian Troopers during the riots, those positions need to be filled."

He turned back to the screen and pushed the button for Itillie, the Director of the city of Isling. Itawnia, her lassie and Keeper of Isling, answered. She was young, nay more than thirty or so, and her brown eyes were worried. It looked like she was forcing a smile.

"Aye, may I assist ye?"

Daniel stared at her. "Where tis Itillie?"

Itawnia took in a deep breath. "There was a bit of trouble on the waterfront, and she went with our Enforcer to make sure all was well. They have things under control."

"If it was a riot, why was I nay contacted?"

"It was but a fight among some early morning drunkards. There tis nay else for them to do here."

Daniel regarded her for a moment. "I did nay see Itillie when I called earlier and left a message. If ye listened to it, ye heard that I am having a meeting of all the city directors, their keepers, and the director and keepers of all the centers here this afternoon at two o'clock. I want a list of what needs to be repaired and how things can be improved." He held up his hand as he saw Itawnia's mouth drop and then start to protest.

"I ken there tis nay funds now, but list all things. We will find ways to start repairing Ishner." He smiled at her. "And if ye both are nay here, there will be a new Director and Keeper of Isling." He ended the call, sat back, and looked at Ishmael.

"According to the screen, tis only the Directors of two Centers in Port Issac that were arrested during the riot. That means I need new Directors and Keepers there. Have the list for me by noon. Now I'm going to call all the Center Directors, and those calls will nay be different than the last calls." He swung around and glared at the screen. Finding StarPaths while in space was far easier than dealing with Thalians.

Chapter 2

The Maca's Home

Daniel saw his counselor to be, JoAnne, Lass of Ayran, waving at him as he landed his fliv on the padport. Her red cape swirled around her. The ceremony uniting them was next week and she still wore the red of Ayran. He could see that Iolan, the Director of Construction, was walking toward her, the woman dressed in the dull black of the Sisterhood.

He hurried over to where they stood. He had noticed Iolan had sense enough to bow to the Lass of Ayran. Iolan turned to him, and her lips were stretched as though trying to smile.

"I am Maca!" Daniel roared. His chest and body seemed to expand.

Iolan's mouth dropped, and she tried looking right then left. There was nay escape or she would lose home and fliv, according to the Director of Iconda. She stepped forward to lay her head on his shoulder and realized she was almost a foot too short. To her horror, she felt his hands on her rib cage, and she was swung upward. The heat in his hands caused a sharp intake of breath as she performed the ancient ritual of first her head on one shoulder, then the next. She realized that she was trembling. She had just met a powerful Maca, her Maca. How could this be? Was the teaching of the Sisterhood all lies? Had she wasted her life and deeply hurt her own parents? She continued to shake as

Daniel set her down. Dear Gar, if his beloved were not here, she would tear off her clothes if he demanded it or even hinted at it.

"My Maca," she murmured and bowed. She looked up into the set face and hard, light-brown eyes that seemed to soften at her discomfort. Iolan was not fooled. This was Daniel, the StarPath finder and Warrior. She kenned she was about to agree to every demand he or JoAnne would make.

Daniel looked at JoAnne and smiled. They stepped together and hugged. "Have ye seen the inside?" he asked.

"Aye, and ye are correct. The bedrooms are hideous." She turned to Iolan. "The main bedrooms are to be repainted in the medium teal as I wish to hang deep teal curtains as befits the Maca of Ishner. One bedroom will be red with royal blue drapery for any visitor from the House of Ayran or the House of Don."

She did nay wait for an answer, but turned back to Daniel. "Who do I consult for the drapery?" A blank look came over Daniel's face. The Director of his Lad of Don home took care of such matters, and his face cleared.

"I will need to check and see who the Director of the Maca's Home tis. Was there nay to greet ye?"

"If there tis anyone in there, they are well hidden." Her voice was sharp. "Tis totally strange. I need a list of other qualified Directors, or I shall bring my own." Joanne was used to running Ayran since her mither was Guardian of the Realm and her brither, Jarvis, Maca of Ayran, was often away at the Warriors Academy or flying into space. Her elder, JayEll, Lad of Ayran, was too busy being the Counselor of the Realm or a Martin for any real assistance.

Iolan cleared her throat. "I believe the Director was detained by the Troopers. She was in Issac during the riots and joined a last-ditch stand at the waterfront."

They were both looking at her. "I thought the rioters were all from Port Issac." Daniel's statement was part question. "If nay, why was there nay more elites from the other cities?"

Iolan swallowed and licked at her lips. "Beauty was becoming too much of a liability. Ye canna run around murdering Thalians for nay reason. In truth, Maca, many of us kenned that Ilyan was nay a true Maca." She shrugged her shoulders. "Many felt it was nay worth risking our lives for her or her position. Ishmalisa had changed too. All she cared about was Ilyan. It was a fool's errand for the Troopers of the Sisterhood to capture Ishmalisa and her counselor." The last burst out, and Iolan realized she had resented the way the Sisterhood had progressed over the last fifty years.

Daniel had a tight smile on his lips, nodded, and turned to JoAnne. "Did ye wish to select the Director and Keeper, or do ye wish me to arrange for them?"

JoAnne shrugged. She was irritated at the absent help. "Mayhap ye best do so. If ye do nay have them within three days, I'll bring in someone from Ayran."

Iolan winced. That meant if she did nay have this place and the Tower under her supervision, they would be bringing in workers from Ayran and Don. "If I could view what needs to be done, I can then bring in a crew. Will the credits be available?"

Daniel led the way inside. "I will pay for the work we require here from my Don credits, but the credits for the Tower will come from Ishner."

* * *

Daniel looked at the assembled group. The meeting with Iolan had concluded in time for him and JoAnne to have caterers bring a lunch to the Maca's home ere she returned to Ayran. He had put off meeting with Issing, Lass of Ishner, till she finished going over the accounts. He assumed her report would be bad. He and Ishmael had met in the foyer of the Tower and rode the lift to the second floor where the meeting rooms were located.

Ilvina, Director of Iconda, stood as he entered, and she bowed. "Welcome, Maca." She kenned the power he had and was nay about to dispute or deny him. Let the others be fools. She heard a couple of gasps from the seated Directors and Keepers.

"Thank ye, Ilvina," Daniel replied. "Ye all ken why this meeting was called. As ye probably ken, the Director of Port Issac and the Keeper were arrested by Thalian Troopers during the riots. They have been sentenced to the asteroid mines. This tis Ivan, the new Director of Port Issac."

He pointed to the man standing by the window. The man bowed and walked to the chair next to Ilvina's Keeper.

"Some of ye may remember him as he was Director ere the Sisterhood replaced him. Like ye, he has come prepared to list what needs to be done. He will select his Keeper."

Daniel noted that the faces of some of the women became flushed while others looked puzzled. How had someone from Don found anyone connected to the House of Ishner and its former Directors?

"All of ye must ken Itillie, Director of Isling and her Keeper, Iltawnia." He didn't bother mentioning that Iltwania was also her lassie. He nodded at the two at the end of the table and proceeded. "If ye dinna ken the names of the Directors and Keepers of the Centers, that tis fine. We need to proceed or we shall nay finish."

"Do ye, Itillie, have anything to add to the list that Ilvina has given to all?"

Itillie stood. "We need that prohibition order rescinded," she stated.

Daniel looked blank. "Uh, what prohibition order?"

"The one imposed on us when Beauty and Belinda were hiding in the Isomatic Mountains. That means nay come for the hiking and picnicking now that spring tis almost here, and will nay be able to come for the skiing when there tis snow. Even the personnel for the camps are forbidden. We need the people that can afford to visit us."

Daniel looked at Ishmael. "Place that on the menu for tonight's cast." He looked at Itillie, and his fingers moved over the circles on the desk in front of him. "The ban tis removed. Anything else?"

Itillie took a deep breath. "Thank ye, Maca, and, aye, I wish to bring my counselor back as the Keeper of Isling. He kens certain areas far better than I. If he tis there, our lassie can finish her education."

Daniel frowned. "I thought it was already clear that ye had the right to replace the people at working with ye. Ye can also make recommendations for those at the Centers."

"How were we to believe ye when we dinna even ken ye? We have heard so many rumors. Before, rules are made and then changed the next day. If what ye say tis true, ye must ken that the food delivered to our Center tis nay adequate!" Itillie voice kept getting louder. "They seemed to think because we did nay have people enjoying the mountains, we should eat less."

Daniel looked at Ishmael. "How or where do I check the food poundage per population?"

Ishmael was blinking, and then his face cleared. "Issing, I shall ask her." He pushed the com circle in front of him.

Issing's dark hair and eyes appeared on his screen and the far screen. He relayed the Maca's message. "Aye, a moment please." Within seconds, she was back, and her contralto voice filled the room. "The people in Isling are receiving five pounds of supplies less per week than those in the other two cities. Should I increase it?"

"Aye," Daniel snapped and them sat back. "Tis that sufficient for now?"

Itillie nodded. "Thank ye, Maca." Her voice was almost a whisper.

Daniel took a deep breath. "Now, those of ye in the Centers, do ye have yere lists ready, and if so, why have ye nay submitted them to my office?"

All of the fifteen people shifted in their seats. Ileana, Director of Iconda's First Center, spoke. "My Maca, we need Tri clothes in the color of Ishner. Nay of our customers like the dull black of the Sisterhood, which tis all that was issued to us. We also need toys for the wee ones, and being allowed to have bakery items again would be a dream come true."

Her counselor and Keeper of the First Center was on her feet screaming over her words. "How dare ye! What we have tis what tis necessary. Why have ye called that buffoon Maca?"

Daniel's blunt index finger went out, and he pushed a circle. "Issing, cancel Ilflora's right to a lift or a fliv, and the right to unlock or lock the First Center of Iconda." He heard Ilflora's rage-filled words.

"Ye canna do that."

"I just did. Ye are to leave now. If ye dinna leave, ye will be tossed out."

"No!" She started towards him with her fists curled and then realized that Daniel towered over her as he stood.

"I am also rescinding yere right to the locks of the home where ye live. Yere counselor will have to tend to permitting ye in or out."

Ilflora looked at him in disbelief and whirled to Ileana, her counselor. "Why are ye still sitting there? Are ye nay coming with me?"

Ileana swallowed. "I intend to run the First Center as it should be run." She looked at Daniel. "My parents were Director and Keeper there till the Sisterhood evicted them. Now they are too old, but my sister should be my Keeper. She too worked there till the Sisterhood insisted I hire my counselor."

Ilflora gasped.

A tight smile crossed Daniel's face as he asked, "And are yere parents still available to advise others?"

"Aye, Maca, as I intend to ask both how things could be better arranged."

Daniel looked at Ilflora. "Do I call the Enforcers or throw ye out myself?"

Ilflora drew in her breath and stalked out. She was shaking with anger. She would need to use their boat to see Ilarmina, Director of Fisheries, but the boat was in Port Issac. She would need to wait for Ileana.

Those in the room had watched Ilflora leave and turned their attention back to the Maca as he took his seat. "Since I am nay hearing anything from ye, I will appoint Iandy as Director of Port Issac's First Center, and his counselor Ilmyra as the Keeper there." He turned to Ivan. "Do ye have any suggestions for the Third Center that was closed?"

"I will, Maca, but first I must see who tis still alive or in Port Issac." He cleared his throat before speaking again. "If ye will pardon me for asking, has Captain Ishmael told ye about the plating for repairs?"

Daniel eyed the man. "Ye dinna have to ask for pardon when asking a question and what plating? Ishmael, did ye nay say there was nay enough to repair your troller?"

"So I was told, Daniel, er, Maca." Both Daniel and Ishmael were staring at Ivan.

"Where tis the plating located and who else kens where it tis?" Daniel asked.

"Any that listen to street rumors in Port Issac ken where the plating tis. It tis in the warehouse the Sisters were trying to empty and transfer everything from there to Captain Issaric's troller the night of the riots. I believe ye have reclaimed that plating from the troller."

"Aye," Ishmael responded. "Ikea reported that we were short but two sheets for a complete repair. I instructed him to find the welders and fitters and begin the process." Inside, Ivan winced. Mayhap he should have waited for the Maca's approval.

"Why nay from the warehouse?" Daniel's voice was mild.

"We were nay sure the Sisters guarding it would let us remove any," Ivan answered.

Daniel stood. "How many guard it?"

"Three or four, Maca. The other person tis just the attendant who accepts or signs for release. She tis younger and I dinna believe armed." Ivan took great pleasure in reporting the Sisterhood's behavior. He wanted them gone.

"I take it the others are armed, tis that correct?"

"I would be surprised if they were nay armed," Ishmael answered. "It tis why I spent most of my nights on my troller or in Medicine with Melanie and our wee ones."

Daniel reached down and touched a circle. "Issing, dinna let any com calls go out of here." He turned to the group staring at him.

He stood as this situation required a Warrior. He snapped out his orders. "Ye are to remain here till I give the clear signal. Ye may use the gym if ye wish. Ishmael, come with me." He turned, and his wide body went swaying out of the room with Ishmael following.

Chapter 3

The Warehouse At Port Issac

Ishmael followed Daniel outside and into his fliv. Once they were inside, Daniel hit the com button on the dash. It was a private com circle to the Guardian of Flight. In theory, it was one of the comlines that the other Houses could nay access.

Ribdan, Lad of Rurhran and Director of Flight, answered, "Aye."

"Ribdan, I need a full max blazer and stunner, plus my warrior suit with the globe. Have at least four Troopers fly it to me. They should be suited up. I will be at the warehouse near the waterfront and fishing trollers in Port Issac. Have them scan the building as I need to ken how many are inside." He showed an image of the area and the coordinates. "Have them land there with my equipment. Do it now." He signed off and went up into the air.

He flew over the warehouse and landed on a padport in the back. The loading doors of the building were massive, down, and locked.

The air carrier with the Troopers and equipment followed within minutes. The first one out was Pillar, Guardian of Army. He and Daniel had practiced being Warriors at the Warrior

Academy from the time they were laddies. He was dressed in the Warrior armored suit and wearing a globe. He ran over to Daniel and Ishmael and handed Daniel his armored suit. Daniel slipped the black warrior's defense suit over his body-tight clothing. Another Trooper arrived and handed him the globe, the stunner, and then the long blazer.

"Thank ye. How many are inside?"

Pillar answered, "I counted five inside. Four are armed and waiting for us." Then he asked, "Are ye ready?"

"Aye, Captain," the Troopers answered.

Daniel did have one request. "Pillar, would ye station one of yere men back here in case they try to run out the back?"

The Warrior called Pillar grinned and nodded at the others. "Stay close to the fliv just in case." He then followed Daniel to the front while securing his globe. The windows were high and nay open.

"The receptionist may be armed, Maca," Ishmael said. "Ivan could be wrong."

"Aye," Daniel replied. He took out his com and turned the speaker to high. "All are to come out now without the weapons and yere hands raised." There was no answer.

Daniel could have disabled the lock from his Maca's office, but he lifted the blazer and burned around the door again and again. By the fifth time, there was no door. Just the entry into the processing room and teal flames poured out. Daniel and Pillar advanced with red flames spewing from their blazers. The two looked at each other, and both moved to the side and went running towards the wall. Daniel beat Pillar by two steps and jumped high in the air and twisted through the door with his blazer blasting.

Pillar was right behind him, except he had dropped down and rolled through the door while firing his blazer. The desk in the front was smoldering, and two burnt bodies were crumpled in the doorway leading to the back. Two did not account for the four blazers they had heard.

Daniel was up and walked around the desk. A young female was huddled behind it. She looked up at him, terrified, and quickly shifted her eyes toward the door into the back. They heard the doors in back sliding upward, and a scream came from the back. Daniel grabbed the woman's dropped stunner. "Guard her," he yelled and ran towards the back, leaping over the two forms in the doorway.

Inside were stacks and stacks of the precious metal for ships and fliv building. The only being standing on the loading dock was the other Trooper holding a com. One Sister knelt on the floor beside a bleeding companion. The Trooper looked up at Daniel.

"Her legs are almost gone. I have called Medicine."

"Aye. Stay there with them till Medicine arrives." He hurried back towards the front. At the doorway, he debated moving the two, but decided he should leave them for Medicine and the transport to the appropriate House Byre Berm. He stepped over them.

"Yere Trooper has taken two prisoners. One tis down and he called Medicine."

Pillar nodded. They both turned their blazers toward the door as another female form appeared.

"What have ye done?" Ilarmina voice cried out. "Why didn't ye contact me? I could have stopped this." Her physical appearance said she was close to three hundred as grey hair wisped at the sides, and her muscles did nay look whip hard. Then she saw the two burnt bodies, covered her mouth, turned, and voided the contents of her stomach. This was not what she had expected or wanted when she had set up the guards.

Daniel and Pillar removed their globes. "And who are ye?" Daniel asked.

The woman turned back, anger blazing in her eyes, and then, she shook, closed her eyes, and swallowed. She then looked up at Daniel. "I am Ilarmina, the Director of Fisheries."

"Then ye kenned the Sister were hiding and storing the metal here instead of using it for repairs as they were to do." Daniel's voice was harsh.

"Aye, Maca. I was ordered to set this up by the Sisterhood." Her eyes were hard and her voice brittle. "I ken ye are going to take away all that I have, but dinna blame Ivy for the actions of the others." She pointed to the forlorn young woman in dull black standing beside the Trooper. "She tis but thirty-five and has just had the Adult Confirmation rite."

"She tis House?" Surprise was in Daniel's voice.

"Of course not," Ilarmina snapped. "A Captain of the Sisterhood performed the ceremony."

Daniel blinked his eyes at that statement when suddenly he understood. "The Sisterhood considers itself a House, aye? How many of Ishner have that belief?"

"I canna answer that question, Maca, for I dinna ken. I do ken she would have left that warehouse had I told her to do so."

"Would the other four have permitted that?" Daniel's voice was mild.

Ilramina looked at him. "They should have," and realized that she had implied they would have obeyed her.

"Who told ye I was here with Troopers?" Daniel's voice was as demanding as his question.

Inside she cringed. This man was clever and nay easy to confuse. "I assumed ye would wish to inspect it." She left out that she hadn't anticipated the extra Troopers. "I just did nay think ye would be here till after we met this afternoon and ye had appointed someone else."

There was an almost smile on Daniel's face. "And how many Sisters would have greeted me?"

She took a step backward. "I had nay power to call in others to guard the warehouse. I direct the ships, the processing, the plants, and any construction on or off the ships. I dinna command Troopers or Enforcers." Half of that statement was true. She did nay have any Troopers under her direct command anymore. They had been arrested after the riots.

"According to the records, ye were the Director of Fisheries before the Sisterhood became so prominent."

"Aye, Ishmalisa appointed me while she was still Guardian of Ishner and Ilyan but a wee one."

"Then we do need to meet this afternoon at my Tower office. I will expect ye at four." Daniel turned and pressed his com button for the Maca's Meeting Room in his Tower.

"All are free to leave now. Report any problems to me. I shall be in touch regularly."

He then turned to Ishmael. "Ishmael, I need to meet with my counselor-to-be. She expects me back at the Maca's home. Will ye tend to things here while I am gone?"

"Aye."

"Pillar, I thank ye for yere assistance. I will keep the blazer and armor for now."

Medicine had arrived, and one Medical in purple approached him. "Ye have murdered two Sisters."

Daniel, Ishmael, and Pillar all stared at her, but Daniel answered. "Ye are mistaken. I gave an order that they disobeyed and fired at me. I answered their fire."

She stared at him for a moment. "I shall report this to my Maca." She whirled and returned to the Tris loading the three dead women and one wounded one into the Med Carrier.

Chapter 4

Another Meeting

It was a hurried meeting with the construction/painters that Ilvina had sent over. The women assured JoAnne, Lass of Ayran, that they could procure the needed teal blue and aqua paints to change that dark walls and obliterate the sex graphics that Ilyan had someone portray on the bedroom walls. It should be finished by nightfall tomorrow.

JoAnne frowned at them. "Why so long? There are but three rooms."

The two looked at each other. They had heard how the new Maca locked people out of their homes and flivs. Idante bowed. "It will be finished by noon tomorrow. Tis that acceptable?"

JoAnne nodded. "Aye." She turned to Daniel. "There tis nay proper sheet material for beds in Ishner. I shall bring the red bedding of Ayran if there tis nay in the storerooms here. I have the new Director and Keeper of this home searching."

Daniel smiled at the woman he had loved since their first bedding eighty-some years ago. "Efficient as always, my love. Where do ye wish to grab a brew? I have two more meetings this afternoon. Then I have to visit the manufacturers, if there are any left here, that tis. That information does seem to be a bit hazy. If nay, Rurhran may have the material Ishner needs to replenish the colors of Ishner."

"Do ye ken of any decent brew hall here?" JoAnne suspected there was none for Ishner had become isolated over the years. Nay of the Houses had wished to visit or shop here.

"Nay, but some of the smells from the quays and blocks lining the ocean at Port Issac were quite tempting."

"We should visit the waterfront here. This tis where our home tis. There must be someplace that tis nay dreary around here." As she spoke, the overhead cloud shifted and a shaft of sunlight moved over the landscape, making the teal Maca's Home sparkle.

JoAnne laughed. "I do believe I have my answer. There tis a pleasant spot out back by the pool. I have brews in the cooler."

* * *

Daniel sank back in his Maca's chair. The time spent with JoAnne had restored his good humor. He was certain it would nay last until the evening meal.

"It tis Ilarmina, Director of Fisheries, to see ye, Maca," came over the com.

"Aye, send her in." He swiveled the chair to face the door. He still wasn't certain whether he would retain her or not, although he had to admit the list she had sent over was complete, or at least it looked complete to a Warrior accustomed to space and fighting rather than running the fishing port and operations of the major economic area. He would have to check with Ishmael.

Ilramina stepped through the doorway. She had found a teal cummerbund somewhere, and it rested on her hips. Daniel realized the woman looked as old as the personnel records reported. She was nearing three hundred, close to the age of decline. She bowed and took the seat across from him and waited.

Daniel nodded and brought up the list she had sent. "Since we have secured the metal, why tis it still there on the list? I thought ye kenned that was stocked in that warehouse was to be used."

"I was nay certain ye would release it."

"Ahh, do ye ken that I have ordered Captain Issaric's ship to be cleaned and sent out. It will be captained by Ikea per the suggestion of my Counselor of Ishner, Ishmael."

"Good, we need the fish and the protein it provides, although I do need the information for my records." She hesitated a moment. "I dinna what the directors of the different cities told ye, but the previous Maca was nay interested in fish or trade. There tis a shortage of food in certain areas. Particularly in Isling. Fish are nay the protein problem as most are able to fish in their localities. It tis the grain and vegetables that dinna grow in our harsh climate, and the pina pods for tea. I suggest ye set up a trade with Rurhran and mayhap with Troy. That tis nay on the list, but I realized I should have included it."

Daniel blinked. The woman had rattled on, and how did she ken about the food shortage and how could there be a shortage of tea? It was a wonder the people of Ishner had nay rioted sooner.

"How could there be a shortage of pina tea? There was a bumper crop last year."

"First, ye must have the funds to pay for it." Her voice seemed to come through clenched teeth.

"Why tis Ishner so broke when all the other Houses are doing so well?"

Her laugh was harsh. "As I said, the previous Maca did nay care for trade or for production. As she seemed to draw farther away, Ishmalisa and Ilnor grew more and more concerned about their lassie, and they neglected what they once did for the trading and the accounting." She hesitated a moment, and suddenly, anger seemed to convulse her face.

"Everything they were doing meant their ideas and procedures would fail and Ishner be ruined." She leaned forward. "For years, I have suffered a loss whenever funds were available. I knew they were taking it, but I dinna ken how they used it. Now people in Ishner hunger because of their neglect and thieving ways."

"Missing funds?"

"Aye, Maca. The Directors of the Center had the same problem, but Ishmalisa ignored us."

Daniel swallowed. What had he gotten into? He had directed Issing, Lass of Ishner, to go over the accounts and give him a report. Now it looked like he and/or Ishmael would be going on a trading mission on top of meeting with the school officials and the remnants of any manufacturing in Ishner.

Ilramina continued. "I have traded with Rocella, Lass of Rurhran, for cereals, dried fruit, and/or vegtables before. We have kenned each other since childhood. I am willing to meet with her after we are through. Rurhrans are fond of our smoked fish."

A smile tugged at the corners of Daniel's mouth. "This tis why ye have been Director of Fisheries so long, aye? Ye became valuable to the Maca who did nay have time."

Ilramina sat straighter. "Nay inhabitant of Ishner should hunger when we have so much."

Daniel's huge body seemed to relax. "Tell me, were there nay others to do the trading or buying?"

"Ishmalisa once took care of it all. Then she became so wrapped up in her grown lassie that she neglected everything else, and the Sisters took over. They cared more for their Warrior training than for the people of Ishner. That was a huge mistake," she hesitated before adding, "on their part."

Daniel's smile was still there, but the eyes were hard. "In other words, if the Sisters had run Ishner as it should have been run, ye would nay have objected."

Ilramina felt her stomach clutch. The man was more than a Warrior. She should have kenned. "Maca, anyone that would have managed Ishner as it should be managed would have been acceptable after years of debacle." She rose.

"If there tis nay else, I will return to my office and wait for yere orders to vacate."

"And why would I give such orders?"

She gritted her teeth, but tried one more time. "I thought ye had rejected my offer to negotiate with Rocella and had someone else picked for Director of Fisheries."

"I have nay rejected yere offer. I would need to approve such a trade before it tis valid. As for Director of Fisheries, there tis but one candidate. At the present, he tis my Counselor of Ishner and has nay desire to sit in an office on land. He wishes to return to the seas with his troller and crew."

Ilramina drew in her breath. Of course, Ishmael was the only true candidate, and as this man just said, Ishmael nay cared to be landside. She bowed. "Then I shall contact Rocella. If she agrees, I will be there within the hour. How much sustenance tis needed?"

"According to the Director of Isling, they lack at least five pounds per person a week. There are twenty thousand within the city and another five thousand around or close by. Have ye discerned any shortages here or at Port Issac? Nay mentioned any."

"It tis nay always the best or what one desires, but I ken of nay going hungry. If the directors of the other cities did nay mention it, I doubt if it tis a problem."

Daniel nodded. "So how do ye convince Rocella that ye are a valid negotiator if I dinna arrange it?"

Ilramina stood. "It would nay be the first time, Maca. Ilyan was remiss about such things." She bowed and started to leave when she saw the Rurhran Export/Import logo and then Raffer, Director of Rurhran's Export and Import, saying, "Aye."

"Good afternoon, Raffer. My Director of Fisheries, Ilramina, will be there to discuss trade matters with Rocella, Counselor of Rurhran. She has my permission for certain trade arrangements. She assures me that she will be welcomed."

“Of course, she will be welcomed, Maca of Ishner.” He grinned. “Will ye be at the Arena for more battles once ye and JoAnne Walk the Circle?”

Daniel returned his smile. “Oh, nay, JoAnne would have her revenge if I were to win and choose a different lassie.” He closed the circuit and looked at Ilramina.

“Give my greetings to the Counselor of Rurhran.”

“Thank ye, Maca.” Ilramina bowed and left. Inside she was seething. She had forgotten how close House members could be and how the Sisterhood had strangled that asset while here. It was difficult to decide who to damn most: All men, or the ones who had led the Sisterhood on Ishner.

Chapter 5

Manufacturers and Schools

Daniel watched Ilramina leave and heaved himself out of the chair. It was time to visit the Manufacturer of Materials and then the heads of the schools at the Ishner Academy. He was nay looking forward to either. It was much easier to sail through the Stars and find the perfect route to their destination. It was the reason his elder Fither, the Guardian of Flight, Llewellyn, had dubbed him the StarPath Finder.

He nodded at Linda sitting at the welcome counter of Ishner. He had let her retain her position. Mainly because it was nice to hear a familiar Don name. All the names starting with I in Ishner were confusing him and he kenned a Maca should nay err.

"I should return to do my nightly cast from here. If I have nay returned by nightfall, ye may close the Tower. I will reclose after the casts."

"Aye, Maca. Should I tell anyone where ye are if they ask?"

"I dinna how long I shall be at each place. Just page my com if it tis important. If nay as important, make an appointment for tomorrow." He smiled and left through the side door where his fliv was parked on the padport. It took but seconds to hit the outskirts of Iconda and the sprawling buildings that theoretically manufactured the teal and aqua material for Ishner's House and

Tri populace. Clothing and furniture once were a booming business in these plants. Now the place looked deserted.

A nervous Tri in the dull, black uniform of a Sister stood at the door. For a minute, she looked like she wanted to challenge him and then changed her mind.

"The Director tis expecting ye." She stood aside.

Daniel nodded and walked inside. At least the place was lit, but there was no sound from all the machines, and nothing was moving, nor was there anyone manning the board above the cabinet where the crystals were embedded in their sockets to control the machinery below.

"Welcome, Maca. How can I help ye? I am Idonna, the Director of Manufacturing."

Daniel looked at her. She was tall for an Ishnerite, and her black hair was a short bob, combed straight back.

"Ye do nay seem overly busy." His voice rumbled out.

"Ye did order us to stop making the black Sister uniforms." She tried to keep any sound of criticism out of her voice. The news of those losing their homes and flivs had traveled swiftly.

"And where tis the teal and aqua material ye need to make the clothes, the bedding, and the furniture of Ishner?"

"We were nay allowed to order any. Now I have bales of the black material, but nay any other color. I suggest we continue with what we have as I have nay credits to buy other colors."

"Ye dinna make any fabrics from raw materials? It was my understanding that Rurhran sells both the plant and leather material. Don sells leather and some plant material to all who wish to purchase. Even Troy offers plant material for dying."

Irritation filled her voice. "There are nay credits. We have a warehouse filled with the black outfits and furniture."

"Have ye offered them to the Warrior's Academy for their students and dorms?"

For a few seconds, she stared at him with her mouth ajar. Then she almost whispered, "But most there are males."

Daniel frowned. "Are ye telling me there are nay but lassie's clothing? Were the men of Ishner to go naked?" It took all his control to keep his voice normal. "It should nay matter who sits or sleeps on the furniture and bedding." The last was roared out.

She bowed her head and looked up. "I was told what to do. They had nay kenning on how to run a manufacturing plant. Our employees, our friends, I had to let them go."

Daniel shook his head. "Dear Gar, did ye nay suggest the proper way?"

"Aye, Maca, but they threatened to replace me as they had my fither."

"So everything tis gone, including the credits. Tell me, tis yere fither still living?"

"Aye, Maca. Since I was named as Director, my parents could at least live in my home."

"How eld are yere parents? Does either ken anything about manufacturing?"

Hope surged in Idonna's dark eyes. "They are but two hundred and thirty-three years, and they ran both plants."

"Call them, and hand yere com to me."

Idonna did as bid and handed the com to Daniel.

"Ye are reinstated as Director and Keeper of this plant and the furniture plant. Sell the dark material and furniture for what ye can and," he hesitated a moment, and Innodad, the father, interrupted.

"I ken what to do, Maca, but I have nay the ability to open any of the doorways."

"Yere lassie does. Come by the Maca's Tower in the morn and all will be changed."

He handed the com back to Idonna while both could hear the man thanking Daniel. "I dinna care what position they give ye as long as these buildings start producing again." He smiled at her.

"I am due at the Director of Schools next. I dinna wish to disappoint them." His huge form strode out of the building. It seemed every encounter with anyone brought up some pointless injustice that the Sisterhood had inflicted on Ishner.

* * *

It took but five minutes to arrive at the Ishner Academy, where the early grades of schooling and then the training for sailing the seas, the fishing industry and related products were the main subjects. They would send qualified students to the Warriors Academy or any Academy of other pursuits if they were accepted by the different Houses. Ishner, however, had few that qualified as Warriors nay matter what the Sisters had claimed. The people of Ishner were smaller than most of the other Thalians, and few could afford the charges at the Warriors Academy if they did nay qualify, although a number of Sisters had paid the fees. Usually, they, like their counterparts from Medicine, would flunk out when they refused to interact with the males in training for the position of Warrior in Flight or in Army.

Daniel knew he was meeting the Director of Schools and the directors from ten other schools on Ishner. He presumed it would devolve into his removing them, as the director had insisted there was truly nay need for any such meeting.

He walked into a room with a huge, ancient round table of wood from the slopes of their Isomatic Mountains. It gleamed from years of oil and polish. The seated Directors looked at him with hostility in their eyes. One rose and walked toward him with arms open as if to place her head on his shoulders. She took a few steps before realizing that he would need to pick her up. Before she could change her mind, Daniel had lifted her high enough. He wondered if she had a hidden weapon when he felt her head on his right shoulder and her body quivering.

"My Maca," she murmured and placed her head on his left shoulder. "My Maca, forgive me. I doubted ye."

He could feel her body shuddering against his, ready to do his bidding, and he set her on the floor. She looked at him, closed her eyes, and bowed her head. Then she turned to the others. "We were wrong in our assumption. He tis Maca." Het head was lifted high, and she returned to her chair and the stunned faces of the other directors.

Daniel looked at the group, and his deep voice rumbled out. "I have had barely time enough to review the subjects taught, but why tis there two tiers of classes for the same subject?"

The directors looked at each other, and Ilindia, the Director of Schools, stood, trying to match his height and failing miserably. "Ye dinna expect us to teach lassies and laddies in the same room, do ye?"

"That tis exactly what I expect."

They gasped at his answer.

"It would be too difficult for the laddies," Ilindia spluttered.

"It would nay," Daniel roared.

"We would have to dismiss almost half of the instructors," she protested.

"Then do so. How many qualify as fulltime instructors anyway? How many have completed the courses at the Academy?"

"They all have." Ilindia was adamant.

"Then why were so many hired. We are wasting funds."

"They needed an income to participate in the Sisterhood..." her voice died out with realization this Maca would nay consider that a reason.

The one who had placed her head on his shoulder stood. "Maca, she had nay choice, just as we had nay choice at our schools. We were directed to do so."

"Who gave those directions?" Silence greeted his question.

"Well?" Daniel roared.

Ilindia took a step backward, swallowed, and looked up at him. "We were told it came from our leader Beauty."

Daniel frowned. “Do ye mean that this practice has been going on longer than she was free?”

“Maca,” said Idacy, the one who had acknowledged him, “she was giving orders long ere she fled her confinement. The assigned Enforcers from here and the other houses would bring us her orders.”

“She tis dead and so tis the Sisterhood,” Daniel almost snarled. “Ye will teach the same subject to all in the same room. The students will sit in alphabetic order. The laddies will have the same physical activities as the lassies. If any instructor objects, she tis fired, and ye are to let me ken. Any replacement must come from the best qualified, male or female.” He was issuing his commands as he would as a Fleet Commander.

“I canna accept that.” Idana, Director of Port Issac Schools, stood as she spoke.

“Ye are nay longer Director.” Daniel pulled out his com. “Ishmael, Idana tis nay longer Director at Port Issac Schools. She nay longer has access to her fliv or her home. Tell the Enforcers to assist her when she contacts them to clear out her possessions.”

“No, ye canna do that!” Idana screamed.

“I just did.” He looked at her. “Ye will have to be assigned quarters by the new Director of Port Issac. “When ye have a place to live, ye may contact the Enforcers to remove yere personal items from your current home that will fit in your new quarters. The Enforcers will remain with ye to ensure that nay else tis broken. Good day.”

He turned to the others. “Are there any other protests?” His voice was mild again.

Ilindia took a deep breath. “Maca, I am nay sure I will function well with a male as a director or instructor.”

“Ye must have worked with male colleagues before.”

“Aye, but I have grown set in my ways. I had planned to retire at the end of this educational year, but now, if ye fire me, my pension and my home will be gone.”

"Then why don't ye retire now?" Daniel asked. "Ye have served over two hundred and fifty years in this field. The Director's home would go to the new Director, whether I fired ye or ye retired."

Hope filled her eyes. "Then I shall retire."

"Would ye consider staying for six weeks and showing the new Director the functions of this office?"

"Aye, Maca. That I can do." A smile lit her face. "I shall find a home near the sea."

"Good as I have but one name of a man to replace ye. Does anyone here ken or recall Ian of Iconda?"

"He tis a Tri," Ilindia gasped.

Daniel frowned. "And I was born Ab. What difference does that make when a person possesses a talent? Ian's talent tis teaching and leadership." His voice was roaring. He took a deep breath. The frustrations of the day were beginning to rankle him.

Silence filled the room. "Good," Daniel continued. "I have sent all of ye the instructions for integrating all the classes and eliminating the nay needed classes. Remember, if any instructor refuses to operate as a Thalian professional, ye are to fire that person and to let me ken immediately. Are ye all clear on that?"

Silence filled the room. Three of the directors were nodding aye. The others appeared stunned into silence.

"I ken I have spoken as a Commander of a spaceship, but that tis who and what I am. We shall have to become accustomed to each other. If ye have nay questions, that tis all. My office tis always available, and I shall be around to check on the various schools."

He nodded at them and left. All he wanted was a brew and the comfort of JoAnne's arms. This was torture compared to commanding a ship. Instead, there were more chores before ending this day.

Chapter 6

Casters and Accounts

He nodded at Linda as he walked through the side hall entrance into the rotunda area of the Maca's Tower and headed to his office. He snapped on the screen to bring up the show of the evening casters.

On screen was the face of one the women from Medicine that had been summoned to the warehouse. She was pointing to the others from Medicine carrying off the dead Sisters from the inside of the storage warehouse. "Yere false Maca gave them nay warning but blazed them into oblivion."

He hit the control that shut off the equipment for the casters. The faces of the two appeared as he roared, "How dare ye show that without asking for permission to air the opinion of another House?"

"We like to publish what tis available," the older with gray hair spoke. "They are respected Sisters from Medicine."

"They still lie. Ye will investigate and then retract. In the meantime, I have announcements for all of Ishner."

"We take nay orders from ye!" The grey-haired one yelled and turned off the screen.

Daniel punched three different circles and the Casting room returned to the screen. The two casters looked at him wide-eyed. "Ye are officially fired. Yere homes and flivs are locked against ye, and when ye exit the Casting Office will be locked against ye both. I suggest ye head to the Director of Iconda ere she leaves for the evening and there secure different quarters and a ride to wherever that tis. When ye are ready to remove yere personal items from yere homes, Enforcers will accompany ye."

"Ye canna do this," said the grey-haired one. I am senior of all the casters."

"I am Maca," Daniel roared. "If ye are nay out of there in ten minutes, the Enforcers will be there to escort ye out. I dinna care if ye have a place or nay to rest this evening."

He spoke into the transmitter to the Ivonna, Director of Enforcement. "Ye are to go to the Casting Office now and escort the two casters out. They may take personal items, but nay else."

"Aye, Maca," came her voice. "My officers are on their way."

Daniel took a deep breath and then called both of the morning casters. "Ye are now co-directors of the Iconda Casting Office. I will be sending two new casters to ye tomorrow. Ye may decide who runs the morning and who runs the evening casts and the in-between casts. I care nay who does. I have just dismissed the other two. Ye, as the new Directors, will receive their homes and flivs. Next, I am taking over the evening casts from here and will be making the announcements to all of Ishner that they refused to do. Are there any questions?"

They stared at him for a moment, swallowed, and both made instant decisions. "Aye, Maca," both said in almost perfect unison.

"Good." He turned off the com and stood. What he wanted to do after today's frustrations of trying to tame Ishner was to hit the gym and throw weights the way his fither threw rocks when angered. Instead, he heard Linda's voice over the com.

"Maca, Issing and Ishmael are on their way to yere office with the financial reports."

Before he could say aye, the door opened and Ishmael and Issing walked in. Issing.was frowning, and frustration wrinkled her brow. Her dark hair was bobbed and parted in the middle. She at least had on the teal blue of Ishner. She walked over, and she and Daniel exchanged the Thalian greeting of hugging and touching the head to the shoulder.

"Ye will nay like this," she announced.

Daniel sighed. "What have ye discovered?"

"I have been over and over the accounts that the Sisters did after they kicked out Illnor and Ishmalisa. Ilyan nay cared who did them as long as she had her credits. Somehow, even before the Sisterhood took over, every eve there was a discrepancy of two and one-half credits missing. Those credits continue to disappear. That means for over one hundred years, they have been stealing ten thousand credits per year. Gar kens what they are getting from the Centers and mayhap even the directors of the cities' coffers. I canna find the command that robs us. Ye need an expert in here. Someone like Don or Ayran have to track their credits."

Daniel swallowed. "Where do the credits go?"

"That would make it too easy. I canna find that out either. I do know that Don and Betron have nay such discrepancies. I have heard rumors that Troy and Rurhran do, but I find the latter doubtful. Ye need someone like Levin to sort it out."

Daniel nodded, but doubted if the Director of Accounting for Don and auditor for the Guardian of Flight would be interested. "We shall see what she recommends."

"Ye canna say over the com why ye need her." Issing was adamant. "Ye can tell her I wish to spend more time with my counselor-to-be, Tamar." She grinned. "Brenda tis claiming him so he can be the new Laird of Betron ere we Walk the Circle."

Daniel nodded. He was quite aware of how fast rumors could fly on Thalia. It was as though Thalians could send thoughts across the miles like a Justine. He hit the com, and Levin's face appeared.

"I am sorry to bother ye if ye are closing out the accounts for the eve, but we have a slight problem here. Issing wishes to be with her beloved, and there are a few things the Sisterhood entered into wrong accounts. Ishner needs an expert to go over the accounts and offer advice. Would ye be available?"

"I would nay," snapped the slender woman of Don. For a moment, she frowned and her face cleared. "My dear, Daniel, I have the perfect solution. Yere Earth relative, Jerome, Lad of Don. He tis at loose ends and," she hesitated before saying driving everyone mad with his meddling and incessant jabbering; instead, she continued with, "he had special training at the Justine Refuge for working accounts run by crystals. He needs a challenge like that."

She smiled at Daniel. "I shall connect ye with yere elder fither and also with Jerome."

They could hear her saying, "Daniel needs an expert accountant. I have recommended Jerome."

Then the faces of Llewellyn and Jerome appeared on Daniel's screen.

"Ye have a problem?" Llewellyn's voice rumbled out.

It's amazing, thought Issing. *Jerome looks just like his eldest fither except for the blue eyes, and the slimmer, less muscular build.* Their dark hair fell the same way, and the nose and mouth were a perfect match.

"Aye, Elder Fither. It seems Ishner needs the services of an excellent," he hesitated as he was not sure which word to use. He was certain that bean counter, the words his fither used, would leave them blank-faced.

Issing smiled and interrupted. "Maca of Don, Daniel needs an auditor and a competent accounts being that tis able to teach someone else. I will gladly be here early in the morning to show him our Ops Room and setup."

"That sounds like a challenging project," came Jerome's deep bass. "I may have stepped on a few toes here, and a stint at a new place will be a change for us all. I have nay taught a class, but I have instructed others how to complete the books at the MacDonald Corporation several times." Jerome showed no signs of slowing his reminisces when the Maca of Don cut him short.

"Excellent. He agrees then."

"What time tis early in the morning?" Jerome asked.

"Could ye make that seven? That way I will have time to meet Tamar for lunch. Then we have other appointments," was Issing's reply.

"Aye, I shall be there promptly." Jerome favored them with a huge smile.

"Will we see ye anytime soon, Daniel?" Llewellyn asked before Jerome could start again.

"Nay, Elder Fither. I have a full schedule tomorrow. JoAnne and I have to meet with JayEll sometime to see what he wishes to say when we Walk The Circle."

Llewellyn grinned. "Tis good for ye," and he signed off.

Daniel glared at the screen and then remembered how busy his fither and elder fither had been while trying to right Don after the devastation of the Justines and Sisterhood.

"It seems ye have yere replacement," he said to Issing.

She bent and hugged him. "Thank ye, my Maca. Dinna worry. I still have my Ishner formal wear for when ye and JoAnne Walk The Circle and then when Tamar and I Walk The Circle." She grinned at him and turned to Ishmael. "Now ye two can have yere well-deserved brews. I am on my way to meet Tamar." They hugged.

Then she spoke to Daniel one more time before leaving. "I will tell Linda to have the door open at seven for Jerome and me."

Daniel looked at Ishmael. "Would ye like a brew first, or shall we just make the cast about the new Ishner?"

"Let's just do the cast, and then I can return to my Melanie for my brew and ye can join yere JoAnne. Tis been a long day for us both." He rolled the chair over to sit beside Daniel.

"Ay, and tomorrow will be nay different." Daniel reached for the button to bring up the screens to tell the inhabitants of Ishner about their new directors and his edict that the classrooms would now contain both sexes. This was in force for all of Ishner's schools.

Chapter 7

Surprises

Daniel reached the Maca's Tower at seven forty-five in the morning. Last night with JoAnne had been everything he had wanted. She had convinced the Director and Keeper of the Maca's Home to have dinner on when they were ready. The Director and Keeper must have tapped their feet waiting for the two to emerge from the bedroom, but they were Thalians and should ken that need for a proper bedding. JoAnne had readied the main bedroom for their usage with the red linens of Ayran. She planned to transfer them when the teal linens were available.

"I brought the red bedding to remind me of home," she had said.

Daniel had planned to check on Issing and Jerome, but he saw his fither's fliv sitting on the padport and wondered why. Best to check on the office first. He nodded at Linda as he entered. Somehow she had managed to find a teal suit of Ishner to wear.

"How long has my fither been here?" Daniel asked.

Linda's smiled, her eyes bright. "Oh, tis both yere fither and mither. They are in yere office."

Daniel nodded. Why, he wondered? Usually, his mither was still in the gym and his fither out on the prairie or checking all the installations at the Laird's Station.

The door opened as he touched the circle. He stepped into the room, and his mouth dropped open. There was his fither up on a ladder slipping the last pad on the back of the elbenor's hide to the wall frame. His mither was standing there, admiring it, and turned as he entered.

"He tis here," she announced and moved toward her laddie.

The man on the ladder half-turned, nodded at Daniel, dropped down to the floor, and moved the ladder away from the pelt of the snarling beast. Then a wide smile cracked the usually stern face, and the grey eyes lit up. It was as though a total transformation had taken place.

Daniel drew in his breath and realized how much he owed this man from Earth. He had taken both Daniel and his mither into his heart and his House. He had held Daniel and taken his sorrow when nay else would. He had rescued his mither from the Ab camp and saw to it that Medicine made her whole again while she was still an Ab.

He heard his father saying. "Doesn't it look great now that it is home where it belongs?" Lorenz had turned his head to look at the hanging pelt. The next thing he knew, he was enveloped in Daniel's arms along with Daniel's mither while Daniel murmured, "My fither, my mither, I thank ye."

Lorenz spluttered and started say, "Put me down, Lug," when somehow the turbulence of Daniel's emotions broke through his Earth/Justine genes. He let Daniel's emotion of love and thankfulness envelope him. Then he began hugging them both too. "It tis all right, my laddie," he said as he had said so many years before when Daniel was but ten and certain that the Sisterhood had killed his mither.

Daniel again put his head on his fither's shoulder and then on his mither's before he released them. He took a deep breath and gazed at the elbenor he had killed with his knife some forty years ago.

"Where are the casters?" Llewellyn was bellowing in the doorway. "Ye need the casters here!"

Lorenz looked at his Thalian father by adoption and Claiming. "This is a family affair. I didn't want an audience."

Llewellyn looked ready to throttle him. "It tis more than just a House affair. All of Ishner needs to see that he tis Maca."

Daniel was trying to suppress a grin. He had seen the two argue before. Diana was looking annoyed.

Llewellyn pointed at Daniel. "Ye will have the casters here this afternoon, and I shall have mine. Tis a shame mine canna show the elbenor being taken down and transported and then being hung by Tris."

"Oh, hell, Papa, we don't want a parade."

"And ye both," Llewellyn roared, as he pointed at Lorenz and then Diana, "will be in Don's formal attire."

He turned to Daniel. "I suspect that ye still dinna have any clothing of Ishner."

Daniel could now smile without antagonizing his elder fither. "Nay, Elder Fither, I dinna expect one ere the end of the week, if then."

"Harrumph," rumbled out of Llewellyn's mouth. "Then ye shall have to wear the Flight Captain's uniform. I shall be in my Maca of Don uniform. Tis that clear to all?"

"What tis clear?" It was JoAnne. She had come down to see if Issing and Jerome needed any help with the crystals and to be here when Daniel held his Maca's Meet in front. She was in her Ayran red, and her dark hair and eyes gleamed from the contrast.

Daniel put his arm around her as she greeted him. "He tis telling us what we must wear when the casters are here."

JoAnne raised her dark eyebrows, but went to place her head on first the Maca of Don's shoulders, then the Laird's, and then Diana, the Laird's counselor. It was most annoying all were taller than she. Even Lorenz was broader across the shoulders, but she smiled at them all.

"Oh, in that case, bide a moment." She turned and walked back into the hall. "Come this way. Tis for all of Ishner to see."

Llewellyn's eyes widened. This was nay what he had planned. Lorenz was smiling, his grey eyes dancing with light, and Diana was a bit opened mouth and snapped it shut. Unlike most Thalians, her hair was a light brown and wavy. Daniel also had the lighter brown hair of his biological fither, Troyner of Troy, but it was straight.

Lorenz walked over to Diana and put his arm around her. "Shall we pose?" He was still laughing inside at how his father's plans had been thwarted.

Llewellyn turned to see that wide smile on Lorenz's face, and as always, the man softened. JoAnne saw the transformation and wondered what Llewellyn had seen when he looked at Lorenz. She could nay remember seeing Llewellyn relax like that. It was but a moment, and the huge form was almost rigid again as the casters walked in and gasped.

This was a room full of the people of House; Don's House and Ayran's House, but House. They were but Tris, and then they saw the elbenor with the snarling mouth, gleaming teeth, and the upper portion with the legs and claws stretched out ready to descend and stared.

"They are here to cast the opening of the Maca's meeting," said JoAnne and smiled at all. "Now I see they must show the elbenor first." She turned to the casters. "Where would ye like us to stand?"

Idottie turned to look at JoAnne. "Ye did nay mention this."

"I did nay ken it had been returned to my beloved," replied JoAnne.

"Papa, er, the Maca of Don, was just keeping it safe for him," Lorenz growled. "My counselor and I brought it here this morning. It's where it belongs." Then he realized Idottie had recorded him and everything he had just said. Thalian reporters were as dangerous as Earth reporters, he decided.

Idottie smiled at them. "My Maca of Ishner, would ye and yere counselor-to-be stand at one side of the elbenor and," she turned to the others, "if the Maca of Don, and the Laird of Don and his counselor would stand on the other side we will begin the program. When this tis finished, we will show the Maca of Ishner walking out to greet the Thalians of Iconda and his opening words."

Lorenz was shaking his head. "Just get the rest of them. I'm leaving." He stepped nearer his father to give the Thalian farewell and found Llewellyn glaring at him.

"Ye started this. Ye put it up, and now ye must take some of the credit."

Lorenz realized this was no time to argue with Llewellyn. Most of the time, Lorenz would win, but right now, something was going on in Thalian politics that left his Earth mind puzzled even after the one hundred years he had lived here. He nodded and stepped back to leave room for his father to be next to the beast.

He pushed his western hat back and grinned at Idonna. She could not help but think she was looking at one of most handsome male faces she had ever seen. The two Macas were magnificent, but this skinny-bodied male had some kind of electric connection. Was it because he was part Earth and part Justine? Of course, she was recording.

"When and how did ye conquer this beast, Maca of Ishner?" she asked as soon as Daniel and JoAnne were beside the elbenor and Daniel had his arm draped around JoAnne's shoulders.

Daniel shrugged and looked at his elder fither, the Maca of Don. "It must have been about forty, maybe forty-two or- three years ago. I had taken a break from all the studies of being a Warrior and was out on the high prairie of Don. Some Abs had killed a calf and insisted on fighting me when the elbenor appeared to claim the calf. The blood scent must have alerted it. That tis when I charged with my knife."

"How did you happen to have yere knife with ye?" One castor couldn't hide the skepticism in her voice.

Daniel grinned at Lorenz. "My fither had taught me that ye never go out on the prairie without yere knife or yere rifle, uh, blazer. It was a lesson well-learned."

"And where has it been since it was so many years ago?" She asked the question, but all Thalia kenned that Llewellyn had hung the pelt beside the one he had brought from the place called Earth.

"My elder fither, the Maca of Don, had it hanging beside the Earth equivalent to the wild elbenor that he had dispatched with a knife. It was a magnificent gesture on his part."

Once again, Lorenz missed the subtle connotations of Thalian politics. Daniel was telling all of Thalia that his elder fither did nay fear that he would try to wrest Don away, but bide his time for his own continent.

"And now," Daniel continued, "I must bid my family thank ye and farewell as the people of Ishner are expecting me." He removed his arm from around JoAnne, and gave the Thalian farewell by laying his head on the shoulders of his parents and elder fither and walking out the door, his wide shoulders swinging. The casters, of course, continued with the cast and mentioned how they were accompanying the Maca to the outside to greet the people of Ishner.

The couple from Manufacturing were there, and Daniel stopped, turned to Linda, and ordered. "This couple deserves a cup of pina tea while waiting. Since this may take longer than I wish, tell Issing to grant them all the rights of the Director and Keeper of Manufacturing. They are to have their home returned and their fliv." He nodded at the couple and continued out through the glass door onto the steps leading down from the Tower. The casters missed nay.

Daniel found his chair set in front of a roped-off section. He had allowed for fifty people to greet him. To his amazement, at least quadruple that number was out in front, and not all fit into the roped-off section. They flowed out over the tarmac and the green grass,

"Good morrow, my fellow Ishnerites," his Star Flight Captain's voice rolled out. The casters both increased the range on their units as Daniel continued. "This tis the recreation of an ancient Thalian custom. Ye, or others of Ishner, will see me every week for ye to bring yere concerns. Since there are nay Maca's Towers in Port Issac or in Isling, I shall be at the Director of the City's office in those towns."

"We have more than just concerns," one man shouted, then looked around to see if an Enforcer was coming for him.

"That tis why I am here, and I will take the first in line." Daniel's voice was becoming a bit strained.

"Medical refuses to treat men," the man shouted. Others in the crowd shouted, "That's right."

"What?" Daniel was looking at the man. "Where? Here on Ishner or at Medicine?"

"Here," several shouted.

"And our laddies are nay taught in the schools as they should be," a woman yelled.

"If ye had listened to last night's cast, ye would ken that the schools are changing that policy today. If that tis nay true for yere laddie, call here and let us ken which school has disobeyed my orders."

He looked back at the man who had brought up the Medical issue. "Was it here that ye were denied by Medical?"

"Aye," the man answered. "My tooth has split, and I needed it mended. She refused."

Daniel pulled out his com and hit the symbol for Medicine. Marita, Maca of Medicine, appeared, and Daniel began speaking.

"Yere Medical here tis refusing to treat the males. Did ye give such an order?"

Her black eyes widened, and she almost sputtered, "That's ridiculous. The entire charge is made up."

"Would ye like to see or speak with the man who was refused?" Daniel roared back. Inside he wondered how the Sisters had infected Medicine with their folly.

"I'm on my way. Keep that person there." Marita disappeared.

Daniel looked at the man. "Well, we managed to get her attention. Please wait till the Maca of Medicine arrives." He turned to the group by the ropes, who were staring at him as if he were a miracle worker.

One man stepped forward, "I would lay my head on yere shoulder."

Daniel opened his arms. His elder fither had warned him at the Council of the Realm meeting that this would happen. The warning had been right. Men and women, one after the other, were there to greet their Maca in person. JoAnne was getting edgy when the Maca of Medicine walked around the corner from the padports.

The purple of Medicine clung to her young, bulky figure as she was but seventy-nine years. Her hair was cut short, but seemed to stick out over the ears. Behind her came two Medicine Tris in their lilac-colored clothes, but their faces showed they were worried.

"Welcome to Ishner, Marita," Daniel used the standard Thalian greeting, and so did Marita. First, she greeted Daniel, but she had kenned him all her life. Timor, her brither, had kenned him as a laddie. Timor had almost told Daniel what she, Timor, and Logan were planning. After Daniel, she greeted JoAnne, Lass of Ayran.

The court duties finished, Marita put her hands on her hips. "Well, where tis the man my Medicine refused to treat?"

Daniel motioned the man forward. "This tis the man. If ye use the scanner on the mouth, we will see the nay-treated tooth."

She frowned, but lifted the flap on her medical bag and moved the scanner across the man's face. Her face registered surprise, then anger. "Where tis the Medical located here?"

Daniel showed her the coordinates on his com. "Come with me, all of ye," she snapped at the two at her side and nodded to the man with the dental problem.

"I feel there should be someone from Ishner there with me instead of just Medicine. That way, if I go missing, there will be an outcry." The man had a stubborn cast to his face.

Marita was staring at him with open mouth. Daniel was almost as surprised. "Dear Gar, tis it really that bad?"

"Aye, Maca, tis a valid request." Not only was it the man with the complaint, but the others standing close enough to hear answered him.

It began to occur to Daniel that the sweep of Sisters after the riots may not have been complete, but why would there be Sisters from another House? He hit the com swirl. "Linda, assign two Enforcers to accompany this man of Ishner to Medicine." He waved the com in front of the man. "Let me ken when all tis finished."

He turned back to the crowd. "That tis all for today. The next Maca's Meet will be at the Director of Port Issac next week."

By the time they started to move off, two Enforcers landed at the front. One stepped out of the fliv and came over to salute Daniel.

Daniel looked at the woman and said, "This man tis to be taken to Iconda's Medicine. When the Maca of Medicine tells ye all tis taken care of, ye are to return him to his home."

"Aye, Maca." The Enforcers and man traipsed off.

"*I will need to start hiring male Enforcers*," Daniel thought.

Chapter 8

Thalian Accounts

Jerome looked at the screen in the Ops Room. He and Issing had gone through multiple years and multiple screens of the Maca of Ishner's accounts. Jerome, at least, had pinpointed the problem of missing funds dating to the fiftieth year before his eldest fither, Llewellyn, Maca of Don, had defeated the Justines and the Sisterhood.

"That tis the year that Ilyan's mither was made Guardian of Ishner. I believe it tis even prior to her wedding Illnor," Issing explained.

Jerome continued to stare at the screen as though that could resolve his problem. "That means that she and Ishner were under the control of the Sisterhood," he said and turned to Issing. "Why was this nay ever reported to the Council of the Realm?"

Issing gave a short, bitter laugh. "The Sisterhood and all of Thalia were under the control of the Justines at that time. Ishmalisa would nay do anything to imperil her rule and later her lassie's. I had nay seen the accounts until seven years ago. Then it was too late as that would have endangered Ishmael or me while we were here in Ishner. It gets worse, Jerome." She paused, shrugged, and continued.

"The minor thefts hit all the Directors of the City and all the directors of the centers in all three major cities."

Jerome straightened and looked at her. "Dear Gar, do ye ken how many credits have been stripped from here?"

She nodded.

"Okay, let me review. All your accounts and entries, whether debit or credit, are controlled by two crystals. They are connected with all the major income-generating facilities here on Ishner, whether retail or manufacturing. They can also connect directly with other continents and all of their economic activity, but there is no way that they can add or take funds from here without the Maca's approval."

His Earth speech caused Issing to raise her eyebrows, but she answered, "Aye."

"The other income/expense entities here have been granted the right to deposit their percent of profits, but any request for credits must be approved by the Maca. Tis that correct?"

Issing looked at him as though he were mad. They had been over this, but she answered, "Aye, or the Guardian if the Maca tis absent."

"All the other Houses are set up like this one; there are but two crystals to encode or transmit all information, credits, and/or debits. The other crystals are for communications and buildings."

"Jerome, I've been over that. Why are ye repeating it?" She stood.

Jerome stood also. "One thing tis nay clear. Tis the theft order encoded in one of the crystals, or does it come from a separate crystal or station?"

Issing shrugged. "I dinna. I suspect it tis encoded, but all the crystals would need to be removed and examined by Ayran. That can be lengthy and costly or nay. It depends on Jolene's or Jarvis's mood. I doubt if either would ken when looking at one. They would have to test its dimensions against the master cylinder or some other method." She smiled at him. "Tis nearing lunch. Tamar tis expecting me. I shall be gone till tomorrow morning."

"One quick question. Are ye certain there are but two crystals for debits and credits? There are more drawers filled with crystals."

"This tis the Ops Room of the Maca's Tower. Of course, there are more crystals. One tis even for defense," Issing snapped, then softened. Why they thought an Earth being, even if he was part Thalian, could solve this was beyond her. "Farewell," she said and left.

Jerome glared at the cabinet of drawers arranged down the wall. He kenned what they were for as he had been at Don's Ops Room and studied the crystal accounting while on the Justine spaceship and then at the Justine Refuge. He stalked to the front and stopped by Linda's station.

"Please tell Daniel that I am going to check something with the Director of the City and at the centers."

"Aye, but why nay just contact them by com?"

"Because," he answered, "I need to look at their ops functions."

The closest was the First Center, and he put his lift down on one of the padports skirting the green, walked across the grass onto the circular walk by the doors, and entered. He saw a tall, muscular Thalian female with the teal sash around her middle denoting her as Keeper.

"Good afternoon. I am Jerome, Lad of Don. The Maca sent a message that I might call. I'd like to examine your, er, yere accounts and Ops area." The woman's dark eyes regarded him.

"Aye, Ileana said ye would be here within the day or two. I am Ieddie, the Keeper here. Ileana tis at the manufacturer's plant badgering for teal or aqua sashes." She smiled. She was fascinated by his broad shoulders and blue eyes. She had nay seen such blue eyes; they were nay light like the morning sky, but deep blue like an evening sky getting ready for night. His hair was coal black, but waved as it was combed back.

"Tis over here." Ieddie walked over to a cabinet with two long doors and opened them. She rolled out the stool used to sit before the screen.

"I am surprised ye dinna have a separate room for this since this tis the First Center."

She smiled. "At one time, Iconda was the only large city on Ishner, and that tis when this was built. All the other centers are newer and have a small separate room. They've talked about enlarging this, but the funds were always short."

"Aye, that tis correct. They are always short." Jerome sat on the stool and checked the accounts. The amount they were losing was two credits a day. A little less, but still considerable considering the number of years it had occurred. "Is it always this amount the store tis short?"

"According to my sister, aye, it tis. Her previous partner insisted it was necessary for the Sisterhood, but I dinna ken how to stop it, and nay does Ileana."

Jerome nodded. "Did your sister mention how many years this amount has been missing?"

Just then, Ileana walked in, and Ieddie breathed a sigh of relief. "Ileana, this tis Jerome, Lad of Don, and he wishes to ken how long the credits have been less each day."

Jerome turned and stood. "Tis good to greet ye."

Ileana bowed her head. This man was from the powerful House of Don and related to their Maca somehow. Then she looked up at him. Dear Gar. His eyes were bluer than the sky. She blinked and finally answered. "This started while the Justines ruled us."

Jerome grew thoughtful. "Did the Justines have ought to do with installing any crystals?"

Ileana shook her head. "Nay, according to our parents. The setup has always been here since the Justines; however, there were times when the Sisterhood took charge of everything."

Jerome nodded. "Thank ye both. Ye have been most helpful." He turned and left, Ieddie's dark eyes watching the swaying shoulders.

His endeavors at the directors of the cities and the other centers were the same. Those in Isling had been installed last, but still during the time of the Justines. It was a morose Jerome that walked into the Maca Tower of Ishner just as Daniel finished his night's cast to the people of Ishner. He waited until the caster had left and gave his report.

"So far all are agreed there is another command coming from somewhere else or tis embedded in one of the main crystals. Nay ken where the command tis located."

"Which do ye think it tis, Jerome?" Daniel stood. Today had been as taxing as yesterday. He wanted his bath and JoAnne, not necessarily in that order, and his dinner.

"I suspect a separate crystal somewhere, as the House of Don and the Guardian of Flight have nay such problems. I also believe Betron does nay have a problem either, but canna say for certain. I have been wondering though, if the other Houses have this same problem, why they would nay report them to the Guardian of the Realm."

Daniel grinned. "Some may suspect that our revered Guardian of the Realm may be involved. The crystals would have been made in Ayran. They would nay wish to upset her."

Jerome pursed his lips. "I had nay considered that. I will dwell on this tonight. Any bookkeeper, nay matter how small the enterprise, would tell ye the answer to a problem can come in a dream. If I should think of something that tis brilliant, do I need to wait for the morrow to return?"

"Put your hand down here." Daniel pointed at the screen on the desk, and Jerome complied.

"Now ye can enter at any time. Just remember to lock the door behind ye."

"Aye, Daniel." Jerome grinned. "Tomorrow then." He and Daniel embraced, and he left. Once outside, he decided a brew and fried fish might help him realize what he had missed, for Jerome was certain he had missed something.

He looked up across the green where the First Center was located. On the other side, nearer the bay, was a place called Fisherman's Club. Brew and fried fish should be there in a place so close to the Tower and the Director of Iconda's office. He hiked over.

The place was busier than he thought it would be. A slender woman at the bar frowned at his blue Don's outfit but handed over the pitcher of brew when he paid with Don credits. "Find a table, and I'll find you when the fish tis ready."

He turned to survey the place and saw Ileana and Ieddie at a table. He grinned and headed over. He had liked the way Ieddie's brown eyes had looked at him, as he had been lonely here on Thalia.

"Good evening, or tis this still yere afternoon?" he asked.

They both looked up, and the smile Ieddie used to greet him made Jerome confident. "Uh, tis early evening," Ieddie replied.

"Would ye mind if I join ye? The brew tis for sharing."

Ileana was puzzled at first, but then realized Jerome was smiling at Ieddie and Ieddie was smiling in return. "Yes, of course,we were just relaxing after a busy day. Manufacturing was able to send some children's clothes and toys they had in a warehouse."

"Did you have any better luck at the other Centers?" Ieddie asked.

Jerome shook his head, "Nay, it was the same. I shall think about it this eve, and mayhap, I can think of a way to resolve it. In the meantime, tell me what Ishner's people do for fun and relaxing."

"Why we go sailing or fishing, of course," Ileana replied. "Plus, there tis always the gym for Warrior training or the pools or oceans for swimming."

"Oh, aye, but do ye nay picnic?" Seeing blank looks, he continued. "That tis taking food for a lunch or dinner somewhere in a cove or a secluded spot for sharing with another or with family, ah, house members."

"Oh, aye, and sometimes we go skiing in the winter. The older ones sometimes play their tower games."

"I have not seen that. Tis that like a board game?"

Once again, the Earth mixed with the Thalian language had left both puzzled.

Ieddie smiled and almost lost herself in those blue eyes. He was too tall and too wide, his hair too black for him to be an Ayana Slavie, the only populace she kenned with blue eyes. "If ye mean a board game tis where a glass tower with different levels, rolling cubes, and placing miniature spaceships on different levels, aye."

Jerome grinned. "Well, nay quite that way. Tis a foldout cardboard piece with different spaces marked in color and words for people to roll dice, ah, dotted cubes, and move a token of any kind to that space." He saw them blinking the eyes and decided to change the subject.

"It might be easier to talk about the different houses or furniture on our planets." He smiled at both, but mostly at Ieddie.

"Are the houses and furniture on your planet different from ours?" Ieddie was curious.

"In most Earth lands, the houses are square or rectangular as are the huge apartment houses where hundreds of people can live. Some are geodomes, but very few are round. The furniture depends on the individual. Those that like Modern, there tis some resemblance to most of the pieces here, especially the desks and the larger chairs. Others prefer the old, elaborate furniture of centuries ago."

Both women were looking at him. "Ye mean people do nay have a clean work area for their desk?"

"Oh, nay, our work-spaces are tidy or nay depending on the individual. Our electronic devices are nay as advanced as Thalia's as we are still using chips to make our computers, uh, consoles work. Most desks are hard plastic, but some desks can be elaborate with wood carvings and inlays. Those would still have a neat working surface, but not too long ago in yere idea of years, there were nay consoles. Everything was done on paper."

Once again, four eyes were blank. Jerome sighed. "Let me try again. There were nay screens, and so they used sheets of paper made from linen, rags, or tree pulp. They used the paper to write their numbers or words on. The desks were filled with drawers and cubicles where the paper, writing implements (what they used to put the words and numbers on the paper), the ink, and sometimes valuables were stored. My one elder had this beautiful, golden oak, uh, let us say a golden wood desk with a rollup cover that revealed all the smaller drawers and compartments." Jerome smiled at them and continued.

"I remember when I was a laddie, he would be delighted to show the children, uh, wee ones, his desk and all he had stored there. He would promise all a surprise, but those that had seen it before had to promise nay to tell…" His eyes widened, and he jumped up.

"That tis it! That tis where they are!" He turned to Ieddie. "Ye are magnificent! I shall repay ye tomorrow." He turned and ran out the door, his wide shoulders swinging.

Ileana and Ieddie stared after him, but Ieddie was thrilled as she thought, "*He called me magnificent.*"

Chapter 9

Crystals For Ayran

Once he was in his lift, Jerome hit the secure Don circle in the console. Lorenz's face appeared.

"Aye?"

"Pawpaw, please meet me at the Maca's Tower in Ishner. I need your pocketknife. I can't tell you why until you get there."

Lorenz raised his eyebrows. "Will Daniel be there?"

"I can't contact him from here without all Thalia kenning."

"Of course, y'all can. He still has his Don com. I'm on my way."

Jerome grinned and poked at the screen for Daniel. It took a few moments, and his face appeared. "Aye?"

"If it tis possible, can ye meet your father and me at your Tower? I am there, and he tis on his way." With that, he closed the circuit, left the lift, and ran into the back entrance to the Tower. He laid his hand on the proper place, and the door slid open. He wanted to dash right to the Ops Room, but decided to wait for Loren,, his Earth great-great uncle.

The royal blue fliv landed on the padport, and Lorenz came striding through the hall. He was in his range clothes, including his boots. At least he had taken the spurs off. Daniel's teal fliv appeared, and soon he and JoAnne had joined them. They all took time for the formal Thalian greeting.

“I need your pocketknife, Pawpaw.” Jerome used the Earth family name for Lorenz.

Lorenz pulled it out of his pocket. “This should be interesting.” They watched Jerome run for the Ops Room. Puzzled, they followed him.

Jerome was studying the drawers on the console, and then a tight smile crossed his face as he went down on his knees and pulled out the drawer with the crystal for sending credits to the Council of the Realm and the other continents. He flipped open the pocketknife and selected the smallest blade. Then he carefully ran it around the back of the cabinet chamber that had held the crystal. Another tray rolled out. It held a medium-sized, teal crystal. On one side was a stream of red, then a dull blackish-grey. He plucked the crystal up and handed it to Daniel.

“That is how they stole ten million credits or more from Ishner.”

Daniel stared at the jewel gleaming in his hand. JoAnne gasped. “That canna be. Give that to me.”

Daniel closed his fingers around it. “Nay, I must ken more.” He looked at Jerome. “What do ye mean or more from Ishner?”

Jerome stood. “I believe that there will be a crystal hidden at each Director of the City’s office and at each console for each city’s Centers. It’s too late to check that out this evening, but with yere permission, I shall visit each one again tomorrow.”

Daniel nodded. “Ye will be assigned two Enforcers to attend ye.”

“Those crystals can’t be there! My mither would nay have Ayran steal from this House or any others.” JoAnne screeched at them.

“I reckon that can’t be verified until y’all figure out when they were put into the consoles. My guess is that the Justines had something to do with it. They were probably extracting funds to repay them for the War and occupying Thalia and Breton.” All were suddenly looking at Lorenz.

"That makes nay sense, Paw-paw," said Jerome. "According to Ieddie at the First Center, this has been going on since the time of the Justines. They would have taken from Don too, or the Guardian of Flight. Has that been happening?"

"The Guardian of Flight was not a House under the Justines. They probably took from the House of Army instead," Lawrence replied. "Neither Don nor the Army has complained of any losses. I haven't heard of Betron complaining either."

Jerome was puzzled. He doubted if the Justines had been so remiss if they were responsible.

A smile slashed across Lorenz's face. "I think they were taking funds once, but those crystals were removed almost one hundred years ago. I always wondered where Andrew got those jewels without visiting Ayran."

They stared at Lorenz after that statement, and Daniel was the first to speak. "Which jewels, fither?"Suddenly, his face cleared.

"Andrew's counselor, Kitten, wears a blue Don pendant and her bracelet tis a black stone surrounded by two smaller black and three smaller blue stones. I remember when Andrew made those for her." Daniel was puzzled, "I thought he had made the crystals too."

"Oh, he did the silver work and set the stones in the settings he created, but he never made the crystals." Lorenz was grinning widely. "Papa didn't discuss the accounting that Andrew was doing. I don't know if he saw the stones before they were set in the silver or not, but I'm guessing he did. He sent Andrew over to give Brenda's Ops people a hand when the Sisterhood was thwarted, and suddenly, Brenda had a green pendant crafted by Andrew. I have no idea what happened to the smaller jewels from Betron."

"Why would nay the Maca of Don have discussed that with Mither? They were friends and political allies. They have remained so over the years." JoAnne was still protesting.

Lorenz looked at her and she shivered when those grey eyes bore into her eyes.

"I reckon that's something you'll have to ask Papa. I have a hunch he is going to insist on going along when everyone descends on Ayran with those jewels." He held out his hand for his pocketknife.

"Paw-paw, I will need this tomorrow. I'll return it once I have all the rest of the crystals. Is that all right?"

"Just as long as I get it back." Lorenz started to leave when Jerome asked a quick question. "What do I give a lassie in this land as a thank you gift? I would nay have figured out where the crystals were if she had nay asked me about furniture in my land."

Once again Lorenz was grinning. "Pastor James's desk, right?"

Jerome nodded. "Aye, if I were on Earth, I'd bring her a big bouquet of roses, but I am nay sure that is suitable here."

"Why wouldn't flowers be suitable here?" JoAnne snapped. "All Thalians love flowers."

"Uh, well in my land, it's considered a woman's gift," was Jerome's embarrassed answer. "I feared it might be an insult here."

"Just pick up a bouquet at the market and a crate of Rurhran's finest brew: Rocket. That would make any Thalian happy." JoAnne acted like she was answering a child. She was still seething at the implication that somehow her mother and Ayran might be part of the thefts.

"When am I allowed to tell Mither that ye and Don believe her to be a thief?" The frost in her voice warned Daniel that she might leave if he didn't mollify her.

"No one thinks she tis a thief. As Fither said, that was done during the time of the Justines. She was young then. I doubt if she even kenned about them or if it was before or after her Rite of Confirmation. I have nay idea who was her Guardian at that time. Do ye?"

"Mither may have been young, but she would have kenned. Of course, I ken who was her Guardian and Guardian Ayran. It was my birth mither." Her voice was pure ice.

Lorenz broke into their dispute. "Once again, we won't know until we ask her. Everyone needs to calm down. Wait until y'all have the rest of the crystals. I suggest y'all send Troopers instead of Enforcers with Jerome when he's extracting them. And you," Lorenz pointed at Jerome, "need to tell everyone not to say why you are at the Centers again."

Inside, JoAnne was still seething. What gave that Earth being the right to order everyone in how to proceed? Worse, he would be her fither-by-marriage soon. A quick look at everyone showed they weren't upset. "I still say we need to take that to Mither as soon as possible."

"I agree, my love. It will be done when we have the other crystals."

"We also need to tell her about the ones that were in Don." She knew she would nay keep it a secret.

"Ye can tell her. I will nay," Daniel replied. Before she could explode, he added. "I'm sure my elder fither will accompany us, and he can tell her. His details would be correct, as I would be guessing."

* * *

Ieddie looked up to see Jerome barging into the Center followed by two Troopers. Then she realized Jerome was carrying a case of Rurhran's Rocket with a huge bouquet of flowers resting on top. He was smiling widely and plopped the case and flowers on the counter in front of her.

"This tis for when ye thirst during the day." If anything, his smile grew wider as he handed the bouquet over the counter to her. "And this tis for helping me solve the dilemma of the missing funds. I left too rapidly yesterday to explain. I hope ye will consider this my apology and will even favor me by joining me for a dinner of fish and brew this eve."

Ieddie pulled the bouquet closer and the heavenly scent of roses and the green of Betron's forest wafted upward. "Yes, of course, I will. I'm through here at five o'clock."

"I should be through with all the Centers by then."

"Do ye mean ye have solved why we are always short, and our funds will nay disappear again?" Disbelief was in her voice.

"As soon as I recover something." He motioned for the black-clad Troopers to stand in front of the door to prevent anyone entering. He went to the end of the counter and opened the doors to their cabinet and went down on his haunches after extracting the jackknife. He flipped the knife opened, pulled out the right-hand drawer, and once again ran the blade along the insides. Out popped another tray. Jerome picked up the crystal and motioned to one of the Troopers. She brought over a small metal box. He dropped the crystal inside. Jerome looked at a wide-eyed Ieddie and smiled.

"When yere sister arrives, ye may tell her the shortages are nay more. Remember. do not, er, nay tell anyone else why I was here."

Ieddie looked at him as though he were mad. "This tis Thalia. It will be all over the land that ye were here with Troopers. The people outside and over by the Maca's Tower must have seen ye enter."

Jerome smiled at her. "But it will all be speculation. Ye can tell them it was a final inspection." They exchanged the Thalian goodbyes, and Jerome and the two Troopers were on their way.

By early afternoon Jerome was back at the Maca's Tower of Ishner and handing Daniel the box with three stones from the Directors of the Cities, and the seven stones from the Centers of the main cities.

"Thank ye, Jerome. Now, I shall call the rest, and we will visit Ayran."

"I dinna believe ye need me there," Jerome stated. "Ye will have JoAnne to verify where the stones have been found. I have a date later this afternoon and dinna wish to miss one minute of it. I haven't met any other lassie that interests me."

Daniel smiled. "It would be best if I keep it to the higher House members. Jolene tis going to be upset."

Chapter 10

Conference At Ayran

Llewellyn, Maca of Don; Lorenz, Laird of Don; Daniel, Maca of Ishner; JoAnne, Lass of Ayran; and Jerome, Lad of Don, all entered Jarvis, Maca of Ayran's;office. Jolene, Guardian of the Realm, was already there waiting for them. Llewellyn had insisted Jerome be with them.

Daniel opened the box of crystals and set them before Jarvis and Jolene. Jarvis tried to look knowledgeable, but knew he fooled nay, least of all his mither, Jolene. She looked at them and shook her head. She lifted the largest and examined it. Finally, she looked at the rest.

"The cuts are of the highest quality. How old did ye say these are?"

"They have to be two hundred or more years old. They could be closer to two hundred fifty years. They would have been created and installed while the Justines ruled. I doubt if the Sisterhood could have fooled the Justines and installed them for the Sisterhood and not the Justines benefit.

"How can ye be so certain, Llewellyn?" Jolene was curious.

"My Ops Room had the blue equivalent to the teal one ye are looking at. The House of Army had a black one. The Guardian of Flight did nay, but that House nay functioned under Justine rule. There was another at Betron, but for some reason, only one, and another one at Troy."

"Why was I nay told about that when they were discovered?"

"Jolene, Andrew removed those while Mither was Guardian of the Realm. He did tell her. Mither did nay request that they be given to her. She just ordered that they nay be used again. Andrew then used them to make jewels for others."

"What?" Jolene rose halfway out of her seat and dropped back down. "When did ye find that out?"

"I reckon Papa knew when it happened. I figured it out when I looked at that crystal last night," Lorenz answered. "I had always wondered why Andrew suddenly developed an artistic desire to create jewelry."

"He could have been prosecuted." Jolene was outraged.

"Mither, tis nay important now." Jarvis stood. "We need to ken who made these and where the funds are." He looked at the group. "Would Rurhran have the same problem?" He turned back to Jolene. "Did Ayran?"

Jolene took a deep breath. "The maker of those had to be Janice, Lass of Ayran. She had the skill."

"Then I suggest we question her," Llewellyn prodded Jolene.

"That will be a bit difficult, Llewellyn. She tis in her decline and rarely wakes. She kens nay when she does waken." Jolene's voice was bitter.

She turned to Jarvis. "Of course, we had a problem. I removed the crystal from my Ops and our Centers the minute I had ye back. As for Rurhran, we shall have to ask them." Her voice was almost vicious.

"Mayhap if ye show this Janice the jewel, it would prod her memory," Llewellyn suggested. Inside he was smiling. Of course, Jolene was clever enough to have figured out where a crystal would be hidden and then nay tell anyone.

Jolene stood. "We can try, but I am nay hopeful. Follow me."

They had thought they would be following her to a home, but instead, Jolene led the way to Ayran's Medical. The building was done in what looked like a deep rose limestone and stretched around two blocks. Inside were shops and restaurants, but also rooms for anyone injured in the mines or elsewhere on Ayran. Years ago, they may have been filled, but now most medical rooms were empty. One held the elderly Janice with a Medicine attendant to watch her.

The Medicine attendant, dressed in lilac, nodded, but did not interfere with such important Thalians entering the room. She moved towards the door as the Guardian of the Realm had checked on the woman's welfare before.

They looked at the wrinkled face, the thin white hair, and the white eyelashes resting on her cheeks. The rise and fall of the chest cavity was barely noticeable. Jolene took the woman's right hand and put the largest jewel in it.

The lashes lifted, and cloudy eyes opened enough to see the gem. A slight smile came and went and the eyes closed.

"Janice, do ye remember when ye made this?" Jolene asked. The woman remained silent and still. The Medicine attendant moved back into the room.

"I'm sorry, Guardian, but she canna hear ye or respond any longer. I expect ye will need to make the Byre Berm arrangements tomorrow."

"Thank ye,"" Jolene replied, retrieved the crystal, and led the way to an empty office. "Well, do ye have any other suggestions?"

"Did this person have an office where she could order and pay for the material she turned into crystals?" Jerome asked.

Jolene looked at him and wondered why he and nay Llewellyn had asked the obvious questions. He was nay exercising good form.

"Aye, she kenned what she needed; plus, she taught the younger ones to create the new crystals as needed, and they filled the orders for jewelry that we would receive." She turned to Llewellyn.

"I dinna ken when or why she did this." Jolene's voice was harsh. "The crystals she created for our defenses were flawless. She kenned they would be used against the Sisterhood. How could she do both?"

"If she were an artist, she could do no less." It was Lorenz. "Who else could create the crystals that she did?"

"No one," snapped Jolene. "I could do them, but somehow her crystals were always perfect. She would nay allow anyone to take one that was inferior." She realized Lorenz was correct. Janice's crystals would always be perfect no matter who they were crafted for and then sent to be installed.

Jerome, however, pressed his point. "Sometimes, an artist will create nay matter any outcome; however, if she had an office that used crystals to transfer credits, mayhap the homing one tis there in her office. Nay in Ayran would suspect her if all the crystalc were so perfect."

The Thalians were looking at him, shaking their heads.

"She has kenned for years she was going into her decline. She would have transferred all of that," Jolene replied with sharpness edging her tone.

Jerome smiled. "I think we should still check. Pawpaw has the tool I need." Jerome inclined his head toward Lorenz.

Jolene was irritated, but one look told her Llewellyn was amused. She looked at Jarvis. "Do we have yere permission, Maca of Ayran, to enter her living and workspace and inspect her Ops Center?" She hoped her wording would make her laddie deny them entry. She was upset with everything and everyone. She was coming off as someone who missed the undermining works of the Sisterhood.

Jarvis nodded. "Of course."

They walked the short distance to the round building where Janice had lived most of her three hundred and seventy-six years. The Maca's touch opened the door, and they filed into the great room. The architecture of Thalia was repetitious, as though an individual building might infringe on the rights of the other Houses. They entered the hall and descended the stairs.

The Ops and teaching space was the first room they came to in the lower region. Once again, the Maca's touch opened the door. The Ops Center was on the other side. Tables and chairs for the teacher and students were lined throughout the room, but the room was empty.

"Is her Ops screen and desk over there?" Jerome pointed at the wall with the larger screen.

"Aye, they are," answered Jarvis.

They walked over, and Lorenz handed Jerome his pocket knife. Once Jarvis had turned on the screen, Jerome knelt and pulled out the main drawer. He ran the knife along the edges, and the secret tray appeared. There nestled the red and dull black stone with the streaks of all the House colors running down from the top facet.

Jerome plucked it up and handed it to his eldest fither. He hoped that was the Thalian protocol.

Llewellyn smiled, nodded, and handed it to Jolene. "May I suggest ye engage Jerome to help straighten out all the finances when ye are ready to do so?"

Jolene and the rest stared at the offending object. Jolene grimaced. "All these years, she had cheated us." She looked at Llewellyn. "How, Maca of Don, will he be able to do what JoAnne or JayEll could nay do before?"

"First, JayEll may nay be available. He tis teaching his Martin classes and, from what I gather, spends less and less time at Ayran and acting as Counselor of the Realm. JoAnne tis about to Walk the Circle and will be spending more time in Ishner; plus, she and Daniel must make ready for their expected wee one."

Jolene glared at him. She kenned Jarvis would nay sit long hours working with crystals and numbers. She, however, regarded anyone from another House less than trustworthy in doing work for Ayran.

Before anyone else spoke, Jerome interrupted. "I do have a date, ah, an appointment with someone, but I suggest ye," and he bowed to Jolene, "have someone design a crystal that is capable of pulling all the information from the one we just extracted without it stealing from the others. It should be in an isolated area of your Council of the Realm. That way, ye do not, uh, nay contaminant the Ops crystals of the Houses."

Jolene stared at him. She did not intend to tell them that she was one of those that could design and create such a crystal. "And just who do I assign to make such a crystal when Janice tis nay able to do so?"

"Didn't she train anyone?" Jerome was surprised.

Jolene closed her eyes and then looked at them. "Aye, but can I trust them?"

"That, Mither, should be up to me. I am Maca, ye ken."

Jolene was about to retort and thought the better of it. "Very well." She turned back to the Maca of Don.

"Llewellyn, if I find we need Jerome when such a crystal and the cabinet to hold the others tis constructed, I shall contact ye. In the meantime, I must prepare for the cast alerting the other Houses what has been going on since the time of the Justines." The hatred could be heard in her voice at the mention of the word Justine.

Chapter 11

The Maca of Medicine

Marita had the young Keeper of Medicine from Ishner in her office. She had ordered another Keeper to Ishner with instruction that all were to be healed as their oath required. Before she stripped this one of the right to dispense any medical, she needed to ken why healing had been refused.

"Why did ye nay heal that man or any other man in Ishner?"

Mattelina stood straight, looking at Marita as though she had asked an inane question. "We are Sisters. We dinna treat males." The scorn in her voice when she said males almost brought Marita to her feet.

"We are nay Sisters!" she roared. "We are Medicine. Our Oath clearly states that we are to heal all who come to us."

Mattelina shook her head, bewildered. "That tis nay what I was taught."

"Who taught ye elsewise?"

"We all had the special classes with Minnay," came the prim answer.

It was like a blow to Marita's stomach. Minnay was one of the last of the House of Medicine that had worked with the previous Maca, her elder Mither, Magda. This could nay be true!

Marita hit the circle to Minnay's office. She had sent the announcement that she would retire come spring as her decline would be arriving in a few years. She wished to devote more time to research while she was still capable, a bit of hiking, and mayhap even some boating. Nay but Maybelle kenned what the research was in her lab as she insisted it would be a surprise to all if it worked. If it did nay work, nay would ken her failure. Marita had always supported Minnay for Minnay had supported Magda when others had turned against her. Marta, Lady of Medicine, her mither, and Melissa, her Elder, had told the tale of the Sister's Challenge to the Death issued to Magda many a time.

"Yes, Maca," came Minnay's voice into the room.

"Would ye please come to my office?"

"I could do so later," was her response.

"I was being polite. Ye will attend now!" Marita's patience had ended. She cut the communications and turned back to Mattelina.

"Ye had best hope that Minnay arrives soon. It might lessen the severity of my sentence, but that tis up to ye right now. Will ye accept a period of probation and swear to treat the males of anywhere ye are stationed?"

Mattelina looked at her as though she were mad. "Nay true Sister would do that." Her voice was almost as stern as Marita's.

Marita was barely fifty years past her Confirmation Rite, but she was Maca. If they believed they could refuse to treat males, did the Sisters still believe in Macas?

Marita's face reddened. "Then ye are barred from practicing Medicine ever again! Ye will now be part of those that keep the park and grounds in shape. Yere home will be assigned to another, and ye will be assigned an apartment near our Center. The Enforcers will accompany ye to what was yere home and watch as ye remove any personal items, but ye will nay ere again wear a purple sash! Yere color tis now lilac."

Mattelina was smirking at her as though daring her to implement such a sentence. The smirk turned to disbelief as the two lilac-clad Enforcers with purple sashes around their waists walked into the room and bowed to Marita.

"Ye are to accompany her," Marita pointed to Mattelina, "to the structure that was her home and let her remove her personal items. She may nay take any purple clothing. That tis now forbidden to her. Ye can stop at the Center, and she tis allowed two sashes of lilac. She is then to be escorted to number one hundred-twelve in the Park complex. If she refuses, lock her into one of the cells below. She will go free when she agrees to this arrangement. Now go." Marita pointed at the door. She was ready to slug Mattelina, but knew such a release of temper would speak volumes about her youth and lack of self-control.

The two Enforcers stepped forward, bowed, and grasped Mattelina by her arms. "Ye canna do this," Mattelina protested. "I am a Sister. She has nay right to be Maca of us. She betrays us!"

Marita rose to her feet. The two Enforcers looked at each other, but before any said a word, Minnay walked into the room. Her hair was iron grey and her face wrinkled. Like most people of Medicine, she was slender and barely six feet in height.

Mattelina tried to pull away from the Enforcers, but they tightened their grip. "Minnay, help me," she cried.

Marita glared at them all. "Get that woman out of here before I make her an Ab and request that she be sent to one of Ayran's asteroids."

Minnay gasped, but the two Enforcers half-dragged Mattelina out through the door.

"Wait," cried Minnay. "We should nay quarrel so."

Marita pushed the circle to close the door. Had she been standing by it, she would have slammed it.

Minnay looked bewildered. "What did Mattelina do to anger ye so?"

"She refused to treat a male while stationed in Ishner. He had a horrible infection in his mouth from a tooth. That could have been prevented or corrected so easily weeks ago. Then she had the gall to claim she would nay ever treat a male because we are Sisters. She also claimed that tis what was taught in her classes with ye. Our Medical Oath meant nay to her." Marita's speech was still rapid and loud. "Do ye ken where this naysense tis coming from? It needs to stop and to stop now."

Minnay swallowed. "If ye will remember, we are Sisters, just as my dear Maca, Magda, was a Sister."

"She did nay deny treatment to males." Marissa was roaring. "She loved Timor, her younger. Why are ye telling falsehoods about my elder Mither?"

"They are nay falsehoods. Magda followed the Sisterhood rules when they became House."

"She just did nay fight with the Sisterhood when the Justines imposed the Sisterhood's rule," Marita snapped.

"Of course, she did nay. That fool Beauty had nay right to pretend to rule. Beauty disobeyed her Maca because she wanted that position. She did nay care about Thalia. Nay did Beauty wish to admit that she had lost to Llewellyn when she was a youth and would nay pay her debt. I canna imagine why so many followed her when Magda or Raven, Maca of Rurhran, were both so much more qualified."

Marita was staring at her. Was Minnay so truly wrapped up into those long-ago years? She took a deep breath. "That tis all very interesting, but I am talking about now. Did ye or any other instructor tell our students and graduates to ignore our Medical Oath and deny treatment to all males? It's difficult to believe that, as Malta took care of all of the injured when our Warriors captured the Draygon on the De'Chin asteroid. She even tended the Draygon to keep him alive for questioning."

"Well, of course she did. All crew members are necessary on a spaceflight like that." Minnay's voice was quite prim.

"Ye have nay answered my question. Did ye or any other instructor tell our graduates to ignore our Medical Oath to treat all?" Her voice was getting louder.

"They were taught to adhere to our Sisterhood beliefs." Minnay's voice remained prim.

"Ye are now retired," Marissa's voice had grown hard and icy. She had the wide chest of the people of Troy like her fither Troyner. Her whole body said the House of Troy, it was wide, heavy boned, and she stood six-foot-five. She towered over the others in Medicine. In her heart, she always believed she should have stayed on Troy, growing, tending, and thinking of new ways to improve or use the pina pods. That was her passion, nay Medicine.

Minnay looked shocked. "Who then will teach the proper way to conduct experiments in testing new procedures or compounds that Marianne has created? I have nay finished my research or the training to instruct others to take over."

"Ye are permitted to do research. Ye will nay teach such heresies to our students again. All Thalians are our patients."

Minnay was glaring at her. "Who will teach my class? Answer me!"

For a moment, Marita was speechless. How dare she? Minnay was House because of her position, nay her birth. It was birth to Marta, the Lady of Medicine, after the eld Maca died that had made Marita Maca. She was well aware that Timor, her brither, would fit Medicine better, but he had been birthed twenty-seven years before Magda passed into the Darkness.

"Ye are nay Maca. I am. Ye are to return to yere quarters now. Ye may keep yere home till I appoint someone else. Ye will then be assigned a retirement cottage. Who I appoint tis nay of yere business!"

Minnay glared at Marissa. She started to pull out her com and thought the better of that. She left the Maca's Tower and hurried across the tarmac into the Medical Resource building. She entered a lift to the second floor where her research room was located. The door responded to her touch, and she walked in.

Maybelle looked up from her position on the floor and then stood. She and Minnay greeted each other, and Maybell caught the emotion of anger still roiling in Minnay.

"What tis wrong?" Maybelle asked.

"I have just been retired from being an Instructor. That fool Mattelina told our Maca that I had instructed her and others to nay treat a male. The Maca felt that made our Medicine Oath taking nay valid. She tis apt to dismiss half the staff and students," Minnay was visibly shaking. "We are so close, Maybelle, we are so close."

Maybelle hugged her. "It will be all right. See, Ma tis almost finished. I am threading some of the nerve wires to the ankle and toes. There tis still a need for more silicone and carbon. We also need the fine, ultra-thin wire leading to the eye nerves and then to the AI unit. Do we have the funds for that?"

"Of course, we do. I will need a list to order the correct amounts, though. Then there are nay questions from Ayran or Don when I order the wire or other items."

Minnay ran her hand down the massive, sloped shoulder. "She will be perfect. Ye canna believe how this has restored me. He twill nay reign as Maca for long." The last sentence was filled with hatred.

"Minnay, I also need more silver and gold wiring. Will our funds cover that too?"

Minnay smiled and nodded. "We will have it by tomorrow. Send me the order amount, and I will return to my office in the morning. I can tell them I forgot to close something out."

* * *

Marita watched Minnay depart, and then she too marched out of the room. It was so confining. How she longed for open fields of pina pods. They did nay defy nature, but flourished with the proper care.

Before Marita could reach her fliv, she saw the incoming flivs of the Guardian of the Realm, Guardian of Don, and the Guardian of Flight. She stepped away from her fliv and greeted them.

"We have a serious issue." Jolene quickly explained what was needed and why the rush as they had to make contact with Rurhran also.

"Tis nay possible, someone would have told me," Marita exploded when she heard the reason for their arrival. Then she remembered that Timor had told her there was a shortage of funds every day. Her mither, however, had assured her all was taken care of, and Timor had nay returned. She led the way to her Ops room, but she could nay believe any such crystal would be found. She stood with folded arms and watched Jerome extract a drawer that seemed to come out of a hidden recess.

She stared at the proof in Jerome's hand after he extracted the one from the hidden tray. She was opened-mouthed as Jolene explained what would happen next.

"We shall return tomorrow with Troopers. At least nay can forward any more funds. Radan at Rurhran tis expecting us."

There was a deep knot in Marita's heart after they had left. Somehow her mither was involved in this betrayal. Marita fled to the one person that could heal her.

Chapter 12

Logan, Lad of Don

Logan frowned as the screen lit up and an auto voice said, "Incoming." Then he heard the words, "This tis Marita. Do I have permission to land?"

A wide smile spread across his broad, sun-reddened face, and he hit the circle. "Of course, my love. I'm in the Experimental Green House. I was about to contact ye."

He set the cup back into the micro and headed out the door to greet her as her purple fliv settled on the padport.

Marita leapt out of the fliv and jumped into his arms, hanging on for dear life. Her Thalian emotions of frustration and anger almost staggered him, and he hugged her as tight as possible. When he felt her relax, he loosened his grip, and she look at him and smiled.

They had kenned each other from childhood. Her fither and his eldest Thalian fither, Llewellyn, Maca of Don, had been boyhood friends during the Justine reign. When his eldest fither returned from exile, he had rescued her fither, her mither, and sib, Timor.

"Thank ye, Logan."

"Why are ye so upset, my love?" His eyes, like hers, were a lighter brown. He had the brown-red hair of the original people of Ayran that were later called Abs and worked as menials for the rest of the Houses, but he was broad-shouldered and as muscular as any Warrior of Don and had grown to six-foot-four; one inch shorter than Marita.

"My House. I am the wrong person to be Maca. I canna control them!"

"What?"

"The Sisterhood. They are taking over."

"Was it so dangerous ye had to run? If so, we must go to the Guardian of the Realm now."

Marita opened her eyes wide. "Nay, they just upset me so I had to get away. I called Timor from my fliv and appointed him as temporary Guardian of Medicine. That should upset and discourage any of the Sisters' plans." She took a deep breath before blurting out, "Logan, Timor should have been the Maca of Medicine, nay me."

Logan's eyes crinkled as he smiled. "Ye were nay born at a convenient time. Yere elder mither still lived when Timor was born."

He turned and put his arm around her shoulder. "Ye must come and see what I was about to do. I did nay bother ye while I felt ye were busy at Medicine."

Marita matched him step-for-step into the experimental greenhouse. She kenned what they had growing in there. She and Timor had nay dared tell their fither. He was far too conventional to entertain such a radical thought as grafting a pina pod plant to an alien plant to create a new species.

Logan opened the micro and removed the cup. "Smell ere ye sip. Then it tis my turn."

Marita's eyes widened. "Have ye tried it?"

"Nay, I just roasted the pods before grinding them. The brewing was finished just as ye were landing," he answered. "I did nay like the beans in the raw form. Mayhap roasting the beans will also make them a great snack or be something more for the bakeries of Thalia, as they tasted better when roasted."

While he spoke, Marita had sniffed and then sipped. Her eyes widened. "It tis delicious. This will be a favorite in a few years. How many of the new plants are growing? We need a name for them. Here, taste." She handed the cup to the smiling Logan.

Logan sniffed at the aroma, then drank. He gave a huge sigh after he almost drained the cup and answered her question. "Nay enough grow now to try to set up a line of new tea or coffee brews, as we need to save some of the seeds and plant them. We also need to be sure this taste will continue with all the new growth. It may be another two to five years before we ken for certain." He shrugged as he kenned an agra's patience was needed for any new seed or plant to become a favorite; plus, they would be competing against Troy's pina pod plants. In his heart, he doubted that Troyner would even approve of this endeavor.

"We need to get our Houses to agree with what we are doing. I invited Kahli over for today's testing." He saw the disappointed look on Marita's face and grinned.

"Dinna worry. Kahli tis buried in the work of outfitting a new enviro section of a spaceship, being the only instructor for the enviro class at the Academy, and parenting the wee one that he and Lania have. He did make a great suggestion, though. He said we should have a small gathering for our immediate Houses. That way, we would have all here, and even yere fither might approve of us continuing our experiment."

"Good, I'm glad nay else are here or coming. I need to get my hands into the earth. I would have gone to the pina fields if my parents wouldn't raise such a fuss while I am there instead of at Medicine."

"Ye are an adult and Maca. Tell them to mind their own business."

"Logan, they would nay be silent." Her voice became fierce. "Nay ken I am here. Let's leave it that way." She smiled at him. "Now, I want to see the plants that are thriving in our special greenhouse, and then I want to visit the fields before we have the night together. Dinna deny me those pleasures."

Chapter 13

Radan, Maca of Rurhran

Radan and Rocella rose to greet the Guardian of the Realm as she, the Maca of Don, Laird of Don, Jerome, and two Army Troopers entered. They were in the Maca's golden office. The huge window looked out at a wide field of golden grain. Both Radan and Rocella were in the gold of Rurhran, but they were wearing their working clothes as there had been no time to change into something more formal for greeting the Guardian of the Realm. Both were puzzled as the Guardian usually had specific appointments for an official visit.

Once the Thalian hugs were over, Radan straightened his shoulders and asked. "How may we help ye, Guardian of the Realm?"

Jolene looked at them, her face set. "We are here to help ye, Radan; ye and Rurhran. Do ye ken how much has been purloined from your coffers over the last two centuries?"

Radan looked puzzled, and he looked at his elder Rocella. Rocella smiled at them. "There has been nay stolen from our coffers."

The others looked surprised, and Jerome's voice rumbled out. "Do ye mean to tell me ye balance each eve when the crystal that was found in a secret drawer on Ayran has your House color on it?"

Rocella looked at him for the first time and her stomach knotted. Another trouble-causing mutant from that planet called Earth. He wore the royal blue of Don and had those odd-colored blue eyes that Earth beings could have.

"We ken exactly where the funds go. We do nay consider it out of balance. It has been this way since the time of my mither." Rocella was adamant, and her dark eyes had darkened deeper. How dare they?

Jolene looked at Radan. "Ye dinna mind the millions of credits that are going to the Sisterhood? I thought Rurhran was loyal to Thalia."

"What?" Radan looked from Jolene to Rocella.

Rocella smiled at Radan as though he were a child. "Mither felt they needed the extra support. We have nay changed anything."

"Enough," bellowed Radan. "Guardian of the Realm, can ye prove what ye just implied?"

"If we find a hidden crystal in your Ops Room, would ye believe it?"

"It would do a great deal to explain your accusations." He waved a hand at Rocella to silence any speech she might make. "I need to see this for myself, and then ye may explain how it works. Please follow me."

Radan led them out of the office and into the Ops Room. The six people working there all looked up in surprise as they trooped into the area.

Jerome pointed at the main bank of drawers under the large screen and said, "That tis where it will be."

"Riddie, these visitors claim there will be an extra crystal in our cabinet. Would you show them where our Ops crystals are located and where the extra one is?"

"Which crystal would that be, Maca?"

"The one that tis hidden behind the main crystal that connects to the Guardian of the Realm's office and the other continents," Jerome answered for him.

"There tis nay such crystal." Riddie's voice was indignant.

Jerome bowed to Radan and to Riddie. "If I may show ye where it tis."

"Ye are nay to touch any crystal or drawer!" Rocella was almost in a panic. Radan had to listen to her commands.

"How can ye be so sure," Radan asked Jerome.

"Because that tis where I found the one on Ishner, at Medicine, and at the office of the Guardian of the Realm. The ones at Don, Guardian of Flight, Army, Troy, and Betron were found years ago by my elder Andrew."

Radan's mouth was slightly open, and he turned to Jolene. "Did he truly find such a crystal in front of ye?"

"Aye, he did," was Jolene's grim response. "He also found a hidden ones elsewhere on Ayran and Ishner."

Radan nodded. He was wide and blocky like the farmers of Rurhran, not the muscular build of a Warrior. His hair was as dark as the ravens his elder mither had been named after. His eyes were a medium brown. "Ye may do yere search."

"Nay," Rocella gasped as she tried to intervene. "It will deprive the Sisterhood of funds."

The rest looked at her like she were crazed.

"Good," Radan snapped. He turned to Jerome and asked, "Where tis it located?"

Jerome pointed to the left cabinet under the largest screen. "It should be in the middle drawer, but it will nay be the crystal ye first see. It tis hidden behind that."

Riddie, who was in the gold Rurhran House colors, and the other workers in the yellow of Rurhran Tris, looked at them in puzzlement.

Radan motioned to the man in the golden Rurhran colors. "If ye would step away, Riddie, this Lad of Don claims he will find a hidden crystal."

Jerome moved in, went on his haunches, and once more opened the secret compartment with the jackknife. He extracted the crystal and stood before handing it to Jolene. That stopped Radan's arm in midair. He had been reaching for the crystal.

Jolene held it up to her eye level and turned it. "Aye, this tis it. Ye can see it tis mostly gold, but the red of Ayran tis there, then the dull black of the Sisterhood. This one, however, tis different. Ye see, in that dull black, there runs a sliver of gold. That means a certain amount tis returning to Rurhran, but nay to yere main deposit. This goes to a separate account."

"How can ye determine that?" Radan asked.

"If it were returning to your main credit holdings, it would merge with the other gold. This does nay. It tis embedded in the black."

"How can I determine the amount?"

"To do so, Radan, would require the skills of Ayran in determining what percent is was taken back from the Sisterhood," Jolene answered. "I can nay determine that before we have more precise figures on how much was flowing from Rurhran each day. That tis why we need all the crystals from the directors of cities, and all the centers in yere towns and cities."

"May I ask how many there are?" Jerome wanted to leave for his meeting with Ieddie.

"There are twelve cities with three centers and another dozen or so with one or two," Jolene replied. "Their populace wasn't as decimated by the Justine War as the rest of us."

"That means it will take all day. Possibly two. I suggest ye find several small blades or knives of your own and have your Troopers do that tomorrow. They will have no trouble locating the hidden one. As I mentioned before, I have an appointment and I must leave." He handed the jackknife back to Lorenz.

Jolene started to object and realized Jerome was correct. Rurhran would be an all day procession across the continent. She turned to Radan. "I suggest ye close all Centers till they have been visited by my Troopers tomorrow. If a crystal tis missing, I will ken that someone alerted them."

Radan nodded, and led the way to the door leading to the padports outside. There they exchanged the formal goodbyes before leaving. He then marched back to his office to confront Rocella, but she had vanished.

He hit the com for the Keeper at the front. "Did the Counselor of Rurhran say where she was going?"

"Nay, my Maca. She looked worried and was headed to the padport. I assumed she was going to one of the bins or fields."

Radan nodded. "Thank ye," and ended the connection. He pursed his lips and hit the com to contact Rocella. An angry-faced Rocella appeared.

"Aye."

"I am assuming ye will nay be returning for a few days. Tis that correct, my Elder?" His face was bland, his address formal, and Rocella kenned exactly why he was saying that. Her days as a Counselor of Rurhran were over.

Radan's assumption was correct. He kenned that Rocella would nay face that humiliation right away.

Rocella swallowed and put a tight smile on her face. "I believe I need to tend to the fields and the reports from the different directors. I will, of course, send the results to ye for compiling." She snapped off the com. It was too much. She needed the solace of a like mind. All her plans and her mither's plans were being shattered by another Earth mutant.

Radan used his lift to reach the huge warehouse where shipments of grain and brew were sent to the other continents and walked into the office of his older brother, Robert. Robert had been warned by the Keeper out front that the Maca was on his way in. He was but three decades older and happily embraced his brither and Maca.

"To what do I owe this visit? Do ye wish to sample the new brew? It tis excellent."

"Aye," Radan grinned and replied. "Pour yourself one also to celebrate becoming the new Counselor of Rurhran."

Robert stepped back and searched his face. “Ye canna be serious. What of Rocella?”

“She tis too steeped in the old ways of the previous Maca. I will nay say more here. I’ll fill ye in when we are in my office. Now, who do ye recommend to take your place here?”

Chapter 14

A Quick Conference

Minnay's distress shocked Maybelle. "What tis wrong?"

"That Don mutant from Earth has discovered where the crystals were hidden. Our funds are gone. Can ye finish without them and then we put our plan into operation immediately?"

"The research tis complete, but we need more silicone, gold, and a few rare metals, and, as I said, the wiring. We also need time to coordinate every movement. That canna be done in a day or two."

The com came on. "Minnay, your patient, Rocella, the Lass of Rurhran, tis here."

Minnay frowned, but thought the better of brushing her off. There was no appointment. Had the mutant gotten to her funds too? She hit the com. "Aye, send her to my office now." She turned to Maybelle.

"I fear that mutant has found her funds too." She ran into the next room and kenned she would nay do that too often anymore. She and Maybelle must finish their project ere her decline became overpowering. She smiled at the screen that showed Rocella at the door, and she pressed the circle to open it.

She and Rocella greeted each other as friends, and as their House standing demanded.

"Welcome, but I fear ye bring bad news."

"Ye are right, Minnay. That new Don Earth mutant tis far more clever as an accounts man than any of us suspected. Like the last one, he has discovered the hidden crystals, but was nay content to keep within his House or the Houses of friends. The crystals this one found were handed to Jolene, and she tis into a galactic war mood. She has all of Ishner's crystals and tis now going after all the crystals in Rurhran and probably Medicine. She has Troopers following in her wake." Rocella collapsed into a chair before continuing.

"Even worse, my Maca has reverted to male thinking. He distrusts anything to do with the Sisterhood. When Jolene pointed out that some of the funds were being returned to Rurhran, but not into the general account, he accused me of stealing. I had to assure him that was my mither's doing as a way to keep the Sisterhood's funds in a viable form. Radan angered even more. I am nay longer Counselor of Rurhran." Tears appeared in her eyes.

"Disgraceful after all ye have taught him," Minnay tried to console her. "Have they stripped ye of the funds?"

"Nay, nay yet. That tis why I am here. Do ye need credits for any project ye are working on for the Sisterhood?"

"Aye, as Jolene has found Medicine's main crystal and impounded it. We can nay send our funds as payment. Ye would have to put it in Medicine's main research fund as a donation. I dinna think our Maca would even think to question such an infusion of credits."

"Good." Rocella pulled out her com and snapped it open before bringing up the information she needed. "What tis the official name of that fund?"

"Research: A project to strengthen the webs of existence."

Rocella raised her eyebrows, but coded the information into her com. "How much do ye need?"

Minnay looked blank for a moment and hit the com for Maybelle. "My love, how much did ye say we needed to complete our project?"

"Between the House of Ayran and the House of Don, we will need at least two hundred thousand credits," came Maybelle's voice.

Rocella smiled and begin hitting the circles. Then she nodded her head in satisfaction and looked up. "There it tis done. I added another fifty thousand just in case the estimate was short. How long will ye be ere it tis finished?"

Minnay sighed. "I dinna. I had hoped it would be ere I retired, but that tis nay to be. My Maca was so upset about our refusal to treat male patients, she retired me today. I will have to come in as a consultant offering my services for free if necessary."

"Oh, my dear, Minnay. Do ye need any funds? I refuse to let a Sister such as ye suffer."

"Thank ye, Rocella, but I already have my little home on the beach. It does need a few more furnishings, but I was planning to retire by Beltayne anyway and had prepared to do so."

"Does that mean that tis when ye hope the Project is complete?"

Minnay smiled, her wrinkled face lit up. "The project will be complete ere then. I will be able to enjoy my retirement."

Chapter 15

Romance On Thalia

Jerome felt he really should have showered, but he was already late when he ran into the First Center of Iconda. Ieddie was at the Ops screen and whirled around the minute she heard someone enter.

"Ye must forgive me for being late, but the Counselor of the Realm insisted I accompany them." He stopped what he was saying when he realized there were others in the Center shopping, gossiping, and going to and coming from the gym.

His mention of someone so important had caused people to turn and look at him. Some were shocked by his blue eyes. How could someone look so Thalian and have blue eyes like an Ayana Slavey? Ieddie, of course, took one look at those blue eyes admiring her and lost her breath. He was magnificent!

She closed up the screen and stood. "I shall forgive ye if ye are still planning on a picnic and/or a sail on the bay."

"Oh, aye. Shall we pick up the food here or from one of the other establishments?"

"Neither, Jerome. I have a basket in the back. We can walk down to the dock from there."

"I was planning on going by Don's Laird's and Lady's Kine Station. We can have the yacht that tis there. My Earth eldest assured me it was ready for us."

Ieddie was staring at him. Didn't he realize she was but a Tri recently made House by becoming the Keeper here? The idea of being on a fancy House boat was overwhelming. Would the food she packed be good enough? Jerome was oblivious to any discomfort that Ieddie might experience.

"Ye go after the basket, and I'll buy some brews. Then we'll be off." He smiled and lowered his head to each shoulder. Ieddie had to stand on tiptoe to reach his shoulders, but breathed a sigh of relief when she managed. At least she hadn't erred in manners.

Jerome had his hands on her waist. "What type of brew do ye prefer?"

"I like the Rurhran's Crème if that tis all right with ye."

Jerome's smile was wide. "I am Thalian and German enough to like all brews." He hurried to the counter.

Ieddie was completely puzzled by the word German, but she ran to the back. *The man does nay care is others think of him as different or fear his blue eyes.* She decided it was because he was House that he was so confident. Plus, the gossip on Thalia now was that the new Earth mutant had impressed the Guardian of the Realm so deeply that she was considering him as a bedding partner. Ieddie dismissed the last rumor as the gossip of Thalia. That type of gossip had connected Jolene with any male or female she came into contact with for any prolonged time, yet that was all it was: speculative gossip.

Within minutes they were stepping out of Jerome's blue lift for two and walking onto the boating area at the bay of Don's Kine Station. A Keeper of the boat was waiting for them. He was an older man dressed in the Tri lighter blue with royal blue sash wrapped around his waist. He bowed to them.

"The Laird told me ye would be here. The boat will accept yere orders. If ye will pardon me, I need to ask if ye have ever handled a boat this large." The man was uneasy for all the Laird had said was to have it ready for his nephew (the man assumed it must mean younger) and friend when they arrived.

"Oh, aye, I had one larger on Earth," Jerome smiled at the man. "Ye have a good day. We should return before dark." They carried their supplies on board and stored them in the small galley. Ieddie was awed at the deep blue colors, the fine-grained woodwork, and the comfortable-looking furnishings. Her sister may have been on such a fine boat, but she had nay.

They went up to the cabin, and Jerome touched the circles while holding onto the helm. They slid out of the mooring and headed into the open Abanian Ocean.

"Where are we headed?"

"To one of the small isles of Ayran. They have beaches, and some a few trees to shade if the sun becomes too much. I doubt if that will happen." He steered to the southeast.

"Ye have been there?"

"Briefly. When I was at odds over what to do, I went out there on Pawpaw's suggestion."

"Who?" Ieddie was puzzled over the strange name.

Jerome laughed. "Oh, that tis the Earth's family name for the man ye ken as Lorenz, Laird of Don."

Ieddie had seen the man on an occasional cast, but she certainly did not know him. It dawned on her that Jerome really wasn't worried about House status or lack of it, but why would he? He was House.

She smiled and looked at the horizon as the isles crept closer. "Oh, there tis sand and trees."

"Ye haven't been here? I would have thought someone from Ishner would have sailed out here just because they have boats."

Ieddie shrugged. "Few have this kind of boat and fewer still the credits to afford one. If ye had employment, ye would do nay to jeopardize it by sailing off on a pleasant day."

Daniel swung in close and cut the motor. Ieddie was ready to leap over the prow of the boat with a rope.

"I can do that," Jerome said. "Ye can steer it behind me. I intend to tie to the tree and then swim back. We can either eat here or on the beach. If the beach, I'll get the rowboat down."

As usual, his words left her speechless. Jerome stood, grabbed the rope, and jumped. His strong legs and arms cut through the water as he towed the boat forward. After tying it off, he returned. Ieddie had the rowboat ready, and they loaded the basket and brew aboard and rowed to the beach.

"Where did ye learn to swim like that?"

Jerome hefted the basket and the brew, leaving her with but the towels and mats as he answered. "Oh, there were the city and school pools on Earth, and, of course, the MacDonald Lodge had its own pool. Later on, my wife, uh, counselor and I had a pool installed at our home. The ranches had creeks or rivers, plus the MacDonald Corporation had its own yacht if we wished," Jerome replied.

The entire conversation left Ieddie befuddled. Only the House members had pools in their homes or on their property, and what in Thalia was a ranch, a Lodge, or a Corporation? What did he mean by MacDonald?

"Oh," was all she managed.

Jerome had set his things down and grabbed the mats and piled the towels on top. "Now would ye like a swim ere we dine?"

Ieddie's eyes lit up. and they went running into the small waves lapping at the beach. They dove, swam, inspected some of the rocks below, and came up gasping and laughing before heading to shore.

Ieddie lifted the basket lids and handed out thick slabs of bread filled with fish and greens. "There tis seasonings there too if ye wish," she said and sat cross-legged and started to eat.

Jerome opened two of the brews and handed her one. Above, birds caused a ruckus about something and kept flying. The blue of the water merged with the blue of the sky, and the warm breezes flowed around them.

Jerome, like Ieddie, grabbed one of the sandwiches. He would have preferred at least one with the smoked sausages of Betron or slabs of roasted kine from Don, but wisely held those words to himself. He sat beside her. "Tis a perfect day for relaxing, but I could nay escape the demands of the Guardian of the Realm. That woman tis a slave driver."

Ieddie didn't really know how to answer that statement. What was she doing with a man that worked for Macas and for the Guardian of the Realm? How could he be so casual about everything?

"Mayhap in a couple of days, we can see each other again. I promised to go along with the Troopers in the morrow, but I need to do the Accounts at Ishner also. When do ye have a free day, afternoon, or evening again? If evening, we could attend some of the more popular taverns along the waterfront. Of course, there tis Daniel's and JoAnne's wedding," he stopped when he saw the puzzled look return to her eyes. "Er, I mean their ceremony of Walking the Circle." He beamed at her.

"Uh, yes, that tis called Walk the Circle here, but ye canna mean to invite me."

"Of course, I am inviting ye. Why would I not, ah, nay invite ye?" Jerome asked. "Ye are a wonderful companion, and I love looking at ye." Jerome berated himself for not knowing how Thalians told a woman she was beautiful in his eyes, but he was certain beautiful was not the correct word.

Ieddie took a deep breath and looked into his blue eyes. She was as captivated as before as she tried to think of some way to tell him that the ruling members of his House would nay welcome someone so close to being nay but a Tri. "Jerome, I am but a Tri in their eyes." There, it was out. No easy way to say that.

Jerome waved his hand in the air. "Bah, what does that mean? My eldest fither says that the U. S. tis a nation of Tris." He smiled at her. "They will take one look at ye and welcome ye."

Was there no way to discourage this man? And she realized she didn't want to discourage him and she still wanted a bedding. She tried again. "Ye will nay doubt be sitting in the Don box, and so will all the important members of Don. They will nay welcome someone like me."

Jerome shook his head. "I am nay an important member of Don. Where would the nay important ones sit?"

Ieddie took a deep breath. "There will be roped off areas in the stands for the members of each House. Those that are more important would be in the front, and the Keepers (like me) and other Tris would be in the higher stands."

"Ye would be my date, or tis companion a better word here? Ye would be sitting with me." It was Jerome's turn to be puzzled. "Ye mean everything tis so formalized that nay protest it?"

"Why would someone protest something that has always been that way?"

For a moment, Jerome stared at her as he thought of all the marches against some policy or other he had witnessed and heard about on Earth and then began to laugh. He choked the laughter down when he saw Ieddie frowning.

"In my world, that would be a reason to protest something. Ye are worried needlessly. If the Don box tis too crowded, we will sit over on the bleachers. It matters nay to me."

"Don't ye realize yere Maca or Guardian might order ye where to sit?"

Jerome shook his head. "Neither would nay do such a thing." He stood. "We need to head back before it tis dark. I'll gather things up, and we can push the boat out far enough to paddle back."

Ieddie gritted her teeth. The man was nay listening, and she realized his manhood had stiffened as the outlines were there in his thong. She stepped closer and put her arms around him. They needed a Thalian bedding before they went anywhere.

Jerome smiled at her. "It tis truly time we left. I have certain matters that require my attention." His voice was husky, and he grabbed the basket and made a run for the rowboat. He wasn't sure how he could explain he was a Christian and that they needed to be wedded before there was a consummation of their growing feelings for each other.

Once again, Ieddie was left completely puzzled and unfulfilled.

Chapter 16

Time To Walk The Circle

Daniel rushed into their home and headed straight to the shower. As usual, his day had been filled with meetings, telling people how to set things up, who to contact, and why it was different from the Sisters' rule and would remain different. Then there was Ishmael's desire to return to his troller and resume his life on the sea. That at least would be settled after tonight's ceremony. JoAnne could then take her rightful place as the Counselor of Ishner.

The water and steam pounding his body revived him and his spirits. He stepped out of the shower to be greeted by a smiling JoAnne holding up two suits of teal. "Which do ye prefer? The one that fits against your skin to show those wondrous muscles or the one with the sheer sleeves that leaves nay doubt ye are built like that?"

A slow smile slid across his face. "Where did those come from? I thought there were nay on Ishner."

"The one tis a gift from me, and the other from yere parents; plus, there are three more sets from yere parents, and another from my House. Ye will be dressed as the Maca of Ishner as the manufacturer here sent over three different sashes." She pointed at them arrayed across the one stuffed chair. "They are proportionate to yere size. The shoes are a gift from yere elder fither."

Daniel stepped closer and lifted her up. "We could take a few minutes to celebrate these wondrous gifts."

JoAnne was still holding the two suits. "We canna. We would be late as I still need to change. I'm in my robe if ye haven't noticed."

The smile was now a broad grin. "Of course, I noticed. I thought ye were greeting me as a proper counselor should."

JoAnne couldn't help but smile, but her words were firm. "Ye will put me down, and we both will don these fancy clothes and meet everyone at the Guardian Compound. Ye did check to make sure it was cleaned and stocked, did ye nay?"

"Aye, and the Keepers were bringing in trays of food and brew."

"Which means it tis time to be there. Now put me down."

Daniel looked like he was considering his options.

"Daniel, we dinna wish to disappoint my mither or your parents. One or more would be quite upset."

Daniel placed her on the floor and grabbed the teal skin-fitting garment. "The idea of yere mither and my fither being angry at the same time tis enough to make the bravest Thalian Warrior surrender." He kissed her cheek and started to pull on the clothes.

JoAnne took her skintight red garment from the closet and also dressed. Daniel barely beat her as he pulled on his shoes. Thalian women did not cover their faces and lips like the Earth women and the Ayanas did. She was ready as soon as the shoes were on her feet.

She smiled at Daniel. "Race ye to the lift." It was a silly thing to say as he caught up to her in one bound as they raced through the home to the padport outside.

They could see the Guardian Compound was filling rapidly with lifts and flivs from every House. All came to honor the StarPath Finder and his counselor-to-be. "We are to wait in our respective House rooms," said JoAnne.

"Aye," he replied, and they waved at others while they hurried into the building. Ayran's box and room were next to the curved wall on the left side. Ishner's were on the right, but almost to the end. The tier seating across from the curved raised Guardians' chairs marked off with House colors were filling with lesser House members and Tris. Daniel heaved a sigh of relief to find no one in the Ishner room and grabbed a quick brew and roll from the food set on the table.

JoAnne too was grateful that her mither wasn't in Ayran's room, but her elder JayEll and Lilith, his counselor, were. Both enveloped her in hugs. "Ye will wrinkle my suit," JoAnne protested.

JayEll laughed. "How? Tis skin tight as it should be, and ye are magnificent, my younger. May Gar bless ye."

"Save that for the ceremony," muttered Lilith as she hugged JoAnne.

"What? I thought Mither and the Maca of Don were conducting things."

"Oh, they are, JoAnne, but I am to give the blessing after ye Walk the Circle," JayEll replied.

The trumpet blared for the Guardians and Counselors of the Realm to take their seats. It was but a few minutes and the screen showed Jolene's face as she stood and her voice came over the com.

"Welcome to all on this auspicious occasion." Her voice boomed out and her face shone. "Tonight, we have the pleasure of seeing Daniel, Maca of Ishner, and my lassie, JoAnne, Lass of Ayran, united as they Walk the Circle." She looked at the crowd and the seated members of the Realm. "If there tis nay other business, the ceremony will commence."

She smiled at Llewellyn, Maca of Don and Guardian of Flight. "Would ye join me below as Daniel was originally from yere House." No one snickered though most kenned that Daniel had been Ab when Llewellyn and Lorenz had arrived on Thalia.

"My pleasure," Llewellyn answered and stood. As they descended the stairs, Daniel and JoAnne walked to the middle of the aisle between the Guardian rostrum and the tier seating. A teal circle had been drawn on the floor, and they stood back-to-back at the portion that looked towards the door entrances on opposite sides.

Llewellyn and Jolene stood in front of the rostrum. Jarvis, Maca of Ayran, joined them. He was in a tight suit of deepest red, with the burgundy sash running from his shoulders and wrapped around his waist and was followed by JayEll. He was in his red Ayran one-piece garment, but he had the brown sash of a Martin running from his shoulders and wrapped around his waist. He carried the long Ishner teal and red Ayran sashes. They bowed first to the Guardians and major House members and then to those in the stands before stepping inside the circle and facing the side view of Daniel and JoAnne.

"Ye did nay ken each other when ye first met, but as ye walked the Life Circle, yere life would float free and easy. Only yere House ties bound ye," Jolene intoned. JayEll handed each scarf to Jarvis as he needed them. Jarvis placed the teal one over Daniel's fist and shoulder, then the red one over JoAnne's fist and shoulder, and stepped out of the circle to return to his seat in the rostrum. JayEll bowed to all and stepped out of the Circle to stand by the rostrum as the ceremony continued.

"We all begin Life's Walk alone." Both JoAnne and Daniel began to walk in opposite directions on the marked circle. When they met at the opposite end, they paused as Jolene began speaking again. "When ye met, ye felt an attraction but continued yere Life's Journey alone."

Daniel and JoAnne stepped around each other as the teal sash went around JoAnne and the red one around Daniel, and they continued on the circle.

"As ye walked alone, ye realized how much ye missed the other and depended on their counsel on Life's Journey." Llewellyn's voice rumbled out.

"When ye meet again," Jolene paused until they met in front of the rostrum before continuing, "ye will pledge to each other and become counselor and counselor."

Daniel wrapped the rest of the teal sash around JoAnne as she wrapped the rest of the red sash around Daniel. They were now facing each other again, and they both recited at the same time.

"I pledge myself to yere wellbeing and depend upon yere counsel to guide me on the last of my Life's Journey."

JayEll stepped forward, and his voice rang out. "We now ask Gar for His blessing." He folded his hands and looked upward.

"Almighty Gar, we ask yere blessings on these newly joined counselors. Guide them through their Life's Journey and bless their uniting with wee ones. Amen."

The seated Thalians rose as one and began clapping. Pillar, from his seat as the Guardian of Army, was shouting, "Daniel, our StarPath Finder."

The tumult died down, and Jolene bowed to all as did Llewellyn. Daniel looked up at the roster and waved as his parents descended the stairs. Daniel, as Maca, was entitled to speak first. He turned to the people sitting across from the rostrum. "All Ishner attendees are invited to stay. The tables will be rolled out for yere dining and seating. My House members are to attend the Arena dining." He turned to the rostrum and announced, "All guardians and counselors of the Realm are invited to the Arena Dining."

It was then JoAnne's turn. She turned to the tier seating. "All of Ayran attendees are welcomed to stay for the evening meal." The wide doors at the back swung open, and tables, chairs, and benches were being moved to the center of the area. "The food tis arriving. My Ayran House members are invited to the Arena dining." The latter all kenned that was but a formal statement. Most of her House members were on the Council.

Llewellyn and Jolene stepped forward and hugged the couple. Lorenz and Diana were next, and then Daniel and JoAnne led the way to the upper Arena Dining area.

Jerome smiled at Ieddie. "Tis time we followed them."

"What?" She could see the people from the Ayran, Don, and Ishner boxes following the guardians and counselors of the realm, but she was nay related. "Jerome, I must stay down here with Ishner."

"Dinna be silly. I have already cleared it with Daniel. Since ye are my companion this eve, ye are welcome."

Ieddie was in shock as Jerome draped his arm around her shoulder and stepped along with those from Don following the united couple. Jerome, like the others, wore a royal blue one-piece garment with a deep navy blue sash wrapped around the middle and the ends halfway down the thigh. Ieddie felt ill-dressed in her Tri aqua garment and only the teal scarf around the waist designating her status as part of House.

Jerome kept talking and waving to others. A burly, young man in royal blue fell in step with Jerome. "Are y'all really going up there?"

"Oh, aye, David. The feast will be sumptuous." A wide, welcoming smile slashed over his face as he greeted his Earth kinsman.

"Ieddie, ye must meet my relative. We have nay figured out if I am his elder or younger, or vice versa."

Ieddie ventured a small smile. As usual, the Earth speech confused her, but she managed a, "Hello."

David's brown eyes smiled at her. "Hello, Ieddie. He's serious. So many generations separate us that it would take a mathematician to figure that one out."

He continued walking beside them. "Y'all don't mind if I tag along. Maybe Ieddie has a sister to introduce to me."

"Oh, she will nay consider a male companion," Ieddie blurted out.

David's eyebrows elevated. "Seems to be my luck. How do y'all rate, Jerome?"

"Oh, I am the most fortunate of men." Jerome grinned. "Ye really should start using ye instead of your Texas speech. I've found that Earth's vocabulary and idioms can confuse those I speak with here. Have ye nay experienced that?"

They jammed into the lift with other lesser House members going to the main wedding feast. Most of the Thalians were greeting each other with hugs.

Issing threw her arms around Ieddie as Ieddie laid her head on one shoulder and then the other. "I dinna expected to see ye here. So this tis where ye have been hiding." They had known each other since they were children. Issing moved to perform the same ceremony with Jerome. Since he was Lad of Don, she laid her head on both shoulders, and Jerome returned the greeting.

The door rolled open to a huge room filled with the food tables covered with teal, red, and royal blue. The tables were set against the rings for the fights. The colorful tables were filled with renowned eating treats from each continent. Another tri-colored table held the mugs and brew kegs. Daniel and JoAnne were standing by the teal-covered Ishner table. It was heaped with fish delicacies of all kinds. It also held platters of deserts made from the wild berries and plums from that cooler continent. Each House had their own table for dining, and those were covered with the House colors.

As the last of the lesser Houses straggled in, Daniel's voice boomed out, "Welcome to all. Join us in our Walk the Circle Feast."

Chapter 17

Dissention

Marita was at the purple covered Medicine table alone. She was dressed in the purple of Medicine, but the orange sash over her left shoulder told the world that she was also Lady of Troy. Logan, as part of the lesser House of Don, had not arrived yet. Her brother, Timor, Laird of Troy, walked over.

He wore the orange of Troy, but the purple sash over the left shoulder told Thalia he was also Lad of Medicine.

"How did things go during my absence?" Marita asked him.

"They were mostly in an ill mood since I am male and toured the grounds as the Maca should. The Tris were all glad to see me as I listened to their complaints."

Marita straightened. "Why would they complain? There tis plenty of food and credits."

"Mainly because their laddies are separated from the lassies and are nay learning at the same level in the schools." Neither noticed their mother approaching the table. Marta wore the orange of Troy, but the purple sash over her right shoulder proclaimed her Lady of Medicine.

"I have been assured by the instructors that all tis well," Marita protested.

"They lie." Timor was adamant. "They dinna teach the laddies the same studies."

"Timor, really, ye are Laird of Troy. What does it matter to ye what Medicine does? They are but following the structure my mither imposed," Marta interrupted their argument. "I'm sure Marita has verified what the instructors have told her."

"Mither, the instructors nay see her. They talk by com. It tis a farce."

"Timor, how dare ye question what Mither did, or what Marita tis doing?"

Timor shook his head. "Elder mither tis dead. Marita is supposed to be Maca." His voice was hard. "It tis too bad she does nay perform her Maca duties." He glared at them and stalked to the orange tables of Troy as more people filled the room.

Logan appeared at Marita's side. "Hello, my darling lassie. May I join ye?"

Marita's face lit with joy, and the two hugged, and she forgot Timor's harsh words.

It was then that Marta realized that neither of her children had greeted her properly. Her mood worsened as she kenned that Marita had every intention of letting this interloper from Don remain with her. Before she could object, Myrtle and Matilda, the Director and Counselor of Medicine's First Center, arrived and the Thalian greeting exchanged. They all turned towards the filled tables set against the Arena Rings as Daniel's and JoAnne's amplified voices rolled over the crowd.

"We welcome our Houses and friends to our celebration. The tables are filled with the finest offerings from each House. Please join us in," a huge smile crossed Daniel's face, "in demolishing it all!"

Jolene and Jarvis were resplendent in red and stood next to JoAnne. Lorenz and Diana, as Daniel's parents, stood next to him. Both wore the royal blue of Don. They all bowed to the crowd and received their filled plates from the Keepers doing the serving. All of the Keepers were dressed in the colors of their respective Houses.

The tables for Don and Betron had been shoved together so Llewellyn, Maca of Don, resplendent in blue, could sit at one end of his table, and Brenda, Maca of Betron, in her forest green, could sit at one end of her table and they still sit side by side. Kahli, Lad of Don, and his counselor, Lania, with their two-month-old wee lassie in her sling, were beside his fither, Llewellyn. Lincoln, Lad of Don, the Laird's laddie, was beside them at Ishner's table. Ieddie was beside Jerome and wide-eyed that they were allowed at the Don table. David, Lad of Don, from Earth, was beside her. The other members of Don numbered fifteen as Logan was at Medicine.

Marta ground her teeth, but returned to Troy's table and her counselor, Troyner. It was time for the Macas of the other continents to come forward for their platters. Together they walked to the front for their plates and took as much as they could. The smoked fish from Ishner, the succulent roasts from Don, the steaming vegetables and cool brew from Rurhran, the special smoked sausages from Betron, and the delicate scented pastries dotted with the chopped pina pod nuts from Troy.

They returned to their seats, and Timor soon joined them with his heaped plate and huge cup of pina tea rather than the brew of Rurhran. Troyner's eyebrows elevated. "Ye do nay need to drink the tea when the brew tis free." To prove his point, Troyner took a huge swig from his mug. Had a stranger walked in, they would have sworn that Troyner was Daniel's fither, nay that skinny bodied male from Earth that sat by Daniel's side.

Timor shrugged. "I'll be returning to Medicine this eve. I'd rather have a clear head."

"Why would ye do that?" Marta asked. "Marita will be there."

Timor looked over at the table where Marita and Logan sat. Both were indulging in the food, but their eyes were on each other. "Even if she returns to Medicine, Logan will be with her. I doubt if that will happen. I suspect they will both return to Logan's home."

Marta straightened. "That tis silly. Marita kens she needs to return to Medicine."

"Nay, Mither. Ye ken that Marita needs to return to Medicine."

She shook her head. "And ye, Timor, need to return to Troy to help with the pina pods."

Timor frowned. "Why? Fither, Trillie, and Theodore do an excellent job of keeping all in order."

"Ye should be there to help with the new experiments." Marta was insistent.

"What new experiments, Mither?" Timor looked at his father. "Have ye started a new strain of pina pods?"

Troyner was baffled. "Why would I do that? All love pina pods the way they are. We are, of course, seeing if they can grow larger, or be grown in a slightly higher elevation. Mount Taline may nay equal the mountains of Don or Ishner, but the climate tis cooler there. Triva tis in charge of those projects." He smiled at those sitting to his left: Theodore, Director of Fields, and Tela, Director of Testing. The two were husband and wife and had remained loyal to Troyner during the time of the Sisterhood. Teresa, their lassie, sat next to them. Triva, Director of Labor, and Trillie, the Director of Shipping, were with them. Triva had handed his friend Llewellyn the key to the miserable shack he and the Laird of Betron had been locked in for two years.

"Ye see, Mither, all tis well on Troy."

Marta took a deep breath and turned to Troyner with a winning smile on her face. "Dinna ye think it would be good to relinquish some of your duties to Timor? Ye, uh, we, could enjoy life a bit more."

Troyner looked at her, his eyes puzzled. "Why? I am barely over two hundred and seventy. That tis far too early to rest, and how could it be we who are enjoying life when ye are at Medicine running it."

"Oh, nonsense, I am merely advising Marita."

"Mither, all ken better. Marita tis nay there." Timor stood. "Ye will excuse me, I must speak with Marita for a moment."

Timor returned to Marita's table and greeted Logan. "How goes the experiment?"

"Ye didn't ask Marita?" Logan voiced his surprise.

"Nay, Mither was standing here." All of them ignored the glares from Myrtle and Matilda.

Logan grinned. Marita nudged his shin. "Why nay stop by sometime this week, and I will show ye. Tis far better than discussing it."

"I will do that." Timor bowed and returned to Troy's table. He would have liked to speak with Teresa, but he feared she might ignore him. Like so many others, Teresa had nay kenned him while he was a laddie. Timor had been a quiet, lonely boy and had grown into a quiet, lonely man.

Radan and Robert approached carrying their brews. The two brothers did not look alike. Robert resembled their fither, Ribdan, Counselor of Flight, but Radan resembled Raven, his eldest mither and former Maca. He looked at Marita. "I've heard that Jerome, Lad of Don, found one of the crystals that steal at Medicine also. Tis that true?"

All looked at him and realized how hard his face and eyes were. Myrtle and Matilda stifled a gasp.

Marita nodded. "I believe the Counselor of the Realm prefers we nay discuss it."

"Bah," Radan snapped. "All Thalia kens. I wish ye to ken that Robert tis now Counselor of Rurhran. Ye may contact him for any dealings with Rurhran." Both bowed and continued on to the table for Guardian of Flight. The noise of clacking silverware, laughter, and talking grew louder.

Radan and Robert greeted their parents Ribdan, Counselor of Flight, and Renie, Lass of Rurhran. "Sit, sit, have a brew," Ribdan boomed while motioning the Keeper server over.

The Director of Flight and his companion greeted the two and moved to make room for the two beside their parents.

"So the Guardian of Flight left ye in charge," Radan noted.

"Of course, he had to be at Don's table. He tis the Maca." Ribdan beamed at his two laddies. "I see ye finally realized that Rocella could be a liability and have chosen Robert as yere counselor. Congratulations to ye both."

"Agreed," Renie chimed in. "I wondered when ye would have courage enough to break that bond."

Radan stared at both. "Ye kenned? Why did ye nay warn me?"

"Ye might have ignored us. She was appointed yere Guardian by Raven, the Maca, ere ye were even born. The influence was difficult to break."

"How could my eldest mither ken she would die ere I was birthed?" Radan demanded. He realized a decline could take years.

Renie shrugged. "She had appointed Rocella as Guardian of the new Maca when she started into her decline. If she kenned, we were expecting the Sisters in Medicine would have told her, and, yes, her decline was rapid. All wondered about that."

Radan nodded. "So once again, Medicine was aligned with the Sisterhood, but their eld Maca was already into the Darkness. Didn't it change under Marta and then Marita?"

Renie shook her head, and Ribdan answered for her. "My laddies, we are here for a celebration. Why nay visit us at home tomorrow eve." He smiled.

Robert stood, and then Radan rose. Radan's face and eyes had grown harder. "We'll be there." Both bowed to their parents.

"We need to make the rounds. Let's visit Pillar next," Radan suggested. They grabbed their mugs and walked towards the table of the Guardian of the Army. He wanted to be better acquainted before Jerome and the Troopers all descended on Rurhran in the morning.

Daniel and JoAnne had finished their meal and brew, and rose to begin their Walk to all the tables of the Macas and Guardians. While not part of the rite of Walk the Circle, it was a well-established custom in Thalia.

Jarvis and JayEll both pounded Daniel on the back, kenning they were safe from retaliation this eve. Daniel was thankful that Jarvis's companion, Aretha, was gentler, though he well kenned the blows she could land. Lilith, the Kenning Woman, JayEll's counselor, was exuberant, but her build was slight in comparison to the others.

The crowd had dwindled when the tong for departure struck. Daniel and JoAnne waved to all and fled to their fliv. Both were ready for their bedding.

Chapter 18

The Crystals

Jolene had called in JayEll and Llewellyn when Pillar advised her they had all the crystals from Rurhran and would be at her Counselor of Realm office in Ayran within minutes. Pillar had arrived as promised, grinned broadly, and dumped all the crystals from Rurhran's centers and directors of the cities' cabinets on her desk.

"Radan tis in a foul mood. He will be contacting ye. He also threatened to bring the whole mess before the next Guardian's meeting if ye did nay have a decent figure on reimbursing Rurhran."

Jolene glared at him. "And how did ye placate him."

Pillar grinned. "I am a Warrior. The only way I ken to placate tis to destroy. I told him I would deliver his message. He will probably contact ye anyway." Pillar bowed and left as JayEll and Llewellyn entered.

Greetings were exchanged, and Jolene pointed to the gold streaked with red and dull black crystals on her desk. "Those are the crystals from Rurhran. How much have the Sisters drained off of them, and where did all the credits go?" It was as though she expected them to enlighten her.

"Jolene, we canna answer that till we ken how much each crystal drained off each day and for how many years. It has to be close to two hundred years or more since the Justines were still in charge when the main ones were installed."

"I believe it was after the Justines pulled their administrator and put a Kreppie in charge." Jolene's voice was filled with anger, and she used the Thalian slur for the Krepyons. "Betta and Beauty convinced the Kreppies that the Sisterhood would need the credits, since all in the Sisterhood were considered Army, nay House status with even one Center."

JayEll's eyes widened, and a tight smile lit Llewellyn's face as he lowered himself into one of the chairs. "I thought ye might ken more about the date since Ayran makes the crystals."

Jolene had nay meant to speak so freely, but all kenned where the crystals were made. "While ye, Llewellyn, did nay warn any of us that the Houses were still being robbed after ye had them pulled out of Don and Betron, and probably Troy. Tell me how soon did ye ken after ye took charge as Maca?"

Llewellyn smiled at her. "Oh, the second day I had Andrew in charge of the accounts. He kenned he had nay made any errors, so there had to be something in the 'machinery' as he called our Ops system. He kenned it was extracting the credits and shipping them elsewhere. He asked what the colors meant after he extracted the crystal in my Ops Room, and I explained. I then asked him to check Don's Centers, and the Guardian of Flight and the Warrior Academy. They were at the Centers, but nay at the other two as those had been closed. I then suggested he check Troy's and Betron's accounts and all directors of cities if any existed. I procured the invitation for him to do so and, of course, he discovered them. Troyner and Brenda were quite grateful."

Jolene stood. "Ye never mentioned it to me. Did ye even bother to mention it to yere own mither who was Guardian before me?"

Llewellyn looked up at her. "My dear, I've already told ye that I informed my mither. We assumed ye kenned since ye did nay bother to mention to me or my mither that ye were nay longer receiving the credits from the three different Houses."

"Dinna 'my dear' me!" She took a deep breath. "Ye are correct. I had removed them from my Ops room, the Directors of the Cities, and all Centers. I thought that would stop the flow of credits from the others. Janice did query me as to why the funds had stopped for the Sisters. I explained we were at war and the Sisters would destroy my laddie. I would die ere I let them do that."

Llewellyn raised his eyebrows. "So, she ignored your wishes?"

"Aye, that she must have for the thefts to continue as nay of my Centers, nay my directors, nay the Mining Director ever complained that funds were missing. She created this gem," Jolene pointed at it, "for her Ops area where she could order material or the large slabs of crystal from Jada. That crystal could then receive the credits from the other continents. She did nay leave any information as to where the credits were stored before sending credits to the various Sister locations."

"Can ye nay track it down?"

"Llewellyn, if I could answer that question, I would." Jolene looked at him. "I think we need a brew, and then I want ye both to venture guesses as to where she might have hidden the funds." She walked to the cold cabinet and took out a bottle of Rurhran's finest and then three cups.

"Guardian of the Realm, I could nay stop the Maca of Rurhran. His sib and Counselor of Rurhran, Robert, tis with him. They are headed for yere door," came Jaffer's voice over the com.

There was a rap at the door, and Radan and Robert entered without being bid to do so. Robert stood about six feet, six inches and, because of his years, a bit bulkier than Radan. Radan was a couple of inches shorter, but his shoulders were broader and his face was set in hard lines. His features were all in proportion with blacked-winged eyebrows. He was a handsome man by any planet's standards.

Radan and Robert bowed to Jolene and tried to ignore Llewellyn and JayEll.

"Ye must have a reason for bursting in on us without an appointment. What tis it?" Jolene was glaring at him.

"Guardian of the Realm, a considerable amount of credits has been stolen from Rurhran over the years. Our people are assembling the amount from the old records. When can I expect the credits to be returned?"

The three looked at him in disbelief. Jolene stood. "First, I too will assemble all the data on that which was stolen, nay that just from Rurhran, but all of the Houses. Then we will try to determine how much was spent out by the Sisterhood during those years. We already have evidence that some of the credits were returned to Ayran and to Rurhran. The problem for both of our Houses tis that nay ken where or how those credits were hid or used. They were nay entered into the General Funds. Before any investigation will begin, a mock set of cabinets and wiring must be created. This will nay connect to any of the Houses. That way, when we run the crystals, it will show on the screen where the connections are and how much was taken, but will nay divert any credits."

Radan took a deep breath. "In the meantime, Ayran will have the extra credits. Is that nay what ye are saying?"

Jolene exploded. "Does Rurhran have the credits that were directed back to Rurhran? The crystal from Rurhran suggests that they received a larger amount than any other. Have ye asked Rocella where Raven hid that account?"

"We do nay ken where the credits are," answered Robert. He laid a comforting hand on Radan's back. "This has been a shock to all of us. Could ye tell us how long this will take?"

Jolene shook her head. "First, it will be measurements for the wire frames to be built. In the meantime, the Ops people in each House should be going over their records to ken how many credits are missing."

"We also need to ken if any of the Sisters had the foresight to transfer their credits to the Justines to hold as Bobinet, the traitor, did," Llewellyn's voice rumbled out.

Radan looked at him. "Why would any do that? Who would want to live near the Justines other than those part Earth/Justine beings that do?" Contempt was in his voice.

Those words managed to rile Llewellyn, and he rose. He still towered over all in this room. "Those beings are my House. They manage most of the Refuge, and it tis open to all. If any Sister felt that Thalia realized what they were doing and in danger of being confined or made Ab, they could hope to flee there, especially the diplomats from Rurhran. That canna happen with Melissa and Margareatha in charge there."

Radan's face turned a mottled red and white. "How dare ye accuse my House?"

"Tis easy when ye consider who has the ability to easily leave Thalia."

Robert was hanging on to Radan's arm, and JayEll stood.

"These words serve nay." He looked at the two angry men. "Right now, we have proof that each House has been robbed of credits and the Sisterhood and the Justines are responsible. Have nay of ye considered that mayhap the Justines were doing their own bit of taxing or skimming and that has nay ended? We should nay argue among ourselves till this tis all sorted out."

His words had the desired effect. Each one in the room considered that possibility, and they looked at JayEll.

"Tis a breath-taking concept, my younger. Why would ye think that?" Jolene asked.

"The Justines claim they have resources from long ago, but do they? We have nay way of checking. Their systems are so different from ours. They may have a share from what the lounge and the room spaces on the Justine Refuge bring in, but tis it enough to feed all of them? We have nay way of kenning, yet they buy whatever foods, drink, or clothing they wish."

JayEll took a deep breath; he knew he had calmed the anger. "Once Ayran's manufacturing has produced the wire cabinet, I would like for Jerome, Lad of Don, to assist with the compiling. He was able to discover all of this and alert us." He turned to Llewellyn. "Tis that possible?"

"I am sure Jerome would be delighted. He would consider it another challenge. Levin will be delighted as this will keep him from disturbing her work."

"There tis one more thing to consider," JayEll said. Jolene glared at him. She was the Guardian of the Realm, nay JayEll.

JayEll realized the others were puzzled. "We dinna ken who has these credits, nay where they have been spent or sent."

"What do ye mean, 'sent,' " Jolene demanded.

Llewellyn answered for JayEll. "The Sisters, nay doubt, used funds to sustain and to free Beauty. How much they paid the guards and enforcers we may never ken. They also used it to furnish and build her hideaways. Did they, like Bobinet, transfer funds to the Justine Refuge as a possible place to flee if they were discovered?"

Jolene's eyes widened. "Dear Gar, tis that what ye meant?"

"Aye, Elder Mither, but also, since the crystals were installed while the Justines were still here or shortly after they left, did they somehow manage to have credits continuing to be transferred to them?"

"Nay possible," Jolene spluttered. "The credits would have to have been transferred to a crystal that was then taken to the Justine Refuge. Nay respectable Thalian would do that."

Llewellyn set his mug down and leaned forward. "Consider, Jolene, Medicine and Ishner; both have harbored die-hard believers. What if someone from there journeyed to the Justine Refuge for a vacation or used a pretense of sending a laddie or lassie there to study the Justine medical techniques? The Justines could easily claim any funds that they brought with them, or claim it was their charge for teaching and providing living quarters. Then there tis also the question of why has Medicine ordered a spaceship for ten, plus training for a crew to fly there?"

Jolene drew in her breath. "How can Medicine afford that?"

"They haven't completed payment yet, nay have they sent enough personnel from Medicine to be trained at flight to be able to pilot or maintain it. They canna take possession till they have done so. I now suspect the funds to pay for it came from the credits stolen from the Houses. Proving all this will take time."

Jolene shook her head. "I can think of nay way to charge a Justine except by finding one of their names in one of the crystals. They possess credits from all the different planets. They dinna have their own. They just possess their storehouses of minerals and gold." Suddenly she turned and focused on Llewellyn.

"Yere laddie, Lorenz, would he be able to make a Justine confess?"

Llewellyn shook his head. "He would be able to if it were but one Justine, but even he canna fight off the minds of all the Justines. Besides, he has this belief that the authorities must prove their charges and a jury decide if one tis guilty or nay. He would nay agree to do so on speculation."

"He forced the Draygon to give us the coordinates to Draygon," she snapped.

"Aye, but he did nay make him confess to a crime."

JayEll stood. "I think our time would best be invested in creating what we need to have to begin this study. The mock wire cabinet should be ready within three to four days, as all the crystals are alike in composition. We will let ye ken."

Chapter 19

The Council of the Realm Meeting

The Council of the Realm Meeting that eve was not the most pleasant. Once they were all seated and welcomed, Radan stood.

"I demand a reimbursement of all funds sent to ye from Rurhran."

Jolene glared at his image on her small screen rather than turn and look at him. He refused to accept what he had been told this afternoon. "The funds were nay sent to me or Ayran. They were sent to a different account of someone from Ayran. From there, they may have been disbursed to other accounts. The secret accounts hidden in the crystals have nay been identified at this time." The various members of the different Houses were muttering.

"Let me explain to all Thalia," she continued and looked out at the assembly of Tris and House members from all of the continents. The casters, of course, were streaming the words and activities to all the screens in Thalia.

"It has been discovered that, at the time of the Justine occupation, certain crystals were installed at all the Ops Rooms, all the operating Directors of City, and all the operating City Centers of each House. Once the Justines were defeated, certain

Houses either discovered or already kenned where those hidden crystals were. Their funds were safe. The Houses that have had funds removed all this time were Medicine, Rurhran, and Ishner. Ishner has been ruled by the Sisterhood. The Maca of Ishner was arrested and made an Ab. With the ascent of Daniel as Maca of Ishner, the theft was discovered with the help of Jerome, Lad of Don." She paused for breath.

"The crystals were brought to my attention. I realized the funds were going to another person, and that person had to be the one in charge of making crystals. We found the crystal receiving funds in her Ops Room."

"Why isn't she here facing charges?" Radan's voice roared out, and people were murmuring the same thing.

"Janice tis in the last days of her decline. According to Medicine, she will nay live out the week." This time Jolene did swivel to the right to look back at Radan. "If ye will be so kind as to let me finish my report to all of Thalia, then I will try to answer yere questions." She turned back to face the others.

"I had removed the one from Ayran's Ops Room when we thought we had won against the Sisterhood. Janice did ask why I was returning the crystal. She thought I was a Sister. I informed her I would nay belong to anything that wished to harm my laddie, Jarvis, or my younger, JayEll. She bowed to me and said, 'I see.' " Jolene took a deep breath.

"There was nay point in asking Medicine or Rurhran to discontinue their crystals. Medicine was still ruled by Magda and Rurhran by Raven. Both were part of the Sisterhood. They had just disagreed with the extremes that Beauty was instituting. I nay ere expected Rurhran to ever request them to be removed. Like many, I made the error that Rocella was still in charge." She nodded at Radan. "I was wrong." Then she looked at Marita and Marta.

"The question remains about Medicine. Who tis in charge? Marta should ken how vicious the Sisterhood tis. They made her and her laddie Abs; however, Marta, who has remained in charge of Medicine, let the thievery continue. Did ye nay ken it was happening, Marita?"

Marita's mouth was slightly open, and her face had a tint of pink as though blushing. "I did question Mither about it once, but she said my elder, Magda, had set it up as a charitable support for the displaced Sisters and that many of them had grown eld. I believed her."

Jolene had a look of total disgust on her face as she turned to Marta sitting in Troy's counselor chair. "Ye could nay have believed that. There were nay Sisters displaced other than those made Abs. Ayran did nay receive any credits or packets of sustenance for the Abs from Medicine."

Marta had her lips in a straight line. "My mither would nay have lied to me. I continued Medicine as she had arranged it. She was a great Maca of Medicine. How dare ye imply otherwise?" It looked like she was going to stand, but Troyner put his hand on her arm before addressing Jolene.

"If ye have more questions, Counselor of the Realm, should they nay be done in private?"

Jolene started to retort and changed her mind. The Counselors quarreling in front of all Thalia was nay the way to inspire confidence. "Ye are correct, Troyner. It will be necessary to have private talks with both Medicine and Troy."

She looked back at the tier-filled section and the screen relaying the proceedings to all Thalians. "It will take approximately three days to set up our mock relay Ops Center, and then we will be able to compile the necessary information from the crystals. We still need to recover all the crystals from Medicine. Our next full Council of the Realm will be held in two weeks, and we should have a report by or even before then. My office will contact Rurhran, Troy, and Medicine for conferences. This tis nay the time to place blame on others without true information."

Radan stood again. "What of Ishner? Who is responsible now? I ken who has part of our funds in Rurhran." He looked at Marita in the Medicine section next to Rurhran's. "I am assuming Marita kens where they are in Medicine." He did nay see Marita swallow. She had nay idea who held any other funds.

"Ishner, however, tis different. May I suggest that Daniel, new Maca of Ishner, bring Ishmalisa or Illnor in for questioning." Somehow his voice managed to imply that Daniel would be as incompetent as Marita appeared to be.

Daniel's eyebrows rose, but he remained seated. "I have already questioned them. They claim they did nay ken funds had been returned to anyone. They assumed Beauty and Belinda were the recipients of the major withdrawals. If any tis being returned, I shall have to wait on Ayran's data and conclusions."

Jolene nodded in approval. "That tis the end of this eve's meeting. It was to inform all of Thalia of the problems that have been discovered and negate any false rumors. Somehow the Sisterhood has managed to steal our credits and cling to their dream of power. It will nay happen." She banged her fist down, signaling the end. An orderly procession began from all sections as there was no arena dining or fighting for the eve.

Chapter 20

The Courtship Continues

Jerome was delighted with his arrangement with Ishner and the Counselor of the Realm. He would meet Ieddie for lunch at one of Ishner's fish restaurants or bring a picnic lunch to share at the waterfront. Then he would proceed to the Guardian of the Realm's Ayran office for the afternoon if needed. Sometimes he and Ieddie would eat dinner in Ishner before he returned to Don, or she would meet him at the Warrior's Haven in Don for dinner. He intended to make every minute of the next three days count.

Ieddie, however, was becoming more impatient each day. How could this Earth being hold out so long without a bedding? It began to worry her.

On the third day, they were on the waterfront and away from the crowded boat area when Jerome opened the brews, but he was frowning. "I dinna quite ken how to put this. Tomorrow I must report to Ayran to help with the data research, which means we have less time."

Ieddie was certain he was about to say, "We had a great time. Farewell." She wondered why he was suddenly smiling at her.

"I think before we dine this eve, we should visit yere parents and tell them that we are considering to Walk the Circle. If they are receptive, mayhap they should dine with us so that we can all become acquainted."

Ieddie opened her mouth to explain, but somehow the words stuck in her throat. Didn't he realize that they had to go to his Maca first? Then it occurred to her that he might not. She forgot that she had nay told Jerome she would Walk the Circle with him.

"Jerome, my love, we canna go to my parents first. Ye are House. We must arrange a meeting with the Maca of Don for his permission."

Jerome chuckled. "Oh, that tis easy. When ye are through this eve, we will go there and then dine at Donnick's Warrior's Haven."

Ieddie stared at him for a moment. "Ye have nay even requested the meeting. How can ye be so certain he will see us?"

Jerome's smile broadened, and he pulled out his com and hit the circle for the Maca of Don. Llewellyn's face appeared. "Aye, tis there a problem?"

"In a manner of speaking, my Eldest Fither. It seems I must arrange to meet with ye and my beloved ere we meet with her parents about the Walk the Circle ritual. I really dinna ken some of yere different social customs, but I am trying to do my best in following them."

Llewellyn interrupted before Jerome expanded on nay kenning their customs. He was familiar with Jerome's ability to drone on about the smallest matter. "I'm busy right now." His lips smiled, and his eyes had a definite twinkle. "Instead, Brenda and I will expect ye both for dinner this eve at Brenda's Maca home." He broke the connection.

Jerome snapped the com shut before asking, "There, ye see how easy that was?"

Ieddie was staring at him. It was nay credible. She was but a Tri and now expected to dine with two Macas? What in Thalia's name was she to say to them?

Jerome put out his hands. "Let us have lunch at the Warrior's Haven like we planned and then we can return here and finish our work before we depart for Brenda's house."

"Uh, I think ye mean home."

Jerome sighed. "Aye, I always forget. House tis family and home tis where one dwells."

"I think it best if I try to figure out what I wear this eve when dining at a Maca's home."

"What tis wrong with what ye are wearing right now? I don't intend to change. There tis nay great fanfare there. Tis just a dinner with my family, and we tell Eldest Fither that we are in love and he gives his blessing."

Ieddie realized that Jerome did nay ken how serious this was. She tried again. "Jerome, we formally ask yere Maca for permission to Walk the Circle. If he or his counselor decide I am nay worthy, the request will be denied. I should at least look like I would fit into House and nay embarrass them."

"Grandpa Mac wouldn't refuse. He will be smiling the entire time." Jerome reverted to his Earth words.

Ieddie swallowed. "Ye call yere eldest fither that?"

"That tis what all the youngers on Earth call him—if they ken who he tis. Many nay longer do."

Ieddie shook her head. It was too much. She swallowed. "These are my work clothes."

"Ye mean yere dinner clothes would be different?" It was Jerome's turn to be puzzled. He couldn't tell any difference in the clothes of most Thalians. They basically wore a one-piece outfit that outlined their muscular structure. There didn't seem to be any of the high fashion he had seen on Earth.

"I dinna have the wide-sleeve formal top. Even if I did, I dinna have a Warrior's biceps. I canna afford the training." Ieddie blurted out the truth.

"We are not, uh, nay attending a formal dinner. We are having our evening meal with my," Jerome hesitated and continued, "with my eldest Fither and his counselor. I will not, uh. nay be in formal wear. Ye Gods, Grandpa Mac would think me crazed, but if it makes ye happy, I will go have lunch at a stand while ye think of something for this eve. I'll be back then to pick ye up." He hugged her, started to walk off, and turned. "I love ye. That tis all that matters."

* * *

Ieddie was beside Jerome as they landed on the padport by the Maca of Betron's home. She was in the same clothes as she wore to work, but it was the clean aqua suit for tomorrow. She had the teal Keepers sash firmly wrapped around her middle and the ends descended to her knee. She kenned this was pure folly, but Jerome was in a grand mood as they walked up the steps to the front as befitted someone coming with a petition.

Before Jerome even had a chance to touch the circle for visitors, the massive door swung open, and the huge form of Llewellyn swept Jerome up and into his arms. At least, thought Ieddie, Jerome tis putting his head on the shoulders correctly.

"Welcome, my youngest! Tis good to see ye." Llewellyn's deep voice was rumbling out after he had laid his head on Jerome's shoulders. "And this must be the lassie ye told me about."

The next thing Ieddie knew, she too was swooped up in the huge arms. Somehow she remembered to put her head on one shoulder and then the next before the Maca set her down and returned the greeting. "Welcome to my heart and to my House," Llewellyn's voice was still booming in her ears. No matter, something must be wrong. She couldn't have heard correctly. They had nay asked the formal question, nor had she been asked her lineage.

"Eldest Fither, this tis my beloved Ieddie. We ask yere permission to wed," Jerome's voice resounded in her head.

She tugged at Jerome's sleeve. "We are to kneel when ye ask that question, and it tis to Walk the Circle," she managed to protest. She looked helplessly at the Maca, expecting the rebuke he was sure to deliver.

"We what?" Jerome exploded.

Llewellyn draped his right arm over Jerome as he spoke to her. "My dear, this American laddie has nay intention of going on his knees to anyone, and I dinna expect it of him. Of course, ye have my permission to Walk the Circle." He was smiling broadly. "We should go in, as my counselor tis waiting for us. Tis this way." He motioned them forward.

Ieddie took a deep breath. This wasn't what she expected, but running was nay a solution either. Jerome put his arm around hern and they followed the Maca into the dining area with the massive table set with fine plates, goblets, and utensils. A huge roast, gravy, vegetables, buns, and butter filled the center.

"My darling, Brenda, this tis Ieddie of Ishner; she tis the young lassie our Jerome will Walk the Circle with when they decide the date."

"Ieddie, this tis my beloved counselor, Brenda, Maca of Betron," Llewellyn finished the introduction.

Ieddie bowed and looked up. Brenda was six-foot-three and heavily muscled as a House Warrior, but the big shock was the fact that she held out her arms. Ieddie walked into them and had to stretch to put her head on Brenda's shoulders, but at least she managed. Brenda finalized the greeting, and then she and Jerome performed the ritual.

"Now tis time to dine." He and Brenda took the chairs on one side so that they were side-by-side. Jerome and Ieddie sat across from them. Ieddie couldn't help but notice that Jerome seemed to bow his headm but it was nay directed at either Maca. Brenda was busy helping herself to the roast.

Once Jerome lifted his head, Llewellyn jabbed a slice of roast and pushed the platter toward Jerome. "Help yereself. Tis from Don's kine, of course."

Jerome grinned, and they all busied themselves filling their plates and eating. The mugs were filled with the butter brew from Rurhran, a golden brew that would have been called blond stout in Jerome's world.

"Aye, of course, the roast tis from Don. Did ye ken that Pawpaw is trying to convince David to take over the carvers or the dairy production and distributing?" Jerome asked. "He tis also insisting I take over the books for one or the other when my stint for the Guardian of the Realm tis over."

"Aye, he claims both have grown considerably in the last century and his time on the prairie tis curtailed." Llewellyn grimaced and shrugged. "I think it tis a good idea. In fact, if ye are like Andrew, ye could just take over the dairy business along with the books."

"Will ye two be going to yere parents when ye leave here?" It was Brenda's turn to ask a question.

Ieddie took a deep breath. "That tis what we planned. Aye, but mayhap I should warn my parents first, and then we would go tomorrow to ask their permission. They have nay met Jerome," she added the last in a rush.

Brenda tilted her head. The lighter brown hair of Betron outlining her cheeks. "Ye have nay warned them at all?"

Ieddie swallowed. "Nay, there hasn't been time. My sister may have, though."

Brenda was puzzled. "Are nay Ilaman and Ilonnie the new Director and Keeper of the First Center of Iconda? Are they well?"

Ieddie was dumbfounded. How could a Maca ken her parents? "They are nay the Director and Keeper anymore, but they are well. My sister tis trying to make an appointment with the Maca to find them better quarters. Uh, the Sisterhood moved them to the fringes of Iconda." She didn't say the broken area.

"That tis outrageous. Llewellyn, ye must speak to yere younger. He should have reappointed them and given them a Director's home." Brenda definitely had their attention.

"Did ye ken them ere the Sisterhood took over?" Llewellyn was curious.

"Aye, he was the one that could arrange the best delivery of the smoked fish and other succulents from Ishner when we held the celebration of Beltayne in the spring," she answered. "I was hoping to contact him for this year's celebration but could nay find them."

Ieddie was shifting in her chair, trying to think of a way to run without divulging more about her parents' plight.

Jerome looked at Brenda then at Ieddie. "What tis wrong, my love?"

Ieddie took a deep breath. "I should have kenned this was folly. I should nay be here. The Sisters made my parents nay for their refusal to part. They dinna exist on the rolls. Nay would they let them work. They were in the poorest section of Iconda till I became a Keeper with a small home of my own." She rose and was about to run out of the room when Jerome stepped in front of her.

Llewellyn's booming voice was heard. "Then tell yere Maca. Daniel will ken immediately. He and his mither were Abs under the Sisterhood. So was Jarvis, Maca of Ayran." He looked at Ieddie.

"Did the Sisterhood nay teach anything about how they almost destroyed Thalia?" Brenda was also standing.

Ieddie was standing with her mouth open, trying to digest the news. She had heard the whispers that Daniel had been Ab, but there had been nay in the lessons other than Llewellyn was a Thalian/Justine mutant and his laddie, Lorenz, Laird of Don, a dangerous primitive, an Earth/Justine mutant who had destroyed the former Kenning Woman. Ileana had once told her that the history the Sisters were teaching was nay truth-filled, but she had kenned it was too dangerous to discuss why.

"Everything the Sisters did to us in Ishner was odious. Nay ken if our new Maca can stop them. We ken the Sisters will still try to stop him. They are more powerful than any ken." Ieddie was sobbing.

"Stop that," snapped Brenda. "We all ken that. The Sisters almost killed my Benji when he was a youth, and then Beauty, my own sib, did when he was mature. They are always trying for a comeback. We won't let them. Ye must nay be fearful and whimper like a wee one."

Llewellyn interrupted Brenda's flow. "Ye need to convince yere parents either to make an appointment with their Maca or attend one of the Maca gatherings so they can explain what happened and tell of their skills. There are many places there that need capable beings."

Ieddie looked at them all. "How can ye make all those years right?" She tore out of Jerome's embrace and started to leave, then turned back.

"I must apologize. I had expected ye to throw me out the minute I walked through yere door. That broke down my defenses. I bid ye all goodbye." She gave a short bow and ran to the outside.

"We will have her parents contact ye on my com. Excuse me for the rush." Jerome tore after her without the formal goodbye and Llewellyn's voice booming, "Aye," behind him. He found her pacing in front of his lift. Her hands were balled into fists.

"Just take me back to Ishner." She turned to the door that didn't open.

Instead, Jerome's arms were around her and he was holding her close. "My darling, my heart, we are going to your parents and telling them of our love. If ye truly must ask them for permission to Walk the Circle at your age, do so, but we are going to Walk the Circle nay matter what they say."

"Didn't they just tell ye nay?" Ieddie asked.

"Of course, they didn't." Jerome was back to using his English speech. "If we do not Walk the Circle, it is because you refuse to walk it with me."

Ieddie buried her head onto his chest. "How can I ever face them again?"

"We could go back in right now, but that will just waste time." Jerome was becoming a bit impatient. Had he chosen wrong?

She looked up at him, a slow smile spreading on her face. "Ye are the most stubborn man I have ever met, and I love ye."

Chapter 21

Wrongs Revealed

Ilaman and Ilonnie were sitting open-mouthed, staring at the impressive looking Lad of Don in his royal blue suit and beaming blue eyes. Their daughter had just said the most preposterous thing after introducing the man. She was frowning at them.

"Dinna ye hear me? I just asked for yere permission and blessing for us to Walk the Circle."

"Of course, we give our permission and blessing," they both stammered, "but what will the Maca of Don think or say? Look at this place. We are the poorest of Thalians."

"Oh, he has already given his blessing. He tis expecting a call from ye," answered Jerome and then noticed that their faces reddened. "I told him ye would be calling on my com to arrange the time."

Ilaman and Ilonnie both stood. "He kens how far we were cast down?" Ilonnie whispered.

"I, I became impatient and told them everything. I thought they would order me out," Ieddie explained.

"Who tis they," Ilaman asked?

"We had dinner with my eldest fither and his counselor," Jerome replied. "Ieddie was wrong in her thinking just as ye are. Eldest Fither is making an appointment for ye with Daniel tomorrow morning. That way things can be straightened out."

The couple looked at each other. "Ileanna or Ieddie will need to transport us. We have nay fliv or lift."

"Jerome, this tis folly." Ieddie was becoming impatient again. "Ileanna and I must be at the center ere then and ready to open."

"Ieddie, I can transport them there at the correct time since I must be at Ishner's Tower to work in the Ops room. Now, uh," Jerome realized he wasn't sure of the Thalian way to address her parents. "It tis time for ye to call my eldest fither." He handed his com to Ilaman.

Ilaman grasped the com in his hand, but was shaking his head. "Tis kind of ye, but I canna offer anything for the celebration." He tried to hand the com back.

Jerome threw up his hands. "Ye gods, man, what would ye normally offer?"

"Why, the smoked and pickled delicacies from the sea, of course. Nay else would have them, and I ken all the perfect markets."

A wide smile split Jerome's face. "Perfect. If ye have nay position by the time we Walk the Circle, I will pay for them."

The three were staring at him. "That tis nay the usual way things are done," Ieddie objected.

"Who cares?" Jerome snorted. "Both Ieddie and I are over one hundred years. This tis my second marriage. Tis nay uncommon for couples to pay for their own wedding in my land."

Of course, all three were blinking their eyes. Except for the 'who cares,' none quite fathomed all of what he was saying.

Jerome took the com, opened it, punched the right circles, and handed it back to Ilaman. "Aye," came Llewellyn's rumbling voice.

"Maca of Don, this tis Ilaman of Ishner. We agree to Ieddie's and Jerome's request to Walk the Circle and joyfully give our blessing." He wet his lips.

"Excellent," boomed Llewellyn. "I can schedule it for two weeks from now. That gives everyone a chance to notify the guests, arrange for JayEll to attend as a Martin, and order the food and brew. Do ye have any preference for a brew from Rurhran?"

Ilaman gulped. "Nay, Maca of Don, order what pleases ye. Uh, my counselor and I would like to bring some of the smoked and pickled delicacies of Ishner."

Llewellyn grinned. "All will appreciate that. By the way, yere appointment with the Maca of Ishner tis at eight o'clock in the morn. I hope that tis nay too early, but he has other appointments."

Jerome was shaking his head "yes." Ilaman took a deep breath, "I thank ye, Maca of Don."

"Tis welcome, ye are. I'm sure we'll be in touch again. I'll let ye ken where and when the delicacies are to be delivered. Farewell."

Ilaman turned the com off and handed it back to Jerome. Before he had a chance to say anything, Ilonnie had thrown her arms up on Jerome's shoulders. "I would lay my head on yere shoulders as our thanks."

Jerome, however, remembered Thalian etiquette and laid his head on her shoulders first. "I thank ye, my mither-to-be."

After the courtesies, Jerome bowed. "I promised Ieddie a brew at the Warrior's Haven in Donnick. Would ye care to join us?"

Ilonnie sighed. "We canna. Ye see, the Sisters took our Ishner clothing. Tis why we are wearing the color of the Sisterhood." She swallowed.

Jerome looked at Ieddie. "Did ye or yere sister nay save anything?"

"There was nay chance. It was all we could do to save one outfit each for ourselves. The only ones wearing teal or aqua were House or someone that might be seen by the other Houses."

Jerome sighed and turned to the older couple. "I will make sure that orders go in for yere clothes for our celebration." He turned to Ieddie. "And now to the Warrior's Haven."

* * *

Jerome woke and realized someone was resting on his shoulder. He almost bolted out of bed and then realized it was Ieddie. She had insisted on coming home with him. He realized he could no longer put off the Thalian manner of courtship, and agreed. The night had proven everything his eldest fither had ever said about a Thalian bedding. He was still in a bit of a shock as she had called him, "Magnificent." He reached over and stroked Ieddie's face and arm.

"Darling lassie, we have a little time if ye dinna mind eating breakfast on the run."

It was doubtful that Ieddie understood "breakfast on the run," but she kenned what he meant by a little time. She wrapped her arms around him as his hand slid downward.

Chapter 22

Wrongs Righted

Ilaman and Ilonnie stood behind Jerome when he led them into the Maca's office. Daniel rose and greeted first Jerome and then realized the couple were on edge, almost ready to bolt out of the door. He spread his arms wide.

"I am Maca and I issue my call."

For a moment, the couple stood transfixed, staring at him, and then stepped into his embrace, murmuring, "My Maca, my Maca."

The formalities over, Jerome gave a half-bow. "The Ops Room is expecting me. This couple will need a transport for returning to their home or whatever ye assign them and also a com."

Ilaman and Ilonnie stared opened-mouthed at Jerome's retreating back as he walked out the door. The idea that their laddie-to-be could tell a Maca what to do didn't really register in their Thalian minds.

"Please have a seat so we can go over some ideas," said Daniel. "I looked for ye both when I reassigned people to the Centers, but could nay find yere names in the register. I have ordered them restored, but I am curious. How did ye receive yere food from the Center without being registered?"

"The Sisters had erased our names off the roll when we refused to separate. Ileana managed to receive our rations through the dole for any Ab passing through."

"I am surprised Ileana did nay tell me ye still lived when her counselor left."

"She feared to do so. What if ye had fallen in a day or two? Then the Sisters would have been after us again," Ilonnie answered.

"Tis nay much confidence ye place in me," was Daniel's mild remark.

"All we kenned was that ye are a Warrior. What happens when the Guardian of Flight calls ye to return? Do ye miss a battle or the training?" Ilaman voice was bitter.

Daniel started to object, but realized this couple did nay ken him. "Since I am still here, let's proceed on the thought that I intend to remain. What other accomplishments do ye have other than running the First Center of Iconda?"

Ilaman leaned forward. "I was the one that arranged Ishner's display at the Beltayne Celebration in Bretta, and all the three cities on Ishner. Although most that live here go to Port Isaac, or did ere the Sisterhood shut down all celebrations."

"I see," said Daniel. "Why would the Sisterhood stop the Beltayne Celebration? It would give people something to do."

"They feared the lassies and laddies would find each other," Ilonnie sniffed.

"If things improve enough, I'll have ye put together a display for Beltayne in Bretta and here. If nay, there will be stands and games here. In the meantime, I suggest yere lassie install one or both of ye as Keepers at the First Center. She and Ieddie have been putting in long hours. I will also assign a lift at your disposal and a com. I believe it would be best if ye lived closer to the Center. Do ye have any kenning of the area?"

"Aye, once we planned on retiring nearer the waterfront. Nay on it, ye ken, but a couple of rows away. We even had the home ready to move into or to take our days off there." The bitterness was back into Ilaman's voice. "We were locked out of that also."

Daniel leaned forward. "Where was this home?"

"Four rows over from the back padports for this Tower and three up from the waterfront," Ilaman replied.

Daniel's finger was busy touching the circles and lines on his desk. An image of a round Thalian home appeared. It was set in the midst of an overgrown weed-filled lot, but one could clearly see the floor level and estimate it to be the usual retirement home of two bedrooms, a great room, kitchen area, an ops room, a gym, and a pool that was half in the back of the home and half into the open. The occupants could close off the pool from the outside in the winter.

The couple leaned forward. "Why tis the yard in such deplorable condition? What tis wrong with those that dwell there?"

"Ilonnie, nay dwell there," said Daniel. "I am going to restore it to ye. I am also restoring yere lift and com." He paused and looked at them. "Ye are still capable of flying one, are ye nay?"

"Aye, Maca," they chorused.

"Fine, once that information tis imputed, yere prints and eyes for controlling the lift and the locks on the home will be done. Ye should examine the home. If vandals have damaged it, I'll either assign another or have it repaired. Ye may move in at any time. Tis that acceptable?"

Both Ilaman and Ilonnie had tears in their eyes. "Aye, Maca," they whispered.

"Good," Daniel nodded at them and hit the circle for the Ops room. "Issing, I am sending Ilaman and Ilonnie to ye. They need to be assigned a lift, a com, and this home. Ye will take care of that?"

Issing's smiling face appeared. "Tis my pleasure, Daniel. Welcome back, Ilaman and Ilonnie."

Chapter 23

Ma

Ma, clothed in the brown of an Ab, strode towards the Maca of Ishner and shouted, "I am Ma. I Challenge ye to the Death."

Daniel turned from his greeting of the Ishner populace around him. This was his morning for meeting the inhabitants at the Second Center of Iconda. He realized that the woman was as tall and as blocky as he was. He inclined his head, "I shall meet ye at the Maca's Tower within the hour."

"Nay, we fight now." Ma roared back and started to remove her tunic. Minnay's gloved hand touched Ma's still clad shoulder.

"He has the right to arrange the time. Then all the Houses will be there to see ye win."

Ma glared at her, then at Daniel. Her brown eyes were swinging back and forth. "Do ye tell the truth?"

"Aye, come bide at the shore. We will await his return nearer the Tower," Minnay answered.

Ma lumbered behind Minnay and Maybelle as they walked to the waterfront. Once there, Ma began doing squats and stretches. She sparred into space as though all the movements were the way to pass time.

Minnay was correct. The Houses were alerted, and they flew in to see the Challenge, as did many of the higher ranking Tris.

Lorenz was out on the range with the kine. Diana spent nearly thirty minutes trying to reach him and finally left a message on his com. "Our laddie, Daniel, tis Challenged to the Death by an Ab from Medicine at nine of the clock."

Lorenz heard her sobs when he touched the com button nearly twenty minutes later. He frowned, shook his head, and sprinted to his fliv to head straight to Ishner. He didn't bother to remove his range clothes or the ancient Colt in his holster.

The crowd formed a circle around the two combatants. Both had stripped down to a thong.

"Do ye concede?" Ma demanded, her face was frozen and her eyes like glass.

"We fight," was Daniel's reply, and the two huge forms bunched their fists and swayed toward each other, both looking for an opening or a weak spot.

Ma threw the first punch which sailed past Daniel's head. He landed a blow against her left temple, and she lunged at him. Daniel went into the leaping spin favored by Don and landed a kick to her side.

He was surprised at the pain shooting up his leg, and he realized he had kicked something more solid than Thalian flesh. Would this fight be his last? Whatever he was fighting was nay as fast as he was, and it was his only advantage.

She lunged at him and missed as he brought his fist down on her back, but she rolled away and was up swaying towards him. Daniel was blinking his eyes. Something was wrong with his thinking, and her fist smashed into his chest, knocking him backward.

The crowd was watching every move. They did not see the blue Don fliv land or the determined man step out of it and draw his blaster from the door's side pocket. They did not see his bowlegged march towards the fight as he pushed people out his way. One look at that set face and blaster was enough to cause the crowd to part.

Ma had Daniel by the biceps and was about to lift him when the man's blaster erupted, cutting a line down Ma's back. One of the Troopers next to the Guardian of the Realm raised her blaster but stopped, opened-mouthed as fire and sparks flew out of Ma's back.

Ma stood, immobile as the sparks and fire raged in her interior. Daniel was able to pry her fingers away and stepped back, a blank look on his face. The crowd was moving away from Ma.

Jolene, Guardian of the Realm, had her hand on Captain Beni's arm to keep her from firing at Lorenz as she yelled, "Lorenz, Laird of Don, how did ye ken?"

Lorenz did not take his eyes away from the robotic droid that had threatened Daniel as he responded, "I was the one that searched those islands around Ayran before Medicine relocated. There were no Abs. The only living mammals were clegs, nay else but birds."

"How can ye be so sure?" Jolene asked.

"I'm sure." The voice was as hard as his face and eyes.

Jolene decided this was not the place for a dispute and turned to Captain Beni. "Quick, arrest those from Medicine that were with that monstrosity."

Beni motioned to two of the Troopers to follow her, and the three took off on a run after Minnay and Maybelle.

Llewellyn had started to move towards Daniel. JoAnne and Diana were already beside him, steadying him.

"Papa, you take those three to Malta at the Warrior's Academy Medical. That thing was probably infected with something to disable Daniel. My wife and his fiancée are probably infected now. Y'all will need cleansing too once you're there." Lorenz's alien voice and words roared across the space. He figured the Guardian wasn't through with her questions yet.

"Stay, Llewellyn," Jolene interrupted. She was wracking her brain to remember what Lorenz's alien words meant. "I need ye at a quick Council meeting. All the Guardians and Counselors of the Realm follow me, and that means ye, Laird of Don." She turned towards the Maca of Ishner's Tower as the closest building with a proper meeting area.

"The hell, I will. I'm taking my son to the Warrior's Medical," Lorenz yelled after her.

Jarvis, Maca of Ayran, stepped forward, a tight grin below his wedge of a nose. "My Laird, I would be honored to take them."

Lorenz looked at the blocky, Warrior son of Jolene and nodded. "I trust y'all. Make sure y'all and your fliv are disinfected too."

"Aye," Jarvis nodded and headed towards the three.

"Jarvis," Jolene yelled after him. "Ye and JoAnne are part of the Council."

Jarvis turned slightly. "Use Jada. Without the Laird, I would be dead." He led the way towards his fliv while speaking into his com to tell Malta what was needed when they arrived.

Jolene glared after him. She could nay break that adulation that Jarvis and JayEll held for the man that rescued them. Captain Beni was returning with the two prisoners from Medicine. Jolene looked at the House members who had gathered to watch the Death Challenge and saw both Marita and her mother, Marta.

"Marita and Marta, ye have questions to answer also," she snapped at them and turned towards Pillar.

"Guardian of Army," she ordered, "appoint Warriors to guard that thing. Nay are to touch it, and then ye are to join us." She led the way into the Tower and up the stairs to the meeting room.

When all were seated except for the Troopers and the two prisoners, Jolene looked at Marita. "Why did ye allow them to build a forbidden droid?"

Marita answered, "I did nay ken they were building a droid. They told me they were working on a breakthrough for Medicine."

Jolene looked at her in disbelief. "Surely ye asked what it was and checked their progress."

"I took them at their word. They claimed it was a surprise."

"What kind of Maca are ye?" Jolene was near to yelling. "They had to have a huge amount of credits for what it took to build what tis illegal."

Marita could think of no words to refute the accusation.

"And just what do ye propose to do with these two that have broken the Thalian law of building robot droids and the one against the killing of Thalians?" Jolene's voice was hard and demanding.

Marita swallowed. "They are now Abs. They are to be stripped of Medicine's colors, and their punishment tis in the hands of the Council. If nay, I will condemn them to harsh labor."

"Y'all are a little late. Daniel could have been killed." Lorenz muttered.

"Very well, then I move that we try these two before the regular Council meeting after we have completed the investigation at Medicine to see if Marita and Marta were cognizant of what they were creating, and to ascertain if anything else tis brewing or being built there that tis nay allowed. Guardians and Counselors, does this meet with yere approval?"

"Nay!" Marta was on her feet shouting. "How dare ye imply that my lassie or I could be guilty of such crimes?"

"Will ye sit down?" Jolene banged her fist on the table. "Right now, it would seem ye are more apt to be guilty than Marita. All ken how negligent of Medicine she has been. Ye are the one that ran Medicine for thirty-one years ere she had her Confirmation Rite. Since then, ye have run it, nay she." Jolene left out, *We all ken that she prefers pina pods or any growing plant to to real beings.*

Marta's face reddened, and it looked like she was ready to shout again, when her counselor, Troyner, grabbed her arm and spoke in a lowered tone, "Marta, sit down. They have to investigate where the credits came from and who authorized them."

Troyner's face was worried as he wasn't sure whether Marta had ordered credits transmitted to them or nay.

Marta whirled on him. "Ye too?" She was ready to fight.

Lorenz's flat voice drawled out. "I have a hunch the Sisters were using the credits they were draining away from the various Houses."

"That may be true, Laird of Don." Jolene was still using the formal address as the man looked ready to start fighting anyone that disagreed with him. "That tis one of the things we will verify."

She turned to the Guardian of Army. "Pillar, I will consult with ye for yere recommendations to help with guarding and with the investigation. I canna spare Captain Beni."

Lorenz stood. "Fine. I vote, 'Aye,' on your proposal to try them at the regular meeting and investigate the source of the credits for Medicine. Now, I'm going to find out how my son and my wife are." He did his bowlegged march out of the room.

Jolene sat opened-mouthed and then looked at Llewellyn and asked, "Can ye nay stop him?"

A smile cut his square face. "I have nay been able to stop him since he turned eighteen. That was long before we came here." He too rose. "Like my laddie, I vote 'Aye,' on all yere proposals. I am going to check on my younger and my laddie's counselor."

At least Llewellyn's words made sense to Jolene. "Well," she asked the remaining members of the Houses, "how do ye vote?"

* * *

Once they were in the reception rotunda, Lorenz and Llewellyn were hailed by Linda. "The Guardian of the Realm was just forwarded the message that all arrived safely and are being decontaminated.

"Are they released and returning here?" Lorenz asked.

“They have nay been released yet,” she answered. She watched both men walk out.

Chapter 24

Discovery

Malta was in the crowd watching the Challenge to the Death and heard the Laird's command to take Daniel to the Warrior's Medical. She ran for her black Warrior's lift. She had to be at the Warrior Academy ere the others reached there. Once airborne, she touched the control to connect to the Medicine Lab at the Academy and ignored the beeping from the sound of Jarvis trying to reach her.

"Have four rooms and/or beds ready for the cleansing procedure. Alert the padport attendant that the fliv of the Maca of Ayran will need to be disinfected and cleansed. Have four Meds in protective suits, globes, and gloves with four floating covered gurneys waiting. Bring my protective suit, globe, and gloves with ye. They will be landing at the Academy's padport for the Maca of Ayran."

She closed that circuit and opened the one from Jarvis. Before he could speak her words tumbled out. "I was at the Challenge. The gurneys will be waiting for us, and they are ready to disinfect yere fliv."

Malta, the oldest lassie of Ishmael and Melanie, looked like her elder Magna, the former Maca. She was short, even for someone from Medicine. Her features were sharp, and her eyes almost as black as her hair.

She piled out of her lift and ran to where the attendants would arrive with the gurneys. She saw the red fliv of Jarvis descending as four attendants with gurneys came dashing up. The lead one with the gurneys handed her the protective suit, globe, and gloves. She donned them as the doors opened and the people stepped out of Jarvis's fliv. JoAnne was supporting Daniel.

"Get him on the gurney and inside," Malta commanded through her mouthpiece. "Jarvis, ye will be cleansed too. Ye were breathing the same air as Daniel. All of ye, on the gurneys."

Jarvis gave a half-bow and sat on the gurney. JoAnne and Diana were looking at her in disbelief and at the gurneys.

"Ye both touched him. Ye could be infected with whatever tis wrong with our StarPath Finder," Malta yelled, using the Warrior's name for Daniel. JoAnne and Diana went on the gurneys as instructed. The attendants pushed their controls to cover the occupants, and followed the gurneys at a run into the building and down to Medical. All the attendants were from Medical, but had been carefully selected by Melanie and Malta.

"I will analyze the vapors as they are extracted," Malta said to them by pushing the control on her suit. "If any have a problem, red button me." She removed the globe and entered her medical cubicle to wait for the cleansing to work. Within minutes the first fumes from Daniel were going through the scanner. The reports on his physical wellness were beaming onto her screen. Malta scowled and half-rose out of her chair. The Guardian of the Realm was nay going to like her report. Marita and Marta, she dismissed as worse than ineffectual.

Jarvis was the first one out of the Cleansing room, and she could hear him bellowing for someone to throw him a thong. She did nay care if he traipsed through without clothes, but realized she needed to order clothes for the Lass of Ayran and the Laird of Don's counselor. "Bring robes and thongs for two women who stand six feet three inches," she commanded to Academy student at the front. "Also, a thong and uniform for our StarPath Finder, Daniel." She hoped they would arrive before anyone else and went back to the scan and her report for the Guardian of the Realm.

Ten minutes went flying, and Malta sent the encoded report to the Guardian of the Realm. She stared at the screen and decided not to send it to Medicine. She would discuss the results with the Guardian of Flight and Guardian of the Realm. If Marita remained free, then she would discuss the results with her. She stood and stepped out into the Medical lobby as JoAnne and Diana were donning their robes.

"How tis my laddie?" Diana's question was more of a demand.

"He tis almost cleansed," Malta answered.

One of the Keepers from the wardrobe room came running in with Daniel's clothes. Behind him was the Laird of Don, his face still like granite, and those huge, grey eyes of an Earth being focused on her as he asked, "Is Daniel all right?" He stepped up to Diana and wrapped his arms around her.

She saw the huge form of Llewellyn entering the room. How was it that the Laird of Don was in front of his fither and his Maca? "I believe they are finishing now," Malta replied.

Jolene and JayEll ran into the room, and Jolene enclosed JoAnne in her arms while murmuring, "My lassie, my lassie."

As if to relieve the tension, a nude Daniel emerged from the cleansing room.

Daniel looked at the four waiting for him, grabbed the thong from the Keeper, and attached it. JoAnne and Diana had almost thrown themselves across the distance; JoAnne was on his right and Diana was on his left.

Malta shook her head and looked towards the Laird. He was smiling that magical smile that transformed his grim features into the most handsome of men. The grey eyes were shining like silver orbs, and she had the greatest urge to hug him as she had done as a child. Fortunately, Daniel prevented any such breach of manners. Somehow with both women hanging onto him, Daniel had crossed the short distance to his father. It was as though the two hanging onto him were no hindrance as he picked his fither up and laid his head first on the right shoulder and then the left. The Laird's arms were around him. Malta noticed that JoAnne was frowning at the others as though they were interlopers.

Daniel smiled at his fither, and swallowed. "Fither, once again, I owe ye my life. I could nay have beaten that thing."

"Hell, no one could," Lorenz growled, and laid his head on both of Daniel's shoulders.

"Now, put me down, Lug," Lorenz commanded and tousled Daniel's hair. Once on the floor, he looked at Malta. "Was I right about the cleansing?"

"Aye, my Elder," she replied, using the childhood term. Her parents, Melanie and Ishmael had been friends with Lorenz and Diana before they were even wed. She had kenned them all her life. "I have sent the reports to the Guardian of the Realm and to the Guardian of Flight, but prefer nay to say what I found where others may hear me." She kenned the gossiping ways of Thalia well.

JoAnne and Diana were now looking at her. "Do ye mean there was something that transferred to us just from touching him?"

Malta decided that much she would answer. "Aye, from the touching and from breathing the same air in the fliv. Jarvis was affected also, but nay as bad. That tis why ye were advised to return here immediately if ye felt extraordinarily sleepy."

"Sleep does nay last after a cleansing," snapped Jolene.

Malta's face remained bland. "Aye, it does nay. Yere Guardian of the Realm office has my report. Ye and the Council of the Realm will decide how much the rest of Thalia will hear."

"Llewellyn and I will hear it now; in yere office," Jolene ordered.

Malta looked at them both. Llewellyn was wed to the Maca of Betron. Why did Jolene just name him her de facto counselor? Yet, he did nay act like the Counselor of the Realm. Were the rumors true? Did Llewellyn really control the Council of the Realm? She would need to check with her fither. Llewellyn was Maca of Don, and Guardian of Flight. In essence, the latter meant he also controlled the Warrior Academy and the Army even though Pillar was Guardian of Army. She smiled at them. "This way, please." Of course, all kenned where Medical's office was. All had trained in this building.

Once in her office, she realized that Lorenz, Daniel, JoAnne, JayEll, and Pillar had followed everyone into the office. She would have liked to order them out, but realized every one of them was on the Council of the Realm.

She took a seat and made sure the door was secure by pressing the circle on her desk. She looked up at them. "Guardian of the Realm, I suggest ye have the Maca of Medicine seal the room those two used to work on that monstrosity and create the cream they used, if they are the ones that created it. The cream they used is an enhanced form of Sleep. No one would have woke up from it." She let her words sink into their brains.

Jolene swallowed. "Do ye mean all would have died, including my laddie and lassie?"

"Aye, Jolene, that tis exactly what I mean. The Laird of Don not only saved Daniel's life, but that of anyone that would have touched him once he was felled. I have already alerted your guards that surround the droid to nay touch it or allow anyone to touch it. Any that do must be cleansed immediately."

"Can I dispatch Troopers to clear everything out of that room now?" asked Jolene.

"I would nay. They would need protective suits. I prefer the Guardian of Army or of Flight give me the names of those that will be going into the room so that they can be supplied with protective suits from here. I dinna trust Medicine." Her voice was harsh.

Jolene stood and looked at Pillar. "I want ye to assign Troopers to guard that door at Medicine. I dinna care if ye make it four- or eight-hour shifts. Bide a moment while I contact the Maca of Medicine."

She pushed another circle on her com, thinking that the poor excuse of a Thalian Maca had best answer.

Marita's face appeared. "Have the room where those two built that droid locked and sealed. I am sending Troopers to guard it until it can be examined by all after Malta assures me it tis safe."

"It is already locked, Guardian of the Realm," Marita replied using Jolene's formal title. "What time will ye be here?"

Jolene looked at those in the room and turned back. "We shall be there at ten o'clock tomorrow morning, but I am sending Troopers to guard the door." She closed the circuit and looked at Malta. "Will that give ye time enough?"

"It should," Malta replied.

Jolene stood. "We shall see each other tomorrow. Daniel, I give thanks that yere fither tis so clever."

A wide grin split Daniel's face. "As do I."

Chapter 25

Changes

Marianne was in her lab working with others testing the properties of certain plants when someone ignored the Do Not Disturb sign and burst into the lab, shouting, "Ye will miss the Challenge!"

She straightened. "What Challenge?"

"Why, some Ab from here has Challenged the Maca of Ishner to the Death!" the young student yelled and dashed back to the viewing screen.

"Nay possible," Marianne muttered, but stripped off her gloves, globe, and protective suit before walking into the study room where the others were. They were looking at the screen and then back at her.

"Dismissed," she snapped. "Write up your summaries and submit them tonight." She sat at the controls to watch the Challenge.

She stared with horror at the unfolding debacle. She had warned Minnay and Maybelle nay to use Ma till more testing had been done. She had also warned against using the new Sleep. What if the droid malfunctioned and hit or touched the surrounding watchers. Now all she could do was remain silent and hope they did nay reveal anything about the Sisterhood here or on Ishner. Rurhran she discounted except for the funds that Rocella probably possessed. She wasn't sure how long she sat there lost in thought while running various scenarios through her mind as to what she should do or not do.

Her com beeped, and she touched the circle. It was Marly, the one instructor that would teach laddies, or men when they were older. Marianne breathed a sigh of relief. This should be a safe call.

"Did ye just see what happened?" Marly asked.

"I doubt if few missed it," was Marianne's response.

"They will be imprisoned or sent to the mines. Minnay tis too old." Marly was one of the old Maca's defenders. "Worse, they will send investigators here." Her voice rose. "Do ye ken that Minnay's research room tis already locked?"

"I did nay. Why would anyone go there now?" Marianne hoped someone was recording this. It would make her look innocent. "How could ye ken so quickly?"

"One of my students ran across the hall to retrieve her papers. She said she had been doing research."

"How foolish. Anything in that room will be examined. I am also certain that the cameras will be checked to see who tried to gain entrance and remove any evidence. As it tis, the students or researchers that worked with Minnay and Maybelle or in their laboratory will be questioned."

Marly's face registered horror. "How can ye be so sure?"

"Ye gods, Marly, they broke two cardinal laws; make nay Thalian being-looking droid and dinna murder another Thalian. That Daniel still lives tis only because of his mutant fither. The Council will make sure that those who are guilty are punished."

She closed her com rather than look at Marly's sad face any longer. She had to think. Had she left anything in that lab room? Would Minnay and Maybelle have her name on file for some reason? The latter was a possibility when it came to funding for that damn droid. Was there anything in their files that said she kenned their plans? She had advised them to nay input any incriminating information on their notes at the start of the project, and to always use caution as to who was in the room when they proceeded to build it. Would they have recorded any com communications? She grimaced. *If I were a praying person, I would pray to Gar that they did nay,* she thought.

* * *

Timor hurried to be by Marita's side when she walked towards her fliv after the brief meeting and as the others left to check on Daniel and the ones with him. "Ye must lock the doors to all of Minnay's and Maybelle's labs, classrooms, and private dwellings," he warned her.

Marita didn't protest. "I already locked the lab and classrooms, but I'll do their dwellings now."

She used her com. Once that was done, she headed straight for Logan, who was leaning against the short wall that circled back around the Maca of Ishner's tower. He put out his arms to welcome her, and they stood there swaying in their embrace.

Marta grabbed at Troyner's arm as they came down the steps. "Stop her, Troyner. Get her away from him!"

Troyner looked at the couple and back at his counselor. "Do ye nay ken that if we try to do that, it will just drive her closer to him?"

Marta glared at him and marched over to the couple. "Ye must come home with us now!" she demanded and grasped Marita's arm.

Marita turned on her. "How dare ye! Timor and I are going to Medicine. If I do nay stay there all evening, I'll be at Logan's home or my own."

Logan smiled at her then looked at Marta. "Ye ken that we are planning to Walk the Circle in about ten years." He paused, shrugged, and said, "Mayhap sooner."

Marta was left with her mouth open. That mutant! That was nay the way the parents were asked. She shuddered. Marita was a Maca. If she asked it would be out of love or courtesy. Marta set her teeth and marched after Marita. Troyner frowned and decided he had best follow her.

Marta caught up with Marita as she was opening her fliv door. "Marita, dear, we need to go to Medicine."

Marita turned on her again. "Nay, Mither, I need to go to Medicine. Ye are to stay away from there. Ye may come if the Guardian of the Realm orders ye to be there tomorrow to answer any questions. Timor and I are going to Medicine to make sure that the Troopers the Counselor of the Realm is sending will be stationed correctly, have water, and/or a place to rest." She stepped into the fliv and the door slid shut.

Marta was left alone. She realized Timor's fliv was already in the air. Marta whirled right into Troyner's chest. He put his arms around her. "My counselor, ye are too distraught right now. We are going home and share a brew."

"I dinna want a brew. I need to straighten things out at Medicine."

"My, darling, Marita tis the Maca. She does nay want ye there. Dinna open yourself to more harsh words."

Marta looked up at him. "Ye dinna ken. Timor should be out in the pina pod fields, nay trying to tear apart what my mither created. I must stop them." She tried to wiggle out of his arms, but his embrace tightened, and he leaned down to say words into her ear.

"Ye are nay Maca of Medicine. Marita may do as she wishes."

"Somehow, I must stop her. Why do ye nay order Timor to home?"

Troyner shook his head. "Ye forget. Timor can decide to remain at Medicine. The first wee one that either have after I die will be the Maca of Troy. I can order him back, but that does nay mean he would return and that would tear at my heart. Dinna cause this break in my House."

Marta stared at him. Why would he become so resolute now? In less pressing issues he heeded her counsel. "Very well, to keep

Thalian tongues in their mouths, I will return, but I intend to visit Medicine."

Troyner sighed. He kenned he could nay stop that. He hoped this ended their quarrel, but that wasn't to be. Once they were inside his orange fliv, Marta began again.

"Ye must speak to Llewellyn and stop that mutant youngest of his from being with our lassie so much."

Troyner set the coordinates for home, and the fliv lifted upward and sped towards Troy. "I dinna ken who ye mean."

Marta took a deep breath. "Of course, ye ken. Why do ye nay acknowledge that Don tis but a House of mutants." She spat the last word out.

Troyner's face was set and hardened. "That tis nay fair, Llewellyn was my only friend ere the Justines exiled him. It was Llewellyn that saved my life when he freed me from the Sisterhood and freed ye and our laddie from the Abs." He turned towards her. "What in the name of space tis the matter with ye today? It was Llewellyn that gave all three of us refuge when the Sisterhood tried to rule Thalia. How tis it ye have turned so?"

Marta sat back and shook her head. "Logan tis nay but an Ab mixed with mutant blood."

Troyner grunted as the fliv descended. "So that tis it. Ye are more upset about his mither's beginnings than him being part of the House of Don."

Marta took a deep breath. She should have kenned Troyner would nay speak against Llewellyn. Their friendship had been too long, and Troyner, while nay a Warrior, was one of the few Thalians big enough to even go into the arena with Llewellyn.

Once the fliv landed, Marta ran into the home and into the Ops Room. She flipped on the screen and hit the circle for Medicine. Instead of Marita, Timor's face appeared. "Where tis Marita?"

"She tis with the Troopers and showing them the doors to Minnay's and Maybelle's lab and study rooms. I'm with the others giving them the coordinates to Minnay's and Maybelle's homes. Ye will excuse me, I have duties to perform for Medicine." The screen went blank.

Chapter 26

Tour of Medicine

Marita returned to her office where Timor was waiting for her. "Tis all settled with the Troopers?"

"Aye, Timor, they have gone to take their positions. Pillar says that the replacements will arrive every four hours."

Timor nodded. "That means I will need to stay here overnight to let them in. Pillar, of course, has the coordinates for the two homes of the arrested Sisters."

"I will stay here overnight." Marita was pacing. "How could they so defy their oaths to heal?"

"Ye let Mither run Medicine while ye played at being Maca."

Marita whirled on her brother. "While ye did everything you could to avoid the pina pod fields."

"Yet, ye did nay heed my advice."

"Putting laddies and lassies in the same classrooms would nay change what happened," Marita snapped.

"If ye had insisted on seeing their project, ye would have stopped them. As for the two sexes in one class with instructors that like both sexes would help stop the destruction of males. That tis what the Sisterhood wants and ye are helping them."

Marita put both hands over her face and swayed back and forth before looking at Timor again. "How do I stop that? The female instructors will refuse to teach the laddies."

"Put all the students in the same classroom and have the male instructors teach them! Ye gods, Marita, Medicine does nay have that many wee ones. Ye are wasting credits and time."

"The female ones are all friends of Mither's," she protested and turned to look out the window at the water lapping against the dock.

"Mither tis nay Maca," Timor was exasperated. "What tis wrong with ye? Have they given ye some kind of drug that makes ye such a whimpering piece of space dust?"

She looked at him bewildered.

"Have ye ever gone against Mither?" Timor asked.

"Nay as much as ye have, but her words and suggestions have nay stopped me from seeing Logan"

Timor took a deep breath. "Then do the same here. I'll walk with ye to each room or sit here in the Maca's office while ye change the seating in the school rooms." He waved his hand at the far building in the First Center complex. "Ye could instruct me which tacher refuses to teach and I could remove them and assign new quarters." He smiled at her.

"Ye make it sound so easy." Marita's voice was bitter. "What happens when Mither finds out?"

"She yells a lot, but what can she do?"

"Reassign the instructors."

"How, Marita? Tis her print there," he pointed at her screen, "and able to override yours?"

"Uh, she has equal rights."

"Why?" Timor exploded.

"It was just easier if there was an emergency while I was in the fields." Marita's voice trailed off. She sighed and moved around to the other side of the desk. Timor watched her as she coded in the information to the main Ops Room to eliminate their mither as the next highest in rank. She looked up at Timor.

"Ye realize this means ye shall have to serve as my Counselor of Medicine for years."

He grinned at her. "Dinna worry, once we have things straightened out, Melanie will be happy to return and serve as counselor."

"She was furious when I refused to move the laddies in with the lassies."

"Of cours, she was, Marita. She loves to work as much as I do in Medicine when things are right."

"What happened that Mellanie left?"

"When our elder mither started into her decline. She changed things and made our mither promise to keep it running as she decreed."

"What?" Marita asked, "Why would our mither do that?"

"Because our elder mither was her Maca," answered Timor. He looked at her. "And who tis your Maca, Marita, since ye refuse to act as one?"

She stared at him and gulped. "I-I have nay Maca. Mayhap that tis why I half-way listened when some of the Sisters insist that there are nay Macas."

Timor put his hands on the desk and looked at her. "Marita, did it nay occur to ye that ye have nay Maca because ye are one?"

A look of annoyance flashed across her face. "And who tis yere Maca, Timor?"

He straightened and gave a bitter grin. "Llewellyn, Maca of Don. I would give anything to serve as Medicine for the Guardian of Flight and the Warrior Academy as Malta does."

Marita stood before asking in almost a whisper, "Nay our fither?"

Timor grimaced. "Ye dinna ken. Llewellyn and Daniel are powerful Macas. When they touch ye as a Maca, ye ken it. When I was little, it overwhelmed me. I did nay ken how to explain it to anyone. Llewellyn would nay do anything to hurt our fither so did nay insist that I serve Don or at the Warrior's Academy. Mither thought it was our elder Mither's touch that drew me to Medicine. It wasn't. I kenned I was nay built like our fither or any Warrior. I felt Medicine would get me into the Warrior Academy at least. In a way it has, as I am the one on call to run it if something happens to Malta or she tis out in space again or when Markle needs a break. Fither just insisted to Llewellyn that he could nay spare me. That tis a lie. He can run Troy with his eyes closed, he kens it so well."

There was something fierce in his eyes and face that Marita had never seen before. "But, Timor, Fither does need ye."

"Bah, he does nay, but ye do. Now, how do ye wish Medicine to be?"

Marita sat and stared down at her desk. Why had nay asked her that before? Why had she nay asked herself? Then the vision of all in Medicine working as a unit filled her eyes. Timor was right. The division of lassies and laddies as youths was wrong. She had let everything that was wrong with Medicine continue. Why? *Because,* she thought, *then ye would need to admit ye are Maca and work here.* The thought surged through her and she stood.

"I am Maca!" She turned to Timor. "Ye are right."

Her finger hit the circle for the announcements into the Academy. "This tis yere Maca. All instructors and students are to be in the Assembly Hall. I have an announcement." She looked at Timor.

"Bring yere com with the link to the Ops system and follow me." She ran out the door, past the woman at the reception cube and the two troopers lounging on the sofas, and on to the outside. She continued running to the Academy which sat just to the side of the First Center. The island's space didn't allow it to be farther away. Lincoln, Lad of Don, had helped design the entire layout and it had been accepted by the eld Maca and her two lassies, Marta, Lady of Medicine, and Melanie, Lass of Medicine.

She ran down the middle hall and threw open the doors as the bewildered instructors and puzzled students followed her into the room. Marita rushed up to the stage and hit the sound circle at the dais so her voice would carry.

"Welcome to all and thank ye for coming on such a short notice. Please find your seats as this tis important." She watched as they all filed into the room and sat. She grimaced when she realized there were so few of the younger ones. It meant that parents were fearful of having a child.

As the last of those entering were seated, Marita looked at them and announced, "I am Maca." It was like a roar coming from her. Some of the Instructors in the front row straightened. "If any here deny that, ye may leave this room and this island." Silence greeted her words. Timor restrained a smile.

"I am ending this naysense of teaching the lassies and laddies separately. From now on all will be in the same class, but the male instructors and female instructors will nay all be out of their position."

Matilda, the instructor for those in the highest level, rose. "I am nay able to teach laddies in a larger class."

"Then ye are nay longer an instructor, Matilda"

She pointed at one of the male instructors with gray starting in his hair. "Melroy, ye now have the highest level of the combined sexes. Matilda may take her personal items from the room but nay else. If ye need an Enforcer to restrain her, please let me know."

"Nay," yelled Matilda. "Ye have nay right to do this. My Maca appointed me."

"That was the previous Maca. She tis dead: I Am MACA! Now, be quiet and sit down or I will have ye removed."

They stared at her opened-mouthed. What had brought on this change?

"Missy, ye now have the third highest combined level." Missy gasped, started to rise, and thought the better of it.

"Malcolm," Marita said and pointed at him, "ye now have the second highest level."

She saw that some were looking in all directions as though getting ready to flee. "I realize this tis a shock to all. I will need the assistance of everyone to make this a smooth transition."

Matilda interrupted, "I ken the easiest way to do this. Ye claim to be Maca now, so ye must prove it."

Marita stepped in front of the dais, opened her arms wide, and spoke the ancient call. "I am Maca. I issue my Call!"

Matilda was stunned and then walked forward. She would prove that the teaching of the Sisterhood was true. Macas were nay more.

She mounted the steps and realized she would need to stand on her tiptoes to even reach Marita's shoulders. She laid her head on the right shoulder and trembled as she looked up. "Ye are Maca." She laid her head on the left shoulder. "Forgive me."

Marita took a deep breath. "Of course," she answered and looked out at the quieted youngsters and instructors. "Now, if ye will let me finish.

"Matilda, ye had interrupted me before. Ye are nearing the time to retire, but we still need yere knowledge. I would like ye to work part time with the Director of Instruction. Ye have taught Timor and me. Yere home, of course, tis yours as long as ye wish it."

The women younger than Matilda rose as one. The one named Missy spoke for all. "We refuse to teach laddies. It tis beneath us."

"Ye are to report to my office now!" Marita snapped. "Wait in the lobby till I arrive."

"The rest of ye," she pointed at the male instructors who would be teaching and their students. "Ye are to decide which classroom ye will use. It will free up space for other studies. Students, ye will be alerted if ye have new rooms tomorrow. Do any of ye have any questions?"

The women instructors filed out as Malcolm asked, "Do our credits increase to what they were paid?"

"Of course, since they are no longer receiving them. Any other questions?"

"Aye, Maca, are ye prepared to the objections of the parents?" Melroy asked.

"If they have questions, they will be answered; objections will be ignored. Ye will excuse me. I need to straighten the others' thinking." She and Timor walked out of the room and proceeded to return to the Maca's Tower.

The female instructors had headed straight for Marianne's study and lab while contacting their friends to join them. Marianne looked up as her office filled to overflowing.

"What are ye all doing here? I have nay demonstration planned."

"Have ye nay heard? The one who calls herself Maca insists that we were to teach laddies and lassies in the same room." Missy was still outraged. "We refused. We are Sisters!" She balled her fist and shoved it upward.

"So why have ye come to me? I am nay responsible for her decisions." Marianne wanted them out of her study room before someone said the wrong thing.

"Surely, ye ken how to refute this." Missy was puzzled.

"We also need to ken the plan for releasing Minnay and Maybelle," someone in the back yelled.

Marianne took a deep breath and placed her hands on the desk. "First of all, there tis nay way to release Minnay and Maybelle. They broke Thalia's law against Thalian droids."

"But Minnay tis eld. She tis going into her decline!" someone in the back yelled.

Marianne took another deep breath. "Also, I teach the plant and drug lab. I have always taught lassies and laddies as there tis nay but me. Now, all of ye out! I have my reports to do."

"Ye are a traitor!" Missy yelled and swung around to the crowd. "We will shun her! Follow me while we make our plans."

Chapter 27

Another Challenge

Once they were out in the courtyard between the Tower and the academic roundhouse. Missy stepped up on the low, circular enclosure of the fountain. "I do nay ken why Marianne tis so concerned about her reports!" She noted that some seemed to back away at the biting reference to Marianne's choice.

"We'll have to take her word for that, but we have a problem. The one who calls herself Maca tis making nay wanted changes, and canna even stop the Council of the Realm from digging into our records tomorrow. I have a solution." She paused just long enough ensure she had their attention.

"We choose our best candidate to challenge her now! Then that Maca can order the Council of the Realm and her Troopers to leave."

Cheers and fist pumping greeted that solution until one called out, "I nominate Molli! She tis a Trooper and kens how to fight."

Missy looked at the woman. "Nay, Molli tis two hundred years old. Marita would name her fither as her champion. The last time I heard only Llewellyn, Daniel, Jarvis, or Areatha could best him. What chance would Molli have? Plus, she tis stationed at the Warriors Academy and nay here to agree."

"Then ye should be the Challenger. Ye are but one hundred thirty years and have had Warrior's training twice," another voice rang out.

"Because Marita tis but seventy-nine, she would choose Timor as her champion. Do ye seriously think I can beat him?" Missy was becoming upset. "Tis there nay here under one hundred that has had Warrior's training and excelled?"

Quiet descended on the group. In truth, the smaller, more slender inhabitants of Medicine weren't as large as those in the other Houses. Only Ishner had the other group of slimmer, less tall Thalians and even they tended to be more muscular.

Mavis stepped forward. "Why do ye ask? Ye ken that describes me. I should be able to take her down, as I had an edge with my speed when in the bout classes."

"Then we challenge her now! Mavis tis our Sister!" Missy yelled and pumped her fist into the air. The group around her following suit. "Follow us," she demanded and jumped down to run towards the door leading into the interior of the Tower.

Marita and Timor were approaching the door. The security at the reception desk had alerted them that there was a gathering of protesters. Marita had alerted her Enforcers to the situation.

"I Challenge ye to the Death!" Mavis screamed as they met at the open door. "We do nay interact with any laddies or males. We are Sisters."

Marita looked at her as though she were mad. "Ye ken that the Council tis considering disbanding the House of Medicine and yet ye wish to Challenge?"

"It tis yere fault for pretending to be Maca and nay a Sister!" Mavis screamed back,

Marita's hand came up and slapped Mavis across the face. "I am Maca!"

Mavis put her hand up to her cheek and stared at Marita while her body shook from the harsh blow, and with the touch came the realization that Marita was her Maca.

"Forgive me, Maca. I was a fool to believe them." Tears were in her eyes.

The Sisters behind her began to mutter. "Ye have forfeited yere life."

Marita put her hands on her hips. "Do ye rescind that Challenge?"

"Aye, Maca, I was wrong." Mavis lowered her eyes, waiting for the next blow. She could nay fight her Maca.

"Then go home. All of ye go home. This farce tis over."

Missy stepped forward. "It tis nay a farce. I Challenge ye to the Death. I will take her place." She stood back far enough that any blow aimed at her would miss.

"She has the right to a champion from House. Ye are more than fifty years her elder." Timor had moved forward.

Marita was glaring at Missy as she started to remove her purple sash. "Stand back, Timor. I can whip this insolent excuse for a being of Medicine. I am Maca." It was true. For the first time since her Maturity Confirmation, Marita felt like she was Maca and they had nay right to Challenge her.

Timor took the sash. "Are ye sure? Ye have the right to name a Champion and the hour."

Marita kept her eyes on Missy. "I am positive that she will nay bear the blows of her Maca any more than the other one did."

"Ye are heavier," Timor conceded as he put his arm out for her to balance as she removed her shoes and started stripping off the one-piece garment. "Just remember all the training and bouts ye have had. Wear her down. She tis nay used to blows and kicks."

They both stood facing each other once they were disrobed. The two Troopers resting in the reception area appeared in the doorway, talking into their coms. A purple fliv had landed and three from the broadcast building ran towards them with recorders. Lilac and purple Medicine Enforcers had arrived on the outskirts. Who kenned who they might favor? The inhabitants of Medicine were gathered in a circle and other lifts and flivs could be seen coming in to land on the padports.

Marita and Missy had their fists balled as they circled each other, waiting for the other to err. Low mutters and murmurs of encouragement grew louder. Missy suddenly swung for Marita's middle as though that were the widest, easiest target.

Marita easily sidestepped the blow and sent two fists into the sides of Missy's face, danced backward, and swung a roundhouse at the side of Missy's head. The blow sent Missy stumbling to the right, and Marita closed in, her fists striking at any exposed area of Missy face as Missy kept backing away, the crowd parting for both fighters.

Missy kept her fists up and tried to block the heavier blows from Marita. Some she could deflect, but before she could land a punch or swing, Marita would pound away at her face or midsection. Missy realized she could not reach or move fast enough to avoid Marita's blows and her right eye started to close as she dived for Marita's middle.

Marita almost escaped the dive, but Missy's arms and hands closed around Marita's ankles. Before Missy could pull her rival's feet out, Marita deliberately fell forward, her doubled fist coming down on each side of Missy's ribs.

"Aarrgh!" Missy screamed as she tried to alleviate the pain by rolling over without somehow losing her grip on Marita's ankles when another blow hit her ribcage and she was gasping for air as she felt her Maca's hands pulling her up to her knees and two hands closed around her neck. Somehow, she heard someone in the crowd screaming, "No!"

Marita was on her knees as she closed her hands around Missy's neck until Missy hung limp. Marita grabbed Missy's head and jerked it up and to the side. Some of those that were closest heard the neck crack. Then Marita was standing and pumping her fists into the air and screaming.

"I am Maca!"

The crowd screamed back, "Maca, our Maca!" The old ritual held everyone in its thrall. Even the Troopers from other Houses were clapping.

Timor stepped forward with her clothes and sash. "I need to attend to any superficial wounds our Maca may have."

He draped the sash over Marita's shoulders and pointed at Missy's body. "Enforcers, transport this body to the Byre Berm." Two of the lilac suited Enforcers moved forward.

"Nay, she may still live. We need to cure her!" Mattelina screamed.

Timor turned on her. "It tis over. Marita tis our Maca. That one goes to the Byre Berm now. Enforcers, do yere duty."

One of the Enforcers was looking wildly at the crowd. It was difficult to tell if she were looking for some kind of reinforcement or for trouble from another quarter, but the majority of the crowd were the inhabitants of Medicine who had arrived to watch the fight and caught only the last part, but they were the ones cheering their Maca.

The Enforcers ran a scan over Missy's prone figure and picked her up before carting her to their fliv. The small group of Sisters looked around wildly for support and spotted a white-faced Marta, Lady of Medicine, staring at the scene and at her daughter and son walking into the Maca's Tower.

As Marta hurried after Marita and Timor, the Sisters surged forward. "Lady of Medicine, restore our status," Mattelina cried as she reached Marta before she mounted the steps.

Marta turned, puzzlement in her eyes. "What status has been removed? The Council of the Realm tis nay due till ten tomorrow."

"We have been removed as instructors if we do nay teach both lassies and laddies in the same class. She tis planning more changes. That tis why we felt we had to issue a Challenge. Now the others in Medicine are on her side. Ye heard their cheering. It must nay be!"

Marta shook her head. "I'm sure all will return to normal. I'll attend to the school instruction situation." She marched up the steps and ran after her adult children.

She found them in the Maca's office, Marita still nay clothed and Timor daubing and then spraying her abrasions with the supplies from his Medical bag.

"Ye need to be in the Cleansing Room," Marta commanded.

They turned to look at her. "That may nay be safe," Timor responded and returned his medical supplies to his bag as Marita started pulling on her clothes.

"Why are ye here, Mither? The Guardian of the Realm wanted ye to stay away. They will call ye if ye are needed once they have searched here." Marita stood while pulling on her clothes and smoothing the suit closed before swinging the sash over her shoulder and wrapping it around her waist.

"Ye did nay expect me to stay away when my own lassie was in danger of dying, did ye?"

"My fither managed to obey the directive."

"He seemed to think ye were in nay danger. Why he thought ye could defeat someone so much older tis beyond me," Marta snapped.

"He wasn't worried, Mither, because he has seen her fight at the Warrior's Academy and at home. He's seen the wimpy way the Sisters from Medicine fight. They are a disgrace," Timor said. "We need to change who we send to the Warrior Academy."

Marta glared at him and looked at Marita as she spoke. "We need to go now and soothe all the instructors and tell them all will be as my mither arranged things.

"Mither, ye forget. The eld Maca tis dead. I am Maca. It tis my way now, and ye are ordered to go home ere the Guardian of the Realm orders the Troopers to escort ye out." Marita pointed at the door.

Marta looked perplexed, then stiffened her shoulders. "Why are ye listening to yere brither? He should be out in the pina pod fields, nay here where he upsets all."

Marita held her hand over a circle. "Mither, leave now or I shall call the Enforcers to escort ye out."

Marta gasped, shot an appealing look at Timor's tight face, and drug in her breath. "Very well, I shall go soothe Marianne." She turned back as she heard Marita's voice.

"Enforcers, ye are to escort the Lady of Medicine back to her fliv so that she may return to her home as ordered. She tis nay to return here except if the Guardian of the Realm requests her presence tomorrow."

Marta whirled, her mouth open, "How dare ye? I must console all." She turned and realized the door was blocked by two of Thalia's Troopers. One inclined his head toward Marita.

"The Guardian has heard yere words as I had our com on." He looked at Marta. "Lady of Medicine," he said, using the formal title, "by order of the Guardian of the Realm, we are instructed to escort ye to yere fliv which tis to return to Troy immediately. If ye resist, we are to take ye to the holding cells at the Guardian's complex in Ayran."

Marta swallowed. There was nay recourse. "Very well, I shall return to Troy." She stalked to the outside past the two purple-clad Enforcers with the two Troopers following. All four followed her to the padport.

"We are to tell ye, if ye try to return ere called, ye will be forced down." The Trooper's face was bland.

Marta gritted her teeth. There was nay arguing with these trained minions from the Warrior's Academy. She climbed into the fliv and headed for Troy.

Marita and Timor watched them march their mother to the fliv. "Thank Gar, I did nay have to call the Enforcers. Mither tis apt to be rather huffy for the next couple of months." She gave a wry smile to Timor.

"Did ye, Timor, have Marianne's name down for the Guardian to check out also?"

"I have wondered about her, but have nay ere heard anything that would implicate her as part of Minnay's droid. Then again, the Sisters dinna confide in me. The young students have nay said anything, but I believe her plant experiments are on a higher level than the lower grades. The young laddies that make it through are often denied entry into the other subjects. They can sometimes get them if they go to the Warrior's Academy and study under Kahli. That tis another area I was hoping ye would change."

* * *

Marianne saw Marta's fliv take off. She wondered what the woman had said to Marita. There was nay doubt in her mind that Marita's report to the Council would show the younger Sisters gathering in here ere that ill attempt to Challenge the Maca. That they had spurned her advice would nay matter. They had come to her for guidance.

She realized a certain amount of cleaning was necessary ere the guardians and counselors arrived. It took an extra fifteen minutes to do what was necessary before closing the room. The plant experiments should be able to withstand any scrutiny. She closed the lab door, walked through the study room, and out into the hall. Just then the last announcement from the Maca's Tower came over the system.

"The instruction complex and labs will nay open till the Guardian of the Realm has finished her inspection tomorrow. Ye will be notified when they reopen."

Chapter 28

The Council Inspects

Marita and Timor were out by the padports when the flivs from the Council of the Realm and the Council's Guardians arrived. They noted that Jerome, the new Lad of Don, was with his eldest, Llewellyn, Maca of Don and Guardian of Flight. The Laird of Don and Diana were also with Llewellyn. Brenda, Maca of Betron, was with her newly claimed laddie, Beaudon, Laird of Betron. All kenned this was Tamar, tossed out of Betron by the Sisterhood. Brenda had appointed him Counselor of Betron. Few remembered his Betron name and still called him Tamar. Jarvis, Maca of Ayran, was with Jada, his Director of the Mines, now serving as counselor. Daniel, Maca of Ishner, was there with JoAnne, his counselor. Even Ribdan, Counselor of Guardian of Flight arrived with Pillar, Guardian of Army. Radan, Maca of Rurhran, was there with his counselor Robert. Only her parents, Troyner, Maca of Troy, and her mither, Counselor of Troy, were nay there. It was almost like an invasion of her small House of Medicine.

Marita bowed to Jolene, Guardian of the Realm, as she moved forward, the wind whipping the flowing white overskirt. Only the Guardian and Counselor of the Realm were allowed that color. Today, JayEll was the counselor, but he still wore his brown Martin sash as though proclaiming this was but a temporary stint for him.

"Welcome to Medicine. I have Land Cruisers for transport to the Instructors Complex, or we can walk there. Tis nay far and tis yere choice," Marita said.

Jolene, who weighed far more than when she was younger, glanced briefly at the Land Cruiser and realized the others would consider it an affront to the preferred walking. They would welcome the exercise. She declined. "We shall walk, thank ye. Lead the way."

The group followed Marita and Timor to the complex. "I presume ye wish to see Minnay's lab and schoolroom first. It tis in this building." Marita's palm opened the double doors into a wide hallway, and she led the way to the first door on the right. The two Troopers standing guard bowed and moved to the side as the Council of the Realm walked inside.

The instruction room still had the ten chairs arranged to see the screen on the far wall. The smaller screen was just to the left of the door they entered and that is where the Ops control was located. Jolene nodded at Jerome.

Marita saw the Laird of Don hand something to Jerome and he flipped it open. She realized it was a small, primitive knife. Jerome knelt and opened the cabinet drawer and pulled out the tray for the main crystal and ran the blade on the inside of the cabinet. Marita had seen this procedure before, but she was startled when another tray slid out and Jerome handed the crystal upward.

JoAnne took the crystal and turned it over. "This crystal, Mither, tis strictly for the transfer of funds. All the documents for the droid must be on the other crystals in this cabinet. I suggest we take them all."

"Aye, do so. JayEll, did ye bring the lined box?"

JayEll's eyebrows raised, but he controlled his voice. "Aye, Guardian of the Realm." He knew using her title, rather than

Elder Mither, would irritate her. He handed the box to JoAnne who transferred the remaining crystals.

Jerome was still on the floor to return the trays into the cabinet. "May I ask if any of those crystals would have transferred the diagrams for the making of that droid?"

"Ye already did. Of course they would," snapped Jolene.

"And would that show who they may have been sent to?"

They stared at Jerome. JayEll nodded and answered, "They should."

Jerome grinned at them. "That means ye will nay ken till ye have another board constructed and examined them, doesn't it?"

"That's what it means, Jerome. I think y'all are on to something." It was the Laird with his Earth speech.

Most looked puzzled as Jerome began to run the knife around the back of every tray. They were shocked as three more trays appeared, each with a crystal, all in the Sister's color of gray-black. JoAnne snatched one and looked at it.

"This," she muttered, "will transfer the contents to another." She picked the second one up. "This tis just for storage." She then picked the third one up. "This too, will transfer to another."

"Who would those two be?" JayEll asked.

"There tis nay way of kenning until on a board, as there tis nay Maca's seal on any of them," JoAnne answered.

Jolene's face was grim. "Tis this whole place a nest of Sisters?" She turned to Marita.

"Did ye receive any reports from Minnay?"

"No, Guardian of the Realm. She claimed she would show me the results as soon as her experiments were finished," Marita replied.

"Then who was she sending them to? Yere elder, Melanie, or yere mither, Marta?" Jolene was frustrated and angry. What kind of Maca allowed such secrecy?

"I canna believe my elder or Mither would ever support such a thing!" Marita voice was emphatic.

"Then who? Dinna ye ken what goes on in yere own House?" Jolene roared back.

Marita's face flushed and she had to make an effort not to clench her fists. One of those Troopers would probably jump her if she did.

"I can think of nay," Marita confessed.

"I suggest ye query, Marianne," suggested Timor. "When Marita rearranged the instructors, those that were offended all gathered in her lab and teaching area before they confronted Marita yesterday."

Marita looked at her brother. "How do ye ken that?"

"I checked the footage from the hall security cameras after ye won yere Challenge. Then ye hurried us off to the school. I meant to tell ye this morning, but the Guardian and her entourage arrived ere I had a chance to tell ye." Timor smiled at them.

Jolene raised her eyebrows and almost asked why Marita didn't do the checking, but realized other Macas might assign someone else to that duty. "Would ye mind playing that for us?"

"We would need to return to my Ops room," Marita replied and turned to lead the way, but Jerome's words stopped her.

"If the others went to her for support, why? Did she accompany them for the Challenge?"

"She did nay appear for the Challenge at all," Timor answered. "She did tell them that Minnay and Maybelle broke Thalian laws and ordered them out of her lab."

Jolene frowned. "Then why did they flock to her as though she would advise them?"

"Mayhap because she tis the same age as my mither and they have been friends since they were wee ones," Marita said. "Mither usually pays her a visit if she has any duties here."

"I still have a hunch it is more than that," said Jerome. "Could we see her Ops area?"

They were all looking at him, but Jolene nodded. "Since ye have proven one thing, I would like to see ye prove another."

They followed Marita and Timor down the hall. At the end, Marita's palm opened the door, and they entered the student room. The screen and desk were at the far end next to another door. "Her lab/plant garden tis in there. The air quality in there tis optimized for plant growth and the door remains closed." Marita pointed at the other door. They noted there were no more than ten desk chairs in here.

"Are her classes that small?" Jolene asked.

"Yes, Guardian of the Realm. The younger, less specialized students have regular classes. Only those exploring the option of making this their life specialty or kenning more about the properties of some of our techniques with plants become her students."

Jerome moved towards the cabinet and discovered the drawers locked in place. "Tis it normal to have them locked?

"Yes, Jerome, for her it tis. She does nay want anyone to disrupt her reports or findings, but I can open it for ye." Marita walked to the desk. She opened the black surface on the desk and pressed the proper circle. "It tis open now."

"Thank ye," said Jerome as he knelt and began to pull out the drawer. He did not disturb the inset crystal, but ran the blade of the pocketknife around the interior. He did the same for the other three trays. Two produced empty trays that rested behind the ones in use.

"The equipment tis there, but there are nay crystals," JoAnne muttered. She turned to Marita.

"What," she asked, "tis saved on those crystals in an instructor's teaching lab?"

Timor answered for his sister. "One would be for the transfer of credits as ye ken. One tis for the names, ranking, results of the students. The other would hold the inventory of plants, equipment, and materials used. The other would be the experiments, the outcome, distribution, and/or any further work to be done. If I am correct, that particular crystal has a life expectancy of about twenty to thirty years before a new one tis required. That may be why there tis another tray behind it."

"And without the crystals behind the others, there tis nay way of kenning why there were there," Jolene snapped. She turned to Marita.

"Do ye have any idea when these trays were installed?"

"Nay, Guardian of the Realm. I did nay ken they were there. Right now, there tis an order for a new crystal to hold the experiments that will be completed or started," Marita replied.

"As the Counselor of Medicine, I was about to ask ye when we could expect it," said Timor.

Jolene shrugged. "Our crystal maker tis in her decline. The lassie in training may or may nay have started it. I will be able to send ye a response when back in Ayran, but I suggest ye do send off the query again as I may be delayed returning."

She turned back to Marita. "Would this Marianne have any kenning when those trays were installed?"

Marita drew in her breath. "She may. Would ye like me to summon her?"

"Aye, I wish to see her face when she arrives here." Jolene had every confidence in her ability to read a person's reaction. If she missed something, then JayEll or Llewellyn would observe the reactions and inform her.

Marita hit her com and asked Marianne to come to her lab in the Instruction Complex. "Tis done," she told the group.

"Do ye ken what experiments are going on in the laboratory portion?" Jolene was doubtful that Marita was cognizant of anything that occurred in Medicine.

"I believe she tis working on a new pain medication for severe burns to any Warrior hit by blast from a stunner or blazer that might take an arm or a leg but leave the Warrior alive."

"Tis she expecting a war here or in the galaxy," came Llewellyn's rumbling voice.

"I–I did nay ask her," Marita admitted. She kenned the other Maca's in the room were looking at her in disbelief, but only the youngest, Radan, said anything.

"Ye dinna ken what happens in yere own House?"

Marita turned on him. "It seems many of us missed what the Sisters were stealing from us." She kenned that shot would hit home. She had heard that Rurhran, as the richest continent, had been hit the hardest.

Radan started to move forward but was blocked by the wide frame of Llewellyn. "Tis nay time for quarrels. That would be what the Sisters wish to happen."

Marianne appeared in the doorway. She seemed surprised at the number of Thalians in her room. Then she saw Jerome over by her desk and frowned.

Marita smiled at her. "Please come in, Marianne. The Guardian would like to ask ye a question or two."

Jolene stepped forward. "Why did the younger ones come to ye for orders in how to defy yere Maca."

Marianne looked straight at Jolene and answered. "They did nay come for orders. They came for advice. It was the afternoon, and I was expecting a class. I told them to wait till after yere visit here today, and then we could all talk with our Maca."

"Did ye nay ken they would challenge her?"

"Guardian of the Realm, that thought nay entered my mind. I thought there would be a class and experiments this morning after yere inspection."

Jolene still looked doubtful. "Did ye, as one of the older Sisters, ken what Minnay and Maybelle were building? Since ye are the one that controls certain herbs, did ye ken about the new type of Sleep they used?"

Marianne kept from gritting her teeth. "I did nay ken they were building an android. I thought they were working on a way to improve the growth of a natural limb should one be damaged in an accident or in one of our wars. Our current method tis extremely slow and often painful."

"How do ye ken that?" Llewellyn asked. "We did nay have any injured in our last war with the Draygons."

Marianne took a deep breath. "We, or rather Medicine, has the chore of healing Belinda's arm. She canna be sent to an asteroid mining camp with but one arm."

"Why not?" Lorenz asked. "What's wrong with the current system?"

"The arm will always be smaller, but we have almost finished connecting the sinews that we produced. Connecting all the nerves tis more difficult as we must do that at each stage of the growth. If we are wrong, the arm and hand will nay function like the other arm does."

Marianne saw the look on their faces and kenned they all felt Belinda did nay deserve a new arm. She took another deep breath. "If there tis another war or someone tis hurt in a mine or any other way, we would be able to heal with the new process. Instead, they were building that—that thing."

She looked straight at Jolene. "I ken ye have taken my crystals. Ye will see that I did transfer some of my funds to them, but it was for the purpose of healing, nay killing." She turned to Marita.

"All of my lab and tech work, plus the ranking of those that work with me, are on two of the others. I will need them to continue. If I start something new, I would need a new storage crystal."

"Why are ye so worried that we removed yere crystals?" Jolene's voice snapped out.

Marianne swallowed. "Why, it's common knowledge that ye removed the crystals from the other Houses. They may have had spares, but I have nay. I need them for my experiments." She turned to Marita.

"Where tis yere mither? Marta can explain this. They canna take my plants, my records. My Maca would nay allow it." Marianne was beginning to sound desperate.

"I am Maca," announced Marita. She turned to Jolene. "Guardian, I suggest we lock her lab and bring in Melanie to go over the contents with me. I am nay as skilled in the herbs, plants, or the fine points of the quality as Melanie tis."

Marianne gasped. "Ye must keep Melanie away from my lab. She tis a traitor. She would destroy what my Maca ordered."

"I have ordered nay from ye," Marita roared.

"Nay ye! Magda tis my Maca." Marianne realized they were looking at her as though she had lost her senses. Inside she shuddered. She had lost control of herself and the situation.

"Marianne, ye are to return to your home and remain there till summoned. There will be a guard there in case ye try to leave." Marita looked at the other Council members. "Tis that acceptable till Melanie and I have a chance to examine her lab and experiments?"

"What if ye find that new Sleep there? Would it nay destroy ye?" Llewellyn asked.

"I've read the report Malta prepared. It can nay be floating in the room. It would affect all, however, just in case, we will be wearing hazsuits," Marita explained.

"I think y'all should scan the hazsuits that are here before any are donned." It was Lorenz, Laird of Don. "It seems like everyone that works here belongs to the Sisterhood."

"That tis something that we as Council of the Realm will need to resolve once we have more information." Jolene turned to Marita.

"Ye and yere elder will have tomorrow to inspect that lab and compile yere report. What ye find or do nay find will determine if this one tis wanted by the Council. Yere Mither tis to have nay access." With that, Jolene led the others walked out, The crystals, of course, went with them.

Marita looked at Marianne. "Ye are to go to yere home now."

Marianne considered defying her, but realized Timor was still there. She could nay take them both down. "I will need to stop at the Center for food." She said through tightened lips.

"An Enforcer will accompany ye to yere home and remain on guard. Ye may call the Center and order something." Marita pointed at the doorway. "Ye are to leave now. I am locking this place against any intrusion.

Marianne held her head high and marched out. She feared her control was gone, but there was no halting what would happen in the next day or two. Thank Gar, she had put the important crystals in her satchel. Nay cared what she had carried out earlier. What was irritating, she could nay call anyone to warn them.

Chapter 29

A Secret Revealed

Jolene was tired, frustrated at not kenning what was on the crystals, and angry with the lackadaisical methods of the Maca of Medicine. What she needed was a bedding, but if she were to summon someone now, all of Thalia would be gossiping again. Living in her palatial Guardian's Home without any of her House members was lonely. She had nay been able to convince JayEll and Lilith to stay here while JayEll tended to Thalia's demands and that of being the head Martin, a position he refused to claim. Instead, he insisted that all Martins were equal before Gar. Her annoyance at the universe in general was spoiling her appetite, although anyone looking at her might find that difficult to give that any credence.

She stepped into the kitchen from the back padport after waving farewell to Captain Beni. The Captain would return in the morning. None felt it necessary to guard the Guardian overnight when she used the Guardian's Home on Ayran. Her mood blackened when she smelled the roast and herbs. What good was a fine meal alone? She walked through the doorway and saw the smiling face of Jada, Director of Ayran's mines. How had he beaten her here?

"I thought ye might need some company this eve after all the events of the last few days."

Tears sprang to Jolene's eyes. "My darling, Jada. I should have mentioned it to ye, but I feared someone might be listening." She tossed the gauzy white overskirt of her Guardian's uniform and rushed into his arms. They hugged while running their hands over each other's back and thighs, and then kissed.

Jolene was a tad shorter than Jada, and she snuggled closer. "I so needed ye tonight."

"Ye have me, my love. It will nay matter if the food cools." Arm in arm they hurried to the sleeping quarters. They had been too long apart. Jolene had somehow kept this part of her life apart from all the gossip. When she was younger, who would question the fact that the Guardian of Ayran would consult with the Director of the Mines? All her other unions or non-unions had been thoroughly discussed by the Houses of Thalia and she did nay care. Let them endow her with all sorts of bedding partners, not that she hadn't had others, but not as many as the rumors specified.

What she didn't know was that her laddie, Jarvis, had invited Aretha home with him after the brief Counsel of the Realm meeting concerning the crystals and state of Medicine. It was decided to question Marta, Lady of Medicine, after more was kenned about the information on the crystals.

* * *

Jarvis was in a grand mood the next morning when he and Aretha entered his mither's home on a surprise visit. He had nay called ahead, as he wanted the announcement to astound her. They walked through the kitchen, and his mouth dropped and Aretha's eyes opened wide. Jolene and Jada were in the hall locked in an early morning embrace.

"What?" he roared. Then he was looking at two people who looked like they wanted to sink through the floor.

"My laddie, I can explain," Jolene began.

"There tis nay need. It tis just an early morning report on the condition of tunnel I-Fifty," Jada began and then realized that they were both still in their early morning robes.

Jarvis had been staring at one and then the other. "Dear Gar, this explains everything," he whispered, and childhood memories of being with this man much of the time swept over him. "Ye," he roared, "are my fither." He let loose of Aretha's hand, and four long strides closed the distance between them. Jarvis flung his arms around Jada and laid his head on first the right shoulder and then the left while murmuring, "My Fither, my Fither."

Jolene was trying to think of something to say, but Jada's words stilled her.

"My laddie, my laddie," Jada was repeating over and over. "I am so proud of ye. Ye are the Warrior I kenned ye would be."

Jarvis looked down at him. "Why, why did ye keep it hidden all these years? There was nay need. Ye should have been there when we were welcomed home with the Draygon prisoner."

"I was there, my laddie. Ye just dinna see me in the crowd." Tears showed on Jada's cheeks.

Jarvis looked at his mither. "Why, Mither, why? All these years people have whispered about an Ab being my fither when it was Jada."

"Dinna blame her," Jada said. "We did it to protect ye both. If the Sisters had kenned we were bedding partners, they might have taken Ayran from yere mither. By claiming it was a night of frolic with a muscular Ab, yere mither was in nay danger."

"Plus, we did it so well, they did nay even ken I was carrying ye." Jolene's voice was gruff. "It was Janet who helped me hide the fact that I had had a baby by bringing JoAnne into the household. She lived with me, and the Sisters almost left us alone, till one became suspicious when they searched for my hidden book of Gar. Janet killed her and fled. Ye ken the rest."

Jarvis shook his head. "I ken why the subterfuge while the Justines ruled, but that was almost one hundred years ago. Why did ye two hide it after they were gone?"

Jada's face reddened. "I feared yere mither would nay love me or be satisfied with a Tri she had named Director of the Mines to hide our earlier activity."

"Why did ye think that?" Jolene demanded. "I thought ye were still angry about when I made Jarvis survive as an Ab to hide him from the Sisters."

"I was angry, but it did work," Jada admitted.

Jarvis looked at the two in utter disbelief. "Enough," he roared. "I am Maca! Ye two will Walk the Circle and I will officiate. I will also acknowledge that Jada, Director of Ayran's Mines, tis my fither, instead of some sentenced Ab to the mines!"

"But, but, he may nay wish that," stammered Jolene.

"And ye, Mither, are ye claiming ye nay wish him?"

"Of course, nay! He tis the most honorable man in Thalia," she roared back.

"I have always loved ye, Jolene, but ye were the Guardian of Ayran, and then of Thalia. I could nay ask ye to Walk the Circle with me." They were hugging each other again.

Jarvis shook his head. "The ceremony will be in five days. That gives ye time to plan for the ceremony that will be held here." His voice was almost staccato as he gave his orders. "Also, Aretha and I are here to receive yere blessings. We, too, shall Walk the Circle."

Jolene recovered first and hugged Jarvis and then Aretha. "Ye are so welcomed into our hearts and our House." The idea of wee ones again thrilled her.

Jada smiled. "That tis wonderful. Congratulations!"

"When do ye wish me to perform your ceremony? We are a bit swamped now with this investigation."

Jarvis had a tight smile on his face. "Mither ye and my fither will present me, just as Aretha's parents will present her. I intend toask the Guardian of Flight to officiate. He tis the only one that can issue orders to the two of us when we are working as Warriors. We need more time for planning than ye do."

Jolene was shocked. "I am Guardian of the Realm. It tis my duty to marry a Maca."

"Nay when yere Maca commands otherwise." He smiled at Jolene. I shall announce the time of yere rite this evening at the cast and announce that Aretha and I are also planning to Walk the Circle. I will formally introduce Aretha to Ayran. When we set the date will depend on what the Guardian of Flight has scheduled."

"Ye ken full well what the Maca of Don does," Jolene snapped.

"I dinna have his schedule, Mither." Jarvis was grinning. He was enjoying this. For once he had bested his scheming mither. Nay many could do that.

"We shall see ye when we return." He draped his arm over Aretha's shoulders, and they walked back outside.

"Jarvis, weren't ye a bit harsh on them?"

"Aretha, ye have nay kenning of the duplicity my mither tis capable of committing. Remember, she avoided the worst of the Justines' harsh rule. Nay else could have done it."

He put his hands on her hips. "We must go to yere parents now. They should be up, even with the time difference, tis that nay so?"

"Of course, they are up. My fither, Lecco, tis nay ere late when it comes to being in his office directing things." She smiled and added, "Although, he may be so delighted at the thought of his lassie marrying a Maca, he might find a reason to linger with us."

Chapter 30

Marita Considers

Marita walked back to her office after Timor left for his home on Medicine. "Are ye sure, ye would nay like to dine with me," he had asked.

Marita had smiled and shook her head. "Nay, Timor, I intend to contact Logan. Ye should find someone of yere own."

"Ye are as bad as our parents," he had laughed at her and kissed her on the cheek before leaving. "Give Logan my greetings."

In her office, Marita pulled up the desk screen and hit the circle for Logan. His ruddy face appeared and a look of relief swept over it. "The Council has left then?" It was both a question and a statement.

"Aye, they will have to examine the crystals they have collected before they return or summon me. That means I have at least a week to work on things here." She smiled at him.

Logan frowned. "There? Ye mean to work there the entire week?"

"Aye, I must. I should have listened to Timor years ago. Would ye like to come and have dinner here with me this eve?" There was hope in her voice.

Logan was still frowning. "I have to be out in the fields in the morning. The seed was delivered today. I have to finish entering everything into the records now. I was worried about ye and neglected things here. I'll have time tomorrow night if ye are still sure ye dinna wish to leave there.

Marita's happiness vanished. It looked like being Maca would be as depressing as she thought. "Aye, do ye wish to eat here or at the waterfront?"

"There with ye." His voice was forceful. "Then nay will stare at us or disturb us."

Her next call went to Melanie. She was at the outside pool with their ten-year-old, Magda, named after the last Maca. Marita hoped having a child would nay keep Melanie away tomorrow. "Melanie, my elder, I and Medicine need your assistance." Melanie's eyebrows went up.

"My Maca," she said, "Why nay come here for dinner this eve and nay say over the com why I am so needed."

"All Thalia will ken by tomorrow anyway. The Council has been here and left. We need to examine the plants and any experiments in Marianne's lab. We won't have her crystals, though, that outlines why she is using those plants, nor will we ken what properties she may or may not have discovered or enhanced. The Council has taken all the crystals. We will need hazsuits till we ken more about them."

"The suits there may nay be safe. Do ye mind if I call Malta and ask her to brings suits from the Warriors Academy and join us? We do have to finish by the time Magda tis out of classes."

"Ye may be right. I was going to scan them before we donned them, but it would be safer to do that with a hazsuit on. I will call Malta. Thank ye for the suggestion as tis what the Laird of Don recommended. Goodnight, Melanie."

Marita took a deep breath. All this politeness and politics when she would rather be bedding Logan right now. She hit the com for Malta, and there was no response. She must be in the shower, Marita thought and quickly left a message outlining what she, Melanie, and Timor would need early tomorrow even if she could nay join them.

* * *

Malta was having a grand time with Pillar. He had invited her to the Warrior's Haven in Donnick to celebrate. There really was no occasion to celebrate that she kenned, but Pillar used those words to bring her there. They had greeted colleagues from Flight and Army and were just finishing a meal of steak with seasoned potatoes and fresh spinach. Pillar, of course, always choose the darker brew from Rurhran.

Pillar leaned forward and smiled at her. "I am tired of this being bound to Thalia. Our two years of grounding after being with Jarvis to find the Draygons ended last week. Now we need a new adventure or a little war."

Malta shook her head. "One war was quite enough. We almost didn't make it back from the scouting flight Jarvis had us on, or don't ye remember?"

"That was nay the war. It was but a preliminary skirmish," he retorted. "The war was conducted by those that were nay on our flight. I have had a long talk with the Guardian of Flight about returning to space."

Malta frowned at him. "And what little war were ye two plotting?"

Pillar sat back with a hurt look on his face. "We were nay plotting a wee war. We discussed taking a contingent of both Army's and Flight's personnel, particularly those that were nay on Jarvis's hunt for Draygons and those that missed the Draygon War, and do an exploration training flight. When and if we find a suitable asteroid, moon, or planet, we could investigate, record, and then return to Thalia. If the asteroid looks promising, Ayran may wish to establish another mining outpost."

Malta had her head cocked to one side. "And who besides ye would lead this expedition?"

"I thought Leman, Lad of Don, might be the Flight Captain since he missed all of the excitement," Pillar grinned. All of Don had heard of the rousing quarrel Leman had had with his parents about his having a bigger share in the Zark Station responsibilities.

"Did Leman agree to this?"

"I dinna," Pillar admitted. "The Guardian of Flight would attend to the space crew. If nay Leman, mayhap Ribdan or Rollo. It tis my job to select the twenty to fifty Army personnel to take with us. The more I think about it, thirty or forty should be about right. I have some newer ones that need to practice off-planet."

"Just how long have ye been plotting this?"

Pillar grinned. "Ever since we were grounded and Medicine decided that I am one of the few Thalians affected when imbibing more than six brews. I had to do something to keep my mind off the next quaff." He sat back, waiting for her comment or next question.

"And just what am I supposed to do?" She wondered how much effort Pillar had put into this project.

"Well, ye, of course, would keep me company on cold nights." He grinned and elevated and lowered his eyebrows before leaning forward again. "Ye would also keep track of the reactions of all the new personnel experiencing outer space for the first time. Conduct any study projects ye bring with ye, and should we find a suitable landing place, ye would have to evaluate the air, the microbes on the surface, the temperatures, the effect on the Thalians, and anything else that Medicine keeps tabs on for their reports."

"How do ye justify taking Army with ye on such a training expedition?"

"Finding an inhabited planet so close to Thalia and Brendon tis nay likely so we would just be doing a training exercise. I would divide them into teams and have them hunt and destroy the other."

Malta raised her eyebrows on that statement.

Pillar smiled as he answered, "The weapons would nay produce real fire in such a scenario, but ye ken that."

"Ye have nay mentioned Lincoln or Lexton being on the flight." Malta inclined her head at the two young Thalians that had just entered and were greeted by shouts from the younger crowd.

Pillar looked at the two. "Lexton may be one, but can ye really see Lincoln tearing himself away from all the buildings he tis designing or in charge of having constructed?" There was a hint of contempt in Pillar's voice for anyone remaining grounded for such reasons.

Malta gave a low laugh. "Who tis he designing for homes now?" Like many others, she wondered about Daniel's brother. All Thalian homes had been built the same for over four centuries, but Lincoln was intent on changing the layouts and the outside architectural lines. He had even convinced some Thalians to try the new architectural forms rather than completely round for their vacation homes. Pillar had even condescended to admit that was quite an achievement for such a young Thalian. Lincoln couldn't be more than sixty-eight or seventy at the most.

Lincoln saw them, and he and Lexton walked over. "Tis this a private party, or may we join ye?"

Pillar looked up. The Warrior's Haven was close to capacity and he nodded. "Be our guests, but first, let me slide in on Malta's side." Once again, that wide grin spread across his face as he stood and moved to be next to Malta. Once there, he draped an arm over her shoulder. "Tis much more comfortable this way."

Lincoln nodded and waved four fingers at the Tri server walking by with the tray. "I have just ordered a brew for all of us."

"We were just talking about ye two," said Malta. "I was curious if ye were planning on joining Pillar's expedition?"

"I dinna think it tis Pillar's, I thought it was a normal thing for Flight to arrange," said Lexton, the youngest laddie of Lumen and Lavina, Director and Keeper of the Don's Zark Station.

"Ye spend too much time on that Zark Station," laughed Lincoln. "As Guardian of the Army, he has to come up with ways to keep the troopers busy and occupied. He wants to test them out on a more rugged, primitive piece of land even if it tis an asteroid." He turned to Pillar.

"Have ye decided where such a place could be?"

Pillar shrugged. "I intend to schedule time with Daniel and pick his brain about the last time he was in space. I have a hunch the StarPath Finder kens where more StarPaths are than the one that led them to the Draygon planet."

Lincoln searched his face for just a moment. "Tis that nay dangerous without known coordinates?"

"It would be if anyone but Daniel had discovered them. He kens when it tis a sound StarPath," Pillar answered. He turned and looked at Malta.

"Are ye ready?"

She nodded and stood just as the Tri server arrived with the four brews.

"Ye must be in a hurry to show Malta your new vacation home." Lincoln grinned at them.

"What?" Malta turned and looked at Pillar. "Why would ye buy a vacation home? What tis wrong with yere Guardian of Flight home?"

Pillar was torn between glaring at Lincoln and explaining to Malta. "It tis like an investment. Lincoln and Logan explained it to me. I can use it now and then rent out the vacation home while we are gone into space. I was going to surprise ye with it this evening."

Malta considered. Either the Laird of Don or Logan's fither must have influenced Pillar to think about an investment. That was such an Earth concept. "Very well, I shall investigate this new home. First, let me check my com." Her next word was, "Damn."

All three looked at her. Malta grimaced. "Tis nay. I just have to be up early to take something to Medicine in the morning."

"Does that mean ye are nay coming with me?"

She hugged Pillar. "I shall see ye tomorrow eve. I must attend to something at the Warrior's Academy this evening before retiring." She waved at the rest as she left.

Pillar flopped back onto the seat and grabbed one of the new brews. "Tis to drown my sorrow," he growled.

Pillar half-listened to the conversation as he finished his mug. Then he bowed at them all and left. He was tired of the House dramas and wanted the exercise gym at Army before sitting at his desk planning the next event practice. At times he wished he hadn't been promoted so rapidly; but, on reflection. realized there weren't that many Thalians left after the Justines were defeated. Thalia's population still had nay recovered in one hundred years. And he definitely had to think of a new tactic to convince Malta to Walk the Circle with him. He had hoped an evening at the vacation home would do the convincing, but she had left too readily to attend to Medicine's problems.

Chapter 31

Marta Before The Council

Jolene was waiting for the members of the Council of the Realm. She had Jerome and JayEll busy with the confiscated crystals. It was the day after Jarvis had made the cast of her and Jada's plans to Walk the Circle. She had endured (actually she enjoyed it) JayEll's booming congratulations and hug for the upcoming ceremony.

She kenned the Keeper taking over for JayEll's duty as counselor for incoming calls while he worked on the crystals was a tad overwhelmed. She rose to greet Llewellyn and Brenda. As usual, they had beat the rest of those who sat on the Council of the Realm.

"What tis this rumor I hear?" He asked after they had greeted. His black eyes were alight with mischief and a smile was on his face.

Jolene almost snapped, what rumor, but knew better. "Tis nay rumor. My laddie casted it all over Thalia. Even if he had confined the cast to Ayran, it would still be all over Thalia."

Llewellyn nodded. "My deepest congratulations! May yere sorrows be as our joys."

"Humph," she snorted as the rest began arriving and the greetings exchanged. Troyner and Marta were the last to appear, and

Marta was furious. She stood with her hands on her hips in the doorway and refused to greet any.

"Do ye really believe I will submit to yere questions?"

Troyner stood just to the side of her, concern flooded over his ruddy face. "We demand to ken why ye think Marta can contribute any knowledge about the traitorous two from Medicine."

Jolene stared at the two for a moment. "Do either of ye intend to convince us that Marita was actually running Medicine these last forty-odd years when she spent more time in Troy's pina pod fields or with Logan in Don's fields?"

Silence filled the room. Marta's face reddened. "Well, of course, she did. She tis Maca. She just gave her orders through me," came Marta's prim voice.

Marita shook her head. "Mither, the Council has us both here for questioning before Minnay and Maybelle are tried before a meeting with all of Thalia attending. This tis an inquiry, and I nay ever gave ye any orders or suggestions on how to run Medicine. I didn't have to bother with any of the problems as long as ye were the counselor and taking care of things. I could work in the pina pod fields or with Logan. The Guardian was nay wrong about that."

Marita turned to the rest of the Council. "I would rather nay be here with the current Counselor of Medicine." She pointed at Timor. "There tis so much we need to attend to at Medicine now. Melanie and Malta will be there in an hour to help us sort through Marianne's lab. I would like to have that report to ye as soon as possible."

Marta balled her fist. "Marita and Timor. Ye are totally out of line. How dare ye imply that Marianne tis somehow involved in the mess that Minnay and Maybelle have created? I forbid it!"

"Mither, there was a new form of Sleep transferred to Daniel from that droid. Marianne tis the expert with the Sleep that the Sisters developed while the Justines and Kreppies ruled." Timor's voice was almost as sharp as his mither's. "Ye ignored what they were doing because ye felt they were doing as yere mither had ordered. Ye would allow nay to say a word against her policies."

"Timor, how dare ye accuse yere mither of complicity?" Now it was Troyner yelling.

"Enough!" yelled Jolene. She glared at them. "Marta, why are Minnay and Maybelle asking for ye to come and explain things to us? They will try to ask ye to explain to all at the trial."

Marta stared back, her mouth half-open. "I dinna ken. I had nay idea of what they were building in Minnay's lab."

Jolene shook her head. "Did ye nay ask them?" She turned to Marita. "Did ye nay ask them why they wanted funds for a project and then nay look at it?" Doubt was in her voice, and the rest of the Guardians of the Realm looked just as puzzled. Why would funds be given for a project with nay knowledge?

"I,-I had nay reason to doubt them," Marta murmured.

"Nay reason?" Jolene was standing. "Ye, and almost all here except the young ones, remember Llewellyn throwing Minnay across the arena floor when she was silly enough to try to stop him from taking his Maca's chair."

Marita was staring at her mither. "Tis that true?"

"Of course, it tis true," Timor stated. "I was but eight, but I remember that huge form throwing a black-clad Sister in the direction of Medicine's box. Nay could stop him."

Marita shook her head. "Guardians of the Realm, I do need to return to Medicine. I will send my report to all. If ye wish to arrest me for negligence, at least let me send Timor back to tend to everything."

Troyner looked at his lassie and shook his head. "My lassie tis nay at fault." He looked at Llewellyn as though begging for the two centuries of friendship to give him another voice.

Llewellyn leaned forward. "My suggestion remains the same. Complete the financial and information gathering before anyone else tis charged. That Minnay and Maybelle are responsible for the android and the attack on the Maca of Ishner tis nay in dispute. I would prefer that both Marta, Counselor of Troy and Lady of Medicine, and Marita, Maca of Medicine, each write out what they kenned about the spending of funds or any other information that they think tis pertinent. They should submit a copy of this to all of us. Then, and only then, we can decide if more questioning or investigating is needed. Remember, Medicine wasn't the only House being drained of funds. So was Ishner and even Rurhran. Too much damage will be done to all the Houses if a Maca tis recklessly charged."

Radan, Maca of Rurhran, nodded his head. He was the youngest of the Macas, but he realized that Llewellyn must have been giving suggestions over the years that Jolene ruled. His elder Rocella had been correct. Some day he meant to have that kind of power. Llewellyn had his own continent of Don, he was Guardian of Flight. Ayran, Troy, Ishner, and Betron were all on his side when it came to a vote in the Council of the Realm. The loss of Ishner meant Rurhran had but Medicine if there were a disagreement, they might nay have Medicine now. It was a bitter fate to contemplate. He needed to repair relations with Don, but how? Rocella had continued the quarrel over the kine, the sheep, and grains since the Maca of Don had returned over a century ago.

JayEll stood. "I agree with the Maca of Don. Now, if ye will excuse me, I must return to the confiscated crystals and the construction of the cabinets to hold them. Jerome tis doing the best he can without me. Jerome will also need to attend to Ishner's accounts if JoAnne runs into problems."

Jolene frowned and then shrugged. "Very well. How soon can we expect yere report?"

"Elder Mither, if I kenned that I would have told ye." JayEll bowed and left.

It was the signal for all to rise and begin their Thalian farewells. Troyner grasped Llewellyn's arm and muttered,

"Thank ye," in a low tone. He had feared it would be another argument with Marta during the flight home. Then he kenned it would be an argument when he heard Marta's question.

"Marita, dinna ye wish me there to examine those plants with ye?"

Marita looked back at her mither. "Nay, ye have done enough damage with keeping all those old regulations of the Sisterhood in place. I want ye nowhere near there as those in Medicine would think all will remain the same."

"Why change? My mither, my Maca, put all those customs to good usage."

"Mither." Marita's voice was controlled. "I am Maca, nay her." She and Timor bowed to the others and left. There were nay hugs for their mither.

Chapter 32

Marianne's Revenge

Marita, Melanie, and Timor were all in the hazsuits and globes from the Warrior's Academy and looked like ghostly figures as they searched through the plants and collection of animal parts in Marianne's laboratory. Marita was slightly embarrassed. She did nay have the knowledge of the tangle wort, elbenor's tail, the wild bush nut from Don, or the properties of the dramble-berry and its leaves and bark that Melanie and Timor possessed. Melanie was frowning at the dark liquid in one vial.

"Without Marianne's crystals, this tis futile," said Melanie. "I can guess that she tis studying the selenium content, but why? Those properties were kenned long ago. Tis she planning to up the content? When does it become an overload on the plant's system? None of the factors are here for us to see; plus, why did she remove the crystals if all this tis harmless?" Melanie looked at the rows of similar plants, but each plant had a slightly different hue, while others had different leaf patterns on the same stalk.

Melanie pointed at a drambleberry that resembled a tree instead of a bush. "Everyone kens the bark tis mildly poisonous and caution tis used when burning if the canes spread too far. Just why would one create a tree from the plant if ye did nay intend to bore into the bark and discover if there were anything different or salvageable? Do the results pertain to Medicine, some sort of commercial venture, or more weapons for the Sisterhood?"

She turned to Marita and saw that Marita was already snapping her com open. "Marianne, ye are to bring those crystals for your research to this office immediately. Ye had nay right to take them with ye."

Marianne's face appeared on the screen. "My Maca, I kenned ye would have Timor with ye. These are nay for a male to see."

"Bring them now, or I will instruct the Enforcers to bring ye and the crystals," Marita commanded.

Marianne gasped and broke the connection. Then she grabbed her chest of crystals. They would nay take them from her, but first, she had to end this travesty of that male-loving Maca destroying everything that her beloved Magda had instituted. She ran for her fliv. She kenned the orders to take her or follow her would be immediate.

As she sped into the sky, she could see the purple lift rising from the ground. She gritted her teeth. At least she was in a fliv, which was much larger and faster than the two-seated lifts. Did they really think she would be so easy to take? She considered her target. If she hit the study buildings where Marita and Timor were, she might destroy one of her own Sisters. That she could nay do. Should she take out the Maca's Tower? That might destroy Marita's credibility as a Maca for the rest of Medicine. Her heart raced as the lift began to fall behind, but then she saw the Enforcers' fliv head towards her. She had to aim for the Tower now.

Marita touched another swirl as soon as Marianne had cut the connection, "Captain, have the two Enforcers follow Marianne. She tis to come here. Ye should also make sure that she tis coming here. If she tries to flee Medicine, let me ken. Do nay let her leave our air space."

"Aye, Maca," came the response, and the line went dead.

Marita turned to Timor and Melanie. "Do ye recommend we dispose of these plants now or wait for the crystals?"

"She may have smashed the crystals. Then there tis nay proof till ye or someone else runs all the tests on them," was Melanie's answer.

"They are probably meant to weaken the male of our species," said Timor. "Have ye nay noticed that the males of Medicine are beginning to be shorter and slighter than the females?"

Marita was staring at him. "How could they get that into our food system? They canna put anything like that in the water or food. Females eat and drink too."

"And if it had nay effect on females?"

"Nay possible, Timor!" Melanie snorted. "Thalians are too much alike. We are nay like the Justines or De'Chins."

"We won't know without her crystals." Timor pushed his point.

Marita's com buzzed. "Maca, Marianne's fliv tis streaking towards your Maca's Tower!"

"Bring her down! Force her to land," Marita ordered.

The Enforcer lift was too far behind Marianne to stop her. The Enforcers in the fliv were racing after Marianne. Her lead gave Marianne an advantage, but an Enforcer's patrol fliv had more speed than the flivs made for ordinary Thalians.

"Marianne, ye are ordered to land," came the Enforcer's words into Marianne's fliv.

She recognized Meagan's voice, but ignored the order. For some reason, all Enforcers valued their position more than being in the Sisterhood.

In her mind, she quickly weighed hitting the front door between the columns, hitting the rear where the Maca's office and Ops room would be, or the top where the purple glass reflected into the sky and the red defense crystal lodged. She swooped the fliv upward. If she impacted the tower correctly, the damage from the defense crystal exploding would be huge and destroy her crystals.

Meagan, the Enforcer in the fliv, tried again. "Marianne, yere counsel to all will be missed if ye persist in this foolishness." She realized she was nay going to force Marianne to land. Flying into her so close to the glass roof would destroy both.

"Hold on!" Meagan screamed at the Enforcer next to her as she pulled her fliv up and away from the glass roof of the tower. The man beside her watched in horror while the metal-impregnated purple glass shattered as Marianne's fliv descended into the tower and the ensuing blast sent their fliv rolling.

Meagan fought the controls and finally brought the fliv level. She took a quick glance at Milan, who was white-faced. Meagan looked towards the tower and saw smoke and flames rolling upwards. "We are needed there." She turned the fliv and glided to the padport in back of the Maca's Tower, all the while issuing orders on the com. Then both went running inside.

The Enforcers served as both police and firefighters as the latter were rarely needed. The smell of burnt metal and chemicals was already drifting downward. "Send the Enforcer crew I ordered up after us," Meagan yelled at the attendant who looked ready to flee. The two Enforcers raced upstairs rather than risk the lift while the upper portion was burning.

At the top, the closet door holding the firefighting equipment opened on entering the code. Five canisters and one hazsuit and globe were there. Milan raced back down to the next level to grab a hazsuit from the closet there while Meagan slipped into hers. As soon as the globe was fastened, she charged into the dome room with the canister firmly in hand. Another Enforcer appeared in the doorway, took one look, and went racing for another container.

The flames gradually subsided, and Meagan saw the head of the Maca at the top of the stairwell. *At least she has on the hazsuit,* she thought, and her eyes opened wide. Marita held a canister, and Milan was behind her. Meagan turned back to fight the flames and rushed to where she saw a companion backing away from the fire consuming the chair and control cabinet. That Enforcer nodded at her and went running for another canister. Meagan advanced and sprayed the foam evenly over what was left of the burning cabinet and the chair resting near it. She saw everyone doing the same, and the flames shrank and died low around the room, but still they licked at the broken fliv. Parts of Marianne's body were gone and black in the sections that remained. Meagan eyed the fliv. So far, so good. If it hadn't exploded on impact, it should be safe, but she motioned for all to leave while she surveyed the room, damage, and decided on the next procedure. At least the fliv had missed the operations cabinet that housed the lone defense crystal. The fliv had taken out the large blazer that could have swung upward and through the circular ceiling. It had crashed downward, and the fliv rested on top of part of it.

Meagan decided the fliv needed to be stabilized and then cut apart. The personnel at Medicine's Byre Berm needed to be contacted, and someone needed to be here to monitor any hot spots. She pulled out her com to snap her orders out.

Chapter 33

Aftermath

Marita rested her head in her hands after everyone left. Melanie had left to pick up her child from school and rush back to Ishner. Timor had wanted to stay, but after the cast to reassure all of Medicine, she had sent him home. She wasn't sure how deeply the Sisterhood was entrenched, but she hoped this was the last of the open hostility.

She heard her fither's voice and looked up at the screen. "My darling, my lassie, I wish ye to ken that I would be happy to lend ye the funds to restore your tower."

Marita gritted her teeth. Medicine was still paying the Council of the Realm for the relocation from Don to these isles off Ayran. Somehow, she felt Jolene had engineered it so the Medicine would be in debt for years.

"Thank ye, my Fither, but I will wait to see how much the Sisters stole from us. Mayhap there tis enough to restore the glass dome and walls around it. The rest tis a debris cleaning."

Troyner smiled at his lassie and shook his head. "Ye may find the floors and walls will need to be restored if that foam went everywhere. The fire could have done damage that ye canna see at this time."

She smiled back, the weariness showing in her face. "Thank ye, my Fither, but I can always use some of my own credits. Love and hugs to ye both."

"Good, does that mean ye will speak with your mither again? She tis devastated by yere silence and rebukes."

"Fither, I love my mither, but I am Maca now, and I will nay go back to the practices instituted by her mither. I ken that she tis honoring her mither, but it is destroying Medicine. I dinna ken who tis loyal to me or to the Sisterhood." She hit the circle to end the conversation. She had told the truth. She felt the everyday workers in most of the Centers, bakeries, and eating establishments were the ones that were loyal to her, but she was nay sure of any director or personnel that had been promoted under Magda's reign and later Marta's years as Guardian. If she wished to be brutally honest, she could blame herself for ignoring Timor's suggestions and letting her mither have her way of running Medicine while she played at being Maca. The fields of pina pods and Logan's and Timor's experiments had held her interest.

It was strange, but she and Logan had been together since their first bedding. She had nay chosen him for her official First Bedding, and she had been too young when he had his. He had won the fight one evening at the Council of the Realm's dinner Arena and chose her. One bedding had gone on to two, and it was with great effort that they had avoided the third one that evening. They both realized they were too young for such a step as Walk the Circle, but both emerged with red faces, and the elders of their respective Houses asked questions to ascertain whether they had committed to Walk the Circle at too young an age. It did nay matter that they held back that evening. No one else had interested either of them since then, and she was still considered too young to Walk rhe Circle. She clenched her fist and then smiled at the incoming message: Logan, Lad of Don, has been given permission to land at yere Maca's padport.

She had given strict orders that Logan was to be welcomed at all times. She began putting the programs to rest, and had almost finished when Logan entered. She looked up and smiled. He crossed the room and gathered her up in his arms. She snuggled into him, letting her weariness and sorrow at today's events transfer into his kenning. They stood there, holding tight to each other.

His hold lessened as she stopped transmitting her feelings. She bent to kiss him. She might look heavier with her Troy build, but Logan had the Warrior build of Don and actually outweighed her with his hardened muscular structure. "Thank ye, my love."

He smiled at her. "Ye are welcome, my love," and returned the kiss. When they broke apart, Logan continued. "I intend to stay here with ye this evening. Ye will have to make the most of it, for I will leave early in the morning. The corn fields for my eldest Earth fither's zarks, the kine, and his strange idea of what makes a good bread to go with his meal of pinto beans need tending." He chuckled. "Plus, he has even convinced other houses this is a delightful addition to the table as a vegetable."

"Tis all right. I could nay refuse the Laird of Don either. He gave me a zark one year as a birthday gift. Do ye think he kenned I might buy the corn as a feed?"

"He may have." Logan shrugged. "One nay kens what his mind can plot. The next time ye are at my home, we need to take a ride. Our zarks need a bit of exercise." It was true, the last few days had interfered with their usual activities and time together.

She hurriedly turned off the equipment and dimmed the lights as they left her Maca's Tower. The Enforcers standing night guard nodded and saluted as she bid them goodnight. Each took their own transport to her Maca's home and they met at the doorway.

"I intend to make the most of this evening. I dinna care if all Thalia proclaims ye are too young to Walk the Circle." Logan's voice was fierce. "From now on, I consider us counselors."

Marita did not argue. She agreed with him. She was just aware that as Maca she must abide by the customs of Thalia. At least as Maca, she did nay need her parent's blessings. She doubted if her mither would ever agree, as Marta referred to Logan as a mutant. She did nay worry that the Maca of Don would refuse. Logan was his youngest and Llewellyn consider her fither, Troyner as his friend from the time they were laddies. She kenned her fither could nay really disagree as Llewellyn had saved his life.

They would wed just as soon as she turned eighty-five in four and one-half years. Logan would be ninety-two, but she had a hunch it was his Earth genes that wanted their lives together recorded as law now. She wondered how he would like being the counselor to the Maca of Medicine. Would he really agree to the ceremonial parts of being the Counselor of Medicine and letting some of the farm decisions remain with his mither or a director? She doubted it, but yet she could nay doubt him.

Marta was raging after the call Troyner had made to their lassie. "How dare she ignore all that Mither did? She is letting the ideas of Don twist her ideals for Medicine. We have to get her away from that–that mutant."

Troyner looked at his counselor and wondered what had happened to her thinking. The Sisterhood had nearly killed him. It was Llewellyn that had rescued him, Marta, and Timor from the Sisterhood. Then after returning to Medicine, Marta had to flee with Timor as she had feared for his life. Those Sisters might have destroyed an eight-year-old laddie. It did nay good to remind her. She would wave it off as something so long ago that it did nay count. Timor had given up arguing with her and just spent more time at Medicine or with Malta at Flight or the Warriors Academy. That worried him as Timor should be out in the pina pod fields.

Troyner stood and looked out the window over the moonlit yard. He had quit listening to Marta's tirades. He realized the only way to get Timor out in the fields was to give him more responsibility, but Troyner was nay ready to relinquish control. He was nay three hundred years yet. If Timor would find a Troy lassie or even a Troy laddie, he might take more interest, but so far, Timor had nay chosen anyone to share his bed on a regular basis. That seemed strange to Troyner, and he sighed. He turned to look at Marta and realized she had left the room. He frowned. He really did nay like an empty bed.

* * *

The next morning, Timor and Marita both met Malta as she arrived at the Medical Complex set near the Maca's Tower. The head Enforcer Meagan and her counselor Milan came in at the same time. Anger was still coursing across Meagan's features.

"Melody needs to be arrested and charged with attempted murder!" Meagan was roaring. "She tried to sicken me."

Marita looked at Malta. Malta was carrying a bag of hazsuits as were Milan, and a student Warrior from the Academy. The suits had been sent out as a precaution after being used to clean the foam-filled dome area and would be needed for the Tri workers today.

"It isn't quite that bad," said Malta.

"I was the one in danger!" Meagan was still roaring.

"She means that someone introduced a minute amount of Sleep into the hazsuit that happens to fit Meagan or any other larger Medicine personnel. It was nay a fatal dose, but it would have slowed one's responses for a good twenty-four hours or more. I dinna if this was done as a warning or an experiment. I believe ye need to test this substance more." She dug out a vapor-filled tube. "From what I could discern, this is a new type of Sleep with the same properties as the one used on Daniel."

"Ye are saying there tis definitely a new and dangerous form of Sleep. Something that should have been banned years ago." Disgust ran through Timor's words.

Malta shrugged. "Some of the Council felt Sleep should be contained in case it was ever needed as a defense."

"Meagan, send a couple of Enforcers to detain Melody. I will question her after I finish here and with the appointments I have set up for this morning," Marita ordered.

"I could do that for you," offered Timor.

"Nay, ye need to finish checking out Marianne's plants and begin the testing." Marita turned to Malta.

"I canna thank ye and the Guardian of Flight enough for all yere help and support. Some of those suits will need cleansing again this eve, and I dare nay trust anyone here other than Timor and those that work at supporting Medicine. I fear we canna even let them treat any ill or injured person on Thalia right now." She shuddered as the urge to call her mither and scream invectives at her surfaced.

Malta shrugged. "Ye may send the suits back this eve, and I'll have someone return them."

They exchanged the farewells and Meagan bowed. "My crew tis waiting outside. How many Enforcers do ye need to go with ye?"

Marita's eyes widened. "I will need nay Enforcers. I am going to see the directors of each Center, and then I will return here. Timor should nay need one following him as there still are Troopers at Minnay's room, aye?"

"Aye, and they are getting bored. When will the Council see fit to clear entry for Medicine's use?" Meagan's mood was nay improving.

"I'm hoping by this afternoon. Now, if there tis nay else, we all need to proceed. Timor, let me ken if ye find anything in Marianne's lab."

Timor grabbed one of the suits and a globe, and then they bid each other goodbye.

Marita decided to use the fliv to the Centers. She greeted Myrtle and Matilda. Both had served Medicine as the Director and Keeper of the First Center since before she was born. They were approaching the Age of Decline, and both were white-headed.

Marita took a quick glance around and saw that there were shoppers and someone using the pool and gym area. "We need to step into the alcove where nay can hear us."

The two puzzled women followed her. When they were all in the Ops alcove, Marita turned. "I admire ye both. Ye have supported Medicine through all our trials, even when the Justines and Kreppies ruled us." Pink tinged Matilda's cheeks.

"Ye supported Medicine when the Sisters revolted against my elder mither, Magda. Such loyalty tis nay forgotten, but Medicine has new land, new buildings, and it tis time for those like ye to rest."

Both gasped, white draining their faces.

"Wait, I have nay finished. Lincoln, Lad of Don, mentioned how ye toured his new beach home. He was building one for a client who refused to consider it when she realized that most of the work was done by males. Nay matter, she can nay longer occupy it." Marita didn't say Minnay, but assumed they knew.

"If ye like the home," Marita continued, "it tis yeres. Both of ye would have yere pension credits and nay worries." She waited.

Myrtle took a deep breath. "Tis generous." She hated to admit that she tired in the afternoon and another Keeper had to be brought in early. "But, Maca, we have trained nay to take over for us. It was shortsighted, but tis the truth."

"Oh, that is nay problem," Marita smiled at them. "I will appoint Maddie as Director and her lassie or laddie as the Director of the Second Center. She can decide how the workforce will be divided or grow."

Myrtle and Matilda were looking at each other with doubt written across their faces. "She does nay ken how to stock and run a busy First Center. If she brings her laddie here, it is apt to disrupt our Trainer in the pool and weight area."

"Then that Trainer is gone," Marita said through clenched teeth. "Have nay any of ye been listening to my casts? There tis nay more separation of sexes at the education or our activity areas. The Sisterhood's reign tis over!"

Shock was registering on their faces and body stance. Myrtle almost started to say, "We refuse to leave," and thought the better of uttering it. Much wiser to accept the beach home and retire. If things changed back, they would be recalled. If the new edict remained in effect, she wanted nay part of it.

"How soon do we have to leave here?"

Marita's smile was tight, but she managed. "I would appreciate it if ye both would show Maddie around here and explain your ordering process and why your displays are always so well arranged." She saw that the compliments were effective. "She should be familiar with the accounting system, but that should be covered also. Ye three can decide how long that will take, and I shall enter both your prints that will allow ye to enter the beach retirement home at any time. I think ye will like its convenience to the park and the Second Center. Ye can even begin moving some of yere personal items there."

Once Marita was outside, she sped to the Second Center. As she suspected, there was less activity as it was a quiet area where people lived and went to the main complexes to ply their trades.

Chapter 34

The Lab

Timor stepped into the front section of Marianne's two rooms. He placed the globe on the desk to don the hazsuit. The door opened as he finished pulling it on.

"What are ye doing here," a female voice demanded.

Timor looked around to see Marlynn, Marianne's associate. "Ye were ordered nay to enter these rooms till they were cleared by our Maca."

"Ye," came the accusing voice, "are nay Maca. Ye are but her male lackey."

Timor's eyebrows raised and he moved to the computer system without sealing his suit. "Since ye disobeyed orders, yere ability to access this system tis ended."

He had forgotten his Warrior training and partially turned his back to her. Marlynn had not forgotten her training. She extracted her plant scalpel from her Medical bag and lifted it upward. "Ye are to leave," she cried as she plunged the scalpel downward.

Timor's index finger had hit the swirl when he turned to meet her onslaught. The scalpel hit his left eye, dragging the eyeball out as she pulled downward. The shock and the pain made Timor lower his head and place both hands against the injured area as he fell to his knees.

Marlynn raised the scalpel again and plunged it downward into his neck area and sliced across his throat.

She hit the circle to close the door and nay happened. Timor had blocked her access to all ports in this room. She drew in her breath and backed away, trying to avoid the blood and fluid coming from Timor's body. She turned and fled out the back of the facility.

Where could she run? Could they prove she did it? She looked down at the bloody scalpel in her hand and started to toss it, before shoving it down inside her Medical bag still hanging from her left shoulder. She couldn't walk around the building and enter as though it was her fist time. The cameras in the front and at the back had already recorded her. The Trooper lounging in the front had nodded at her. Damn. Where to run? Then she remembered the perfect hiding spot, now a shrine for the Sisters. Nay would think to look for her there in the Isomatic Mountains of Ishner.

* * *

Marita was feeling quite pleased with herself. She had brought Maddie and Mercy over to the First Center and all had went well. Myrtle and Matilda had realized their years were nay long. Better to enjoy them together and explore the beaches that always seemed so close and inviting, yet so far away with the busy time at the First Center. The only one truly nay happy was Mollie, the Trainer at the First Center. She was nay happy with the new policy of allowing all in the pool and weight room at the same time. The alternative of losing her position and home was nay pleasing either. She hoped the patrons would object.

Marita headed for her Tower and realized she hadn't heard from Timor. She brought up her com and pressed the swirl for Timor. Strange, she thought. Nay response. She tried the lobby at the Tower.

"Have ye heard from Timor?"

"Nay, my Maca. I believe he tis still at Marianne's classroom or lab," Moria replied.

"He did nay return from Marianne's yet? Has anyone else been here?"

"Nay yet, Maca."

Marita hurried to the Medical building. The Trooper was lounging inside. "Have ye seen Timor, Laird of Troy?" she asked as she dashed in?

The Trooper rose. "Nay since he entered this morning, Maca."

Marita raced down the hallway. Had the fumes in the Lab overcome his hazsuit? She stopped at the open door, her mouth open, but no scream erupted. She hit her com button for emergency. "Send staff now!" she shouted as she ran to him and bent over him. Her brither's, white, cold face stared at the floor, his left eye rested on his cheek. She ran her scanner, but there was nay sign of life.

"Naaay!" she screamed up at the ceiling as she collapsed to her knees beside him.

Within seconds the screeches of the emergency system were alerting all of Medicine. The closest Enforcer, the Trooper from Minnay's lab, and the Medical staff were piling into the room. Marita stood.

"Who else came in here?" she yelled at the Trooper.

"The person that signed in was Marlynn. She said she was expected," replied the Trooper.

"Did Timor leave an order for her to attend?"

The Trooper's face was composed. "There where nay directives to deny or permit. I dinna if he was expecting her. She did nay leave through the front where I was stationed."

"I will contact our Byre Berm, but first, I must make a cast," Marita whispered. Tears were rolling down her cheeks as she hit the com for an emergency cast.

"People of Medicine. We have a murderer loose in our House. Her name tis Marlynn. Report to the Enforcers if ye see her or have seen her this morning. She tis dangerous. Do nay try to apprehend her without an Enforcer present. This announcement will continue every five minutes." She hit the proper swirls.

Next, she hit the swirl for the Byre Berm. She did nay recognize the woman's face. "Send a crew. This tis more than I can bear." She signed off and took several deep breaths. The Enforcer was watching.

"My Maca, I will be happy to stay with ye. Let me call someone to take my place." It was Milan, the Enforcer. Marita realized they thought she would falter or faint.

"Nay, all of ye clear out. Leave room for Meagan when she comes and the ones from the Byre Berm. I want privacy as I speak with our parents." Her face was stone as her eyes swept over the group. "Out," she commanded.

The people more or less backed out as they bowed. Some of them busy on their coms. Marita hit the swirl for the Maca of Troy, and Troyner face appeared.

"My fither, I have the most distressing," she gulped and went silent, not sure she could continue. How she longed to be there or with Logan. "News," she finished in a whisper. She swallowed. "A Sister by the name of Marlynn has killed Timor," the last was a wail.

The huge, ruddy face of Troyner was blank for a moment. She realized he must be at his desk, for someone seemed to be behind him.

"What?" It was as though he had nay kenned her words.

"Oh, Fither, Timor is dead. A Sister by the name of Marlynn has murdered him. Please console Mither. I must speak with my chief Enforcer." She realized Meagan was in the room, snapping the com at Timor's dead form, then kneeling beside him.

"If ye find that creature, let me ken and I will wring her neck," Troyner bellowed. "He comes to House. He tis my Laird of Troy."

Marita swallowed. She realized he was right. As Maca of Troy, he could insist that Timor's ashes be there, nay at the House of Medicine that Timor loved.

"Yes, Fither, please tell Mither." She pressed the swirl,, hid her face in her hands for a moment, and turned to speak with Meagan.

Meagan had finished her examination of Timor and rose to face her. "I heard ye say Marlynn killed him. How do ye ken?"

"She was the only one to arrive."

"Was anyone at the back door?" Meagan asked.

"As a guard, nay," Marita answered.

Meagan pulled out her com and spoke into it. "Milton, scan the cams in Medicine's Complex, Marianne's study, and the back door. Report to me as to who entered and left, and if anyone has left our airspace."

Chapter 35

Marta, The Lady of Medicine

Troyner slammed his fist onto the desk, and then hit the swirl for Troy's Byre Berm. "Ye are to go to Medicine. They are expecting ye."

"And why do we go there, Maca?"

"Ye are to pick up my laddie, our Laird of Troy." Troyner's voice was jagged and he stood. "I will meet ye there."

"Where are ye going?"

Troyner looked at his counselor, who had entered the room. "To Medicine's Byre Berm to help bring my laddie to his House." He pushed past her and ran towards the front.

Marta was left open-mouthed. "What?" She ran after him. She was able to yell at him before he closed the fliv's door.

"What did ye mean?" She had to scream to make sure he heard her.

Troyner glared at her and bellowed, "One of Medicine's Sisters ye trained has murdered my laddie. Dinna be here when I return." The door slid shut, and the fliv shot upward.

Marta pulled out her com and hit the swirl for Marita. An agonized face appeared. "What did yere fither mean that Timor tis at the Byre Berm?"

Marita's dark eyes hardened. "Didn't Fither tell ye? One of yere precious Sisters murdered him. If ye ken where Marlynn would go into hiding, tell me now!"

"Nay, it canna be. Nay my Timor!"

Marita's face disappeared.

Marta tightened her lips, and she ran for her fliv. She would go to Troy's Byre Berm at Templeton.

Within twenty minutes, the orange Byre Berm's fliv with the red flame was landing on its padport. Troyner's and Marita's flivs were right behind them. Marta ran forward, but the Byre Berm workers rushed the coffin into the interior. She did nay see the royal blue lift of Don, nay the black fliv of the Guardian of Flight land on the padports behind her.

"Ye must let me see him," Marta screamed, tears running down her cheeks.

"Why are ye here?" Troyner was still roaring at her. "I want ye gone. Our Circle tis broken and we are counselors nay more! Return to Medicine from which ye fled to keep Timor safe as a laddie. Why did ye build that horrific society into a killing machine?" He turned away from her.

"Troyner, ye canna mean this. Council has forbidden me to enter Medicine."

Troyner paused at the doorway and saw the huge form of Llewellyn walking towards him with his arms outstretched. Like a robot, he walked straight into Llewellyn's arms. He had consoled his friend when a member of the Sisterhood had killed the Lady of Don.

The two huge forms stood there, swaying back and forth while Llewellyn absorbed the sorrow gushing out of the being of Troyner just as Troyner had once absorbed his.

Marta turned toward her lassie's fliv and gasped. Marita was firmly in the arms of Logan, Lad of Don, as he took in her sorrow. Marta gritted her teeth. It could nay be. That mutant couldn't be so Thalian that he could exchange emotions with another Thalian. Marta was shaking. There was nay to comfort her.

She stepped beside Troyner and pulled at his arm and screamed, "Ye must stop them!"

A dazed Troyner looked down at her. "Stop who?"

"Our lassie! She tis in the arms of that–that mutant." Marta was sobbing and screaming at the same time.

The two men looked at the two forms. Logan was a tad bulkier in the shoulders and arms while Marita was bulkier in the hips and legs. They stood almost the same height, but one could see the sun glinting at the red hair mixed into Logan's deep brown hair.

Puzzlement, then anger flashed across Llewellyn's face, and he straightened. "Tis that what ye think of us, Marta? Tis that why ye encouraged the Sisterhood?"

Marta gasped and took a step backward. Llewellyn was wider and more muscular than Daniel. Thalians laid bets on who was the tallest, but no known Thalian had ever beaten Llewellyn in a fight.

She appealed to Troyner. "Tell them to stop! It tis obscene."

Red flushed across Troyner's face. "Llewellyn, my friend, I apologize. I had nay realized how prejudiced she has become. Our circle tis broken. She leaves here now." He turned to Marta.

"Leave, I dinna care where ye go. If ye dinna leave, I will have the Enforcers escort ye to the Council."

The force of his words drove Marta backward and she shook her head. "Troyner, for Gar's sake, it canna end this way. Timor is our laddie."

Her wails finally penetrated Marita's ears, and she turned away from Logan to look at the others.

"Mither, go away. Ye have done all the damage ye can do."

Marta gasped and stumbled towards her fliv. Where could she go? Who would take her sorrow?

She sped for her sister Melanie's home on Ishner. Melanie was there with Magda swimming in the outdoor portion of their pool. Marta ran to them once she was out of the fliv.

Melanie stepped out of the pool with a frown. "What tis wrong?" Marta did nay visit without verifying they were home.

Marta's arms enfolded Melanie, and the pent up sorrow went washing through Melanie's being. Melanie was stunned, then she responded by hugging her sister closer.

"What tis, what tis?"

Marta looked down at Melanie, for she was three inches taller. She cared nay for the water still dripping downward and puddling at their feet. "My laddie, Tim–Timor," she gulped, "tis dead and nay will let me see him or come near."

"What, how? That canna be!" Melanie was shaken.

"They claim a Sister on Medicine killed him." Marta was sobbing the words out. "They are blaming me."

Melanie was staring at her. "Who tis blaming ye?"

"Troyner, Marita." Marta closed her eyes and shook, and her eyes sprung open. "If I close my eyes, I can see Timor looking at me." She stepped back and collapsed on the chair. "Troyner has ordered me off Troy, and Marita will nay let me return to Medicine."

Melanie didn't mention that the Council of the Realm had nay lifted their prohibition.

"Worse, Llewellyn was there when I was trying to get Marita away from that, that Logan, and he heard me call them mutants. He was angry. I fear I am barred from Don. If the Maca here tis informed, he is apt to ban me also. Where, oh, where am I to go?" The last was a drawm-out wail.

Melanie was biting her lips. The shock of Timor's death barely penetrating when she realized Magda was standing next to her, staring at her elder.

"Marta, ye need to go into the gym room and lift weights. If nay that, I am going to give ye a sedative so ye may rest and wake refreshed. I promise that Daniel will let ye stay here." She knew, of course, that might nay be true, but she could nay burden Marta with that now.

Marta looked up at her, her eyes wild. "Sleep?" She burst into hysterical laughter. "I will nay ere sleep again." The words came out between gulps of air and the hideous sounds of her laughter. "Ye are right. I need to go lift weights." She ran off towards the inside.

"Mither, tis my elder all right?"

Melanie drew in her breath and smiled at Magda. "Yes, dear, she just needs to work out now. We'll go in and make sure the room tis ready for her when she tires."

Chapter 36

Refuge For A Murderer

Marlynn ran out of the back of the Medical complex. She would have to find a place to hide before Timor was discovered. She would need food and water, but returning to her quarters was too dangerous. She ran toward the beach area hoping to find Minnay's retirement home unsecured. She was shocked to see a purple fliv on the padport. It meant someone from House was there, but why?

She remained behind the tree to consider whether to dash to the beach for her boat, but that offered no cover. She saw Myrtle and Mattie step out of the fliv and walk toward the home as though considering it. She saw Mattie pointing to the lilac covered bush and then towards the beach. They walked up to the home and pressed the circle. The door slid open, and they walked inside. Did she dare trust them to hide her? They had remained loyal to Magda when the Sisterhood revolted against Magda after the Justine War. Would they choose the current Maca too?

If she could gain entrance, she would have to convince them to hide her. If they didn't, she would have to eliminate them. She shivered. She did nay wish to destroy their lives. That would be wrong. Would they at least give her food and water to take with her?

Marlynn checked the area. A couple with their wee one nestled inside a carrier sling resting on the fither's chest were the only ones out and walking. Nay were boating. This was a workday. She kenned, she needed food if she made it to the hidden shrine on Ishner, and she hurried to the Second Center.

Thank Gar, this one was nay busy. Merry, the Keeper, was the only one there, and neither recognized the other as Marlynn had always patronized the First Center. She bought a huge water container and insulated cooler and filled it with food. She also bought a roller for the cooler.

"Ye must be planning a few days on an island," said Merry as she packaged things and entered the prices before handing Marlynn the com for her finger touch to validate the transfer of credits.

"Aye, I have a few days. Sometimes isolation tis good for thinking." She almost gulped at the price. It would pretty well clear out her credits. What would she do when these were gone? Nay time to think. She had to flee before the announcement came.

She fled to her boat, stored the items in the locker, and roared out into the Abanian Ocean. She would need to use the passage between Ayran and Troy to get to the Eastern Ocean. She hoped it would be before any Enforcer or Trooper were up in the air looking for her boat.

By afternoon her face was fiery red and she was just starting to go between Betron and Rurhran. It would take another two hours or more to even reach Port Issac. There was no way she could make it to the Shrine in the Issing Mountains before nightfall. She decided to head into Port Issac and try to reach Ilarmina, Director of Fisheries, before she left her office at the main bay street.

It was almost nightfall when she pulled into one of the mooring spots for private boats, but it was nay on the main drag for the trollers being repaired, sailing for the fish, or returning with a load. That portion of the docks was closed to private traffic. She hoped no one would notice the lilac and purple boat, but realized only darkness would hide those standout colors, and this area was apt to be lighted. She couldn't afford to lose the food or water. She had to take both with her and reach Ilarmina's office.

Her arms felt like they were breaking when she approached the building with the sign DIRECTOR OF FISHERIES. She almost broke into tears when she realized it was dark. She tried to hurry to the back where the padports were. She saw Ilarmina striding to a fliv. "Ilarmina," she called, but nay too loud. "I need the help of the Sisterhood."

Ilarmina turned and her mouth opened in an "O" shape. She touched the back door of the fliv and it slid open. Then she hurried over to help. She grabbed the water and stowed it in the back while Marlynn lifted the food. Ilarmina swung that on to the front seat and motioned for Marlynn to go into the back. "Bend down," she hissed. "It must look like I travel alone."

Marlynn obeyed after shoving in the roller containing the box of food. Ilarmina hurried to the other side, stepped into her seat, and took off without bothering to see if Marlynn was comfortable or not. They were at her home in the hills overlooking the bay within minutes.

"Stay down," Ilamma commanded. "I will ascertain if my Director and Keeper are still here. If nay, I'll return. If they are, be patient."

"But," Marlynn started to protest, "I need a cleansing room and..."

"Nay are to see ye," Ilamma snapped. "Yere face tis on all the casts." Marlynn heard the door slide shut.

It seemed to Marlynn that she was imprisoned. She would have left the fliv and ran if she had been able to open the door, but only Ilarmina or a Maca's command would do that, and she was reduced to chewing at her lip and taking quick peeps out of the window. Then she saw the lights of a fliv leaving and hoped that the door would open and release her. It seemed like more hours passed, and two lifts arrived. She stayed huddled down. Nay could discover her now, and desperation wanted to make her scream, but she dare not.

When the door slid open, she was relieved to see Ilarmina. There were three others beside her in the dark clothes of the Sisterhood. "Where tis yere craft?" Ilarmina demanded.

Fear almost blocked her voice, but Marlynn managed to stammer, "It tis in the mooring for visitors to Ishner."

"How large and tis it purple or lilac?" Was the next question.

"It tis but a small craft for four and tis both colors. The upper part tis lilac and the bottom tis purple. It denotes…"

"I dinna give a dȧmn what it denotes. Ye and yere provisions will go with Ilflora. She will take ye to a refuge for Sisters. Stay there and stay inside. Those there will explain why they are there and what ye are to do," came Ilarmina's quick instructions. The one Sister extracted the food and water and handed the water to Marlynn.

"Ye two find that boat, and if nay are around, pull it out to the ocean and destroy it," Ilarmina instructed the other two. "If ye have time, bring back the pieces to burn; if nay time to dismantle, let it sink. Hurry!" She turned and almost ran back to her home as though afraid someone might see them.

"Come, we need to go," said the one with the food carton resting on the ground. The other two were already in their lift. They stored the water and the food, and both stepped into the lift and the door slid shut as the other lift ascended.

"Where are we going?"

"To the apartments where the demoted Sisters live. Ye will need to stay hidden before taking your place on the work crews," came the answer. "I'm Illa. I once was a Trooper, but the Council sentenced me to a work crew, and Ishner nay ere changed that before Daniel claimed to be Maca." She guided the lift down behind a three-story bank of living quarters.

"Inside, hurry," commanded Illa as she grabbed the water container. "Ye are responsible for the food."

Marlynn did as directed and followed Illa, a million questions roiling in her mind.

Once inside, Illa pointed to a door. "There tis the cleansing room."

Marlynn hurried and returned to a waiting Illa within minutes. "What will happen to me?"

"For now we are assigning a bed where ye can sleep. There's a sandwich and brew there for ye. Tomorrow, stay hidden. Ilarmina will be by tomorrow to select a work crew and will explain what ye are to do."

The explanation left Marlynn puzzled. She was Medicine and kenned nay about fishing. How could she do anything, but she was alive and mayhap even safe here. She realized the food and water had disappeared. She dutifully followed Illa.

* * *

Marlynn was awakened by a beeping and then the announcement. "Breakfast tis served. Bring any food or beverage containers in your room with ye."

Nay had said where this breakfast was, but Marlynn hurried to the small cleansing room, then grabbed the sandwich plate and brew can, and went out into the hall. She followed the others down the stairs and then into a wide room on the first floor. Everyone was wearing the dull black of the sisterhood. Then she remembered, Ishner had nay enough of the aqua clothes for their Tris. At least she did nay look out of place. She joined the line going through to where each was handed a plate filled with potatoes and eggs. She carried that to one of the long tables and sat. There was a mug of weak pina pod tea at each place and the silverware. No one seemed to chatter, and all were eating hurriedly. The ones that finished first carried their plates to the bar and walked out. It soon became a procession, and another beep-beep sounded and the next announcement came over the speaker.

"Ilarmina, Director of Fisheries, tis here to select the work crew."

Marlynn quickly followed the last departing back. She really regretted the small bits of uneaten potatoes on her plate.

All were standing in the huge hall that the outer door opened into. Ilarmina was at the door and looking over the group. "Today ye will be cleaning the citizens mooring bays and the landing for the returning troller filled with fish. Tomorrow I will need cleaners on the troller and in the processing plant. The list of names is there." She pointed to the screen at the entry desk.

"Next ye must meet Marlynn. I ken ye saw her on the casts last eve. She has struck the first blow for us! Plus, she has the information we need to make our endeavor successful." A look of satisfaction swept over her face.

"Marlynn, ye will be given a sketch tablet. On it, ye are to inscribe the layout of every structure on Medicine, especially the Maca's Tower, the medical facility with the healing rooms, labs, and classrooms; also, any educational facility for the wee ones. Then we need the location and interior of the two Centers."

Marlynn's eyes widened as Ilarmina continued. "We now have a person from Medicine that can go with us and set up the preliminary Med Center." The others were clapping. Ilarmina smiled at Marlynn. "Ishner is too large and has too many Enforcers for us to revolt here again. I hear that Medicine has but five or six Enforcers. Tis that true?"

Marlynn nodded her head. Then realized she needed to speak. "Aye, Director, there are six Enforcers."

Ilarmina smiled. "We will expect yere drawing within two days. We will set up our final plans once it is complete. Our forces are almost ready, and we can attack while Medicine's Enforcers are looking for ye and the rest of Thalia tis involved with celebrating with the Guardian of the Realm as she and Jada Walk the Circle and then Beltayne this coming weekend."

Marlynn was stunned. These Sisters meant to take over Medicine, and she would be an important part of the invasion.

Chapter 37

Timor's Burial And The Search

The Council of the Realm had met by using their coms and ordered Troopers into Medicine to help with the search for Marlynn. The Council members wished to attend Timor's Byre Berm burning the next day.

The Houses were all represented. Troyner had realized that he must relent and allowed Marta to attend when Triva, his Director of Labor, had pleaded with him. "Ye canna be that cruel. She tis his mither."

"I want nay to do with that lassie ere again," Troyner had stated.

"Then let me be by yere side as I was when ye were released from the Sisterhood's confinement," Triva suggested. "She will ken ye have nay feelings for her and will leave with her sib and family." Triva shivered as Troyner's arms went around her. She had longed for this day ever since she had brought the key that freed him and Benji.

Marta collapsed into uncontrollable sobs when JayEll said the closing prayer to Gar and the byre erupted into flames, consuming the body of Timor. Melanie and Malta supported her back to Malta's lift as Troyner had reclaimed Troy's fliv.

The search on Medicine yielded nay trace of Marlynn, and the Warriors and Troopers spread out over the islands of Ayran and across the oceans using their scanners. They finally located the debris of her boat and com in the Eastern Ocean between Betron and Rurhran.

Daniel received a call from Pillar. "We need a submersible and someone who can investigate the wreckage and retrieve the com. I doubt if there tis anything on it, and I doubt if her bones are there." There was bitterness in his voice as he sent Daniel the coordinates.

Once he had the reports, the com, and two samples of the debris, Daniel delivered them to Flight's Office. "There they are" he announced. "We left them for ye to examine, but Ishmael's evaluation of the metal parts brought him to the conclusion that someone had deliberately dismantled the boat by force and by stunner. Nay were in the craft when it was scuttled. He tis putting that in a report for ye and the Council."

Llewellyn looked up and asked, "Did he offer any guesses on where she went?"

"Ye ken the location as well as we did. She could be on Betron, Rurhran, or Ishner. It would depend on who aided her. The com may tell ye, or it may nay. There are more Sisters on Rurhran and my Ishner than on Betron." He slumped into a chair across from his elder fither. "I have my security checking all the surveillance cameras for any night activity or any bay showing a purple and lilac boat. If ye or the Guardian of the Realm could persuade Rurhran and Betron to do so, it may help."

Llewellyn had a slight smile tugging at the corner of his mouth. "Ye are saying such searching will turn up nay."

Daniel heaved himself up. "Aye, my Elder Fither. That tis what I am saying." He bid him goodbye and left. He did nay wish to hear Pillar rage about the lack of security on all the continents. Why would there be such security measures? Thalians did nay fight Thalians except in the arena or if they were Sisters against the Macas. Which was why Ishner had more cams then the rest. The Sisters had installed them for fear the rest of Thalia would attack them.

Daniel's hunch about the cams proved correct. Even worse, Ishmael's estimation of what had happened to the boat was confirmed by the Warriors Academy laboratory. There was no way to prove which continent Marlynn had used as a refuge. Daniel had his Enforcers checking any empty storage spaces, but there were nay reports of a woman hiding or stealing food. It was the same on Betron. There were nay leads. Rurhran dismissed the idea that she would seek refuge there. She would nay have been welcomed. Radan refused to believe that any Sisters were left from Raven's and then Rocella's rule.

Jarvis's efforts to hold a small celebration for Jolene and Jada as he presided over their Walk the Circle was a complete failure. Instead, Ayran was inundated with celebrants and brew. JayEll had to shout the blessings of Gar over the roar of the crowd. Everyone had aided in setting up the tables, the Directors and Keepers of Ayran's Maca, those from the Guardian Complex, and even Jolene's home. Since the weather was balmy, it was a huge outdoor feast. Jolene and Jada fled as soon as courtesy allowed them to retire to their bedroom. The next day, the hunt for Marlynn continued.

Marlynn took three days to sketch out the layout of Medicine on the isle off the coast of Ayran. "Are the number of homes correct?" Ilarmina frowned at the sketch. Could Medicine number such few Thalians? "There does nay seem to be enough homes."

"I doubt if we number over four thousand, if that," explained Marlynn. "I may have missed the exact number, but our birthing rate has remained low."

Ilarmina looked at her. "Tis that because the Sisters are nay bedding a male and any using collected sperm. How did they expect to take over Medicine without producing wee ones?"

Marlynn shrugged. "Bearing a wee one would be so time-consuming without a counselor to assist for thirty years of rearing till the Age of Confirmation."

Ilarmina snorted. "Ye mean that two of ye could nay do that?"

"Well, aye, but if the wee one were male, one would need to abort. Then what if more are male? Why risk such a thing? We felt it better to pull from the Tri populace. They had nay such inhibitions."

"Which is why yere numbers remain so low. I will take the drawing. I dinna want it scanned, and now tis time for ye to join the work crews. Remember to wear that wig till Beltayne this weekend." Ilarmina folded the pape„ stuffed it into her side sling, and left.

Marlynn frowned. Nay even a thank you for the finished work.

Chapter 38

Beltayne

The preparations for Beltayne were almost finished as the official spring month arrived. Daniel had put Ilaman in charge of Ishner's booth at Betron's main city, Bretta. Ilaman consulted with Daniel almost daily in the process. Ilarmina had the Ishner sentenced Sisters decorating three flotillas with a teal banner for carrying any from Ishner south on the Eastern Ocean to Betron or any other continent as a way to celebrate if nay lift of fliv were available for them. When Daniel complained about the number and cost, she looked hurt.

"I thought it a proper way for those from Ishner that have nay their lifts of flivs yet to be able to sail from the ports of Ishner to join other Thalians celebrating. We do have so much more freedom now."

"Thank ye for that, but I would prefer some celebrate at the booths here."

Ishner was not the only continent celebrating. The biggest would be on Betron, where the spring festival was said to have started. Since the truth was hidden in long ago legends, nay disputed the beginning. Betron would outdo all in the booths and games for Thalians to try their skill.

Lorenz had managed to add zark racing to the events on Don. That, too, would be well attended. The Thalians would use flivs, lifts, boats, even air cruisers to visit one continent's display before heading to another.

Medicine was the only House not putting on a display of events or booths. Marita had sent a Medical booth to the other House events with two Medicals at each booth extoling the new open policies for all. She planned to join Logan at Bretta, and then they would go to Don to watch the zark races. Her House would be a bit depleted by afternoon, as most would take in the celebration at Bretta, the main city on Betron, or mayhap Rurhran with their many brew halls set out on a green between the tents or open spaces where agra demonstrations would take place.

Many of the Medicine Tris loyal to the new Maca had left the island when the flotilla of two boats from Ishner sailed into the bay of their island. Milan was near the bay to keep watch over any activity. He stared in disbelief at the disembarking Sisters in black from boats flying the teal of Ishner.

Milan realized one was raising a stunner in his direction and took to his heels around the Maca's tower and dashed inside, locking the double doors and then the other one from the console. "Attack!" he bellowed into his com's universal circuit. "Send Troopers, we are under attack from the Sisters."

Meagan came running from the gym holding her clothes in one hand, while the com and front desk scre-en lit up with incoming calls. "How many?" The question came from Army.

"Two boat-loads with at least fifteen to twenty in each; plus, some of Medicine may join them," replied Milan as the first of the stunner's blasts could be heard scorching the doors in front and the one down the side hallway. Meagan bounded up the stairs and pulled open the door to their armored outfits and blasters. She grabbed all and ran back down to her counselor. They both struggled into the tight-fitting armored garments and globes.

"How are they armed?" was the next question from Army.

"With stunners that I saw, but nay blasters. They are trying to storm the Maca's Tower."

Meagan saw the desk button from the First Center light up. "They've killed Malcolm. He was coming into the Center. I've locked the doors, but they are burning them with stunners," Merry's voice was frantic. She was manning the First Center as a favor to Myrtle.

"Did ye hear?" Meagan had taken over the console and yelling at Army. "Milan and I are the only Enforcers here today. The rest are at Bretta, Rurhran, or Donnick. Send Troopers now. I dinna how long we will last."

"On their way in five minutes," came the voice.

"I'm on my way," Pillar's voice rang out. He didn't bother to mention that he and Malta had slept late, and both were just drying off from the cleansing room when the universal call came through. He always kept armor, globe, and blasters at his home. Malta was trying to pull on her clothes.

"I'm coming."

"Nay," he yelled back at her as he ran out of the room. "Ye go to the Warriors Academy's Medicine. That tis where we send the wounded."

Marita was almost at Donnick for the zark races when she heard the announcement and swung her fliv back towards Medicine. That was her House!

Logan saw her fliv heading back towards Medicine and gave pursuit in his slower lift. He could nay let her face them alone. "I'm headed to Medicine," he shouted into the com for his eldest fither, Lorenz.

"Don't be a fool. Y'all don't have any weapons," Lorenz yelled and realized the Logan had turned off his com. "Lavina, Lumen, take over the contest. That fool Logan will get himself killed." He was into his fliv and headed to the Warriors Academy where his armor was stored. He sent a direct message to Llewellyn. "Fire in the pan at Medicine. Wear armor and bring your blaster." Then he was running into the Academy as the first Troopers stormed out, headed for their flivs and air cruisers.

* * *

Two black-clad sisters ran into the Maca Tower's round reception room from the hall as smoke billowed into the room. Meagan and Milan ducked down behind the round console table raining fire from their blasters at the attackers. Two more took their places and met the same fate. "Go back," they heard someone scream as more smoke billowed out of the hallway.

"They've set the hallway on fire!" Milan yelled as the scorching from the stunners began crackling the metal-impregnated glass doors.

"Or we did with our blasters," Meagan muttered. She turned in the direction of the glass doors and saw the purple fliv of the Maca descending. "Dear Gar, that tis our Maca!" She stood as another Sister appeared in the hallway opening and firing her stunner. Meagan went down, holding her arm, while Milan's blaster took down the Sister and flames began eating at the clothing on downed ones.

Marita's fliv aimed straight at the Sisters massed at the double doors and spilling down the marble steps. She had to pull up before striking any, but it caused them to leap from the steps or duck down and fire their stunners at her. She turned the fliv and flew back over while firing at them with the stunner kept in the fliv. She pulled up and saw the others at the side entrance and smoke coming from the hall, and anger surged through her. She had nay time to count them, but between those at the side and the front, she estimated it was near twenty. How she needed a blaster and remembered that Meagan had given the other three Enforcers the day off for Beltayne.

She soared upward and realized that Sisters clustered around the First Center had run up a black flag signifying they controlled it. They encircled a group of lilac-covered Tris, and

Marita aimed her fliv straight at the edge of the Sisters. Too late she realized that one had a blaster, and the flame stabbed upward into the control portion. The fliv rolled, and the Sisters and Tris went running as the fliv plowed into the green grass.

Marita's left side was singed, but the fliv had landed on the passenger side and the control still slid her door open. She pulled her stunner out and prayed her fliv had struck the one with blaster. She rolled out, firing her stunner at the black legs and hearing satisfying screams. No one noticed the royal blue lift aiming downward toward the purple fliv.

One of the Sisters stepped around Marita's fliv and aimed her stunner at her, scoring a hit on the shoulder. Marita's stunner dropped, and she started to rise as more Sisters appeared.

"No!" It was Logan's bellow as he ran for Marita. The yell diverted their attention, and they aimed their stunners at him as he threw himself over Marita to protect her.

Five stunners aimed at the two on the ground, scoring direct hits on their heads and bodies. The heads exploded into burning masses of hair, and the flames swept downward to meet the flames coming upward through their clothes as more raked their fire along the burning bodies.

The Sisters raised their fists and stunners into the air shouting, "We have won! The Maca tis dead!"

Wails came from the lilac-clothed Tris, but there was no escape. At least six others had their stunners pointed at them. One of the Sisters pulled out her com and looked towards the bay where Ilramina had remained to direct her forces.

"The Maca tis dead! We are in control."

The black fliv headed towards the Maca's Tower soared in front of the fliv, and an air carrier from the Warrior Academy and Army as Pillar contacted his Troopers. "Ribdan, are ye there?"

"Aye, Pillar, twenty Troopers are with me and several more in flivs."

"Have them attack the front and back of the Maca Tower and send the flivs to each Center." He pulled his fliv up and saw the purple and blue vehicles and the burning lump near the purple fliv. The exultant Sisters formed a semi-circle around them. Rage poured through him. He wasn't in time.

"I'm going down. Get here fast!" he yelled into the com and swung his fliv down towards the green. He had but one advantage. His blaster. He noted which Sister held one, and he zoomed in lower. The Sisters scattered, and he turned the fliv, skidded into a landing, and rolled out, his blaster firing at first the one with the blaster and then swinging it in an arc to take out the Sisters with the stunners. He was a seasoned fighter and they were but amateurs. They dropped screaming, their legs and torsos ablaze.

Pillar stood, but remained in the shadow of his fliv and yelled at the Tris that huddled together in front of the Center. "Are there any inside?"

"I dinna," one of the women yelled back.

"Then get out of here if you can," Pillar commanded as he climbed back into his fliv.

"Incoming," came over his com and Ribdan, Director of Flight, landed his black aircombo by the Maca's Tower and Troopers filed out of both sides, firing at the Sisters on and by the steps of the main door. One black fliv landed at the back, and two more headed for the Centers.

Pillar went back into the air and after the boat he saw pulling out of the bay. This boat wouldn't elude him. He caught up with it in seconds, rolled down his window, aimed the blaster at the cockpit, and smiled with satisfaction when windshield, helm, and body parts went flying.

"Ishner, ye have a boat that tis nay manned roaming the waters of Medicine."

"What?" It was Idana. He had nay been given the day off.

"Ye heard me. Roust a couple of your sea Ishnerites and have them confiscate it."

He gave the coordinates, and then Pillar zoomed back to where the burned remains of Logan and Marita were. Ribdan, in full armor and globe, carrying his blaster, approached. "What happened, Captain Pillar? That looks like Marita's fliv, and the other belongs to Don."

"Aye, Director. The blue one tis Logan's. He tried to save Marita." He pointed at the blackened mass. One of Logan's blue shoes could still be seen covering the purple foot of Marita.

"Dear Gar, how do we tell our Guardian?" Ribdan's voice had sunk to a whisper.

"We'll manage," came Pillar's angry voice. He looked at the Troopers who had landed and walked up, their blasters aimed at the Center.

"I want ye four to come with me," said Pillar. He looked at Ribdan. "Well, ye have the other four. Do ye want the front or the back?"

Ribdan nodded. "I'll take the front. "I've ordered the others to clear the Maca's Tower."

His com came alive. "We found two wounded Medicine Enforcers in here. They put up a brave fight."

"Contact Malta. Tell her we will be bringing them." Ribdan nodded at Pillar. "We'll meet inside."

* * *

The search netted them two more live Sisters. They had not put up any resistance. They looked with horror at the dead and burned bodies of Sisters and House. Pillar looked at the fifth black fliv and a royal blue one that had arrived. Then he saw the Laird of Don on his knees by Logan and Marita. The Laird had his head bowed and his hands folded. He also saw the huge forms of Llewellyn and Troyner running towards them.

Troyner dropped to his knees. “Nay, it is too much! My lassie, my lassie, my darling wee one.” His voice broke into sobs, and he rocked back and forth on his knees.

“I’ll march these back to the aircombo and find out what else they’ve destroyed. I suggest a full sweep of every building and anyone dressed in black be arrested,” said Ribdan.

“Do so,” replied Pillar. “Tell them I’ll be there directly.” Pillar then called Medicine’s Byre Berm and told them they were needed here. “There tis more than one. Ye should alert Don’s Byre Berm also.”

Next, he called the Byre Berm at Ishner. “There are at least a dozen, mayhap two dozen that belong to Ishner.” There was dead silence on the com. The woman at Ishner was staring at him with blank eyes, unable to comprehend the number of dead. Finally, she spoke.

“That canna be. How could ye? Ye male pervert.” She broke the connection. Pillar made a note to warn Daniel about her, and then he turned to those that were grieving.

Chapter 39

Marta, Lady of Medicine

Ishmael, Melanie, their lassie Magda, and Marta were at the Donnick Beltayne booths. They planned on seeing the zark races. They all had a pina pastry and a container of pina pod tea. They had greeted Lorenz and his counselor, Diana, with a flurry of hugs.

"And which should I wager on this time?" Ishmael asked.

"Y'all are on your own." Lorenz smiled that brilliant smile that drew people to him.

"Even Daniel has been too busy to check them out and give me a hint," Diana almost pouted. "Now, I shall probably lose credits."

Amid gossip and chuckles, all but Lorenz had climbed up to the tier seating. When they turned to look, they saw Lorenz running for the Warriors Academy. They looked at each other, now what?

The zarks were coming towards the starting gates when the announcer's voice changed. Instead of reading off the names of the riders and zarks, she launched into an announcement.

"Citizens of Donnick, Don, and all visitors. Ye are forbidden to go to Medicine. They have been attacked by the Sisterhood. All Troopers that are here are to report for duty. When we ken more, we will tell all."

Marta gasped and started to rise. Melanie clamped her fist around her heavier and taller sibling. "Nay, Marta. Ye must stay here. Let the Troopers do their duty."

Marta yanked her arm away. "My lassie, she will go there if she tis nay already there. She tis all I have left."

"Stay here till we hear more. It will help nay if they shoot ye down," Ishmael ordered.

"I am going down at the front of the stands. The minute I hear, I am going to her." Like all of Thalia, she kenned the Troopers would win.

Fifteen minutes and one race later, the announcer's voice came again with news. "Ye are still ordered to stay away from Medicine. The rebellion tis o'er and our Troopers are in command, but they are doing a sweep of every building there. It was a united effort of Sisters from Ishner and from Medicine. Many have perished in their folly and the rest are captives." There was a pause. "It tis my duty to tell ye that Marita, Maca of Medicine, Logan, Lad of Don, and Merry, a Keeper at Medicine, were the only House members killed. May Gar have mercy." The last was almost a sob. Marta and Kitten could be heard screaming. Marta ran for her fliv. Nay could stop her, and she fled through the sky.

She saw Troyner's orange fliv beside the black fliv of Llewellyn's and landed beside them. The Trooper met her as her door slid open.

"Ye must leave," he ordered.

"Troyner tis here to see our lassie. Why am I denied?" Marta raged. She could see Llewellyn supporting Troyner and sharing their sorrow as they moved slowly to their flivs.

"Mayhap it would be best if ye waited. Tis bad," said the Trooper.

"What do ye mean? Of course, it tis bad. They just announced her death. Do ye mean she still lives?" Hope had sprung back into her voice.

"Nay, Lady of Medicine. She tis nay more."

"Let her go," snapped the other Trooper. "We all ken she encouraged the cult of Sisterhood. Let her see what they did to loyal Thalians." The Trooper glared at Marta.

"She tis on the burned patch of the green by the First Center." There was something vicious in the Trooper's voice, and Marta realized he was from Marita's age group, but she put the thought out of her mind as she raced past the Maca's Tower to the area of the First Center.

Troyner was so lost in his grief, he did nay see her. She heard Llewellyn's shout, "Dinna, tis bad," as she continued running. She could see the fliv of Medicine's Byre Berm and two of the people carrying a body bag and stretcher.

Marta came to an abrupt stop when she saw the Troopers surrounding a band of black-clad Sisters and the Laird of Don rising from his kneeling position. His face was like stone, and he looked ready to kill all the captured Sisters. Then the Sisters spied her and screamed.

"Lady of Medicine, help us!"

Marta was staring at the blackened lump on the ground that looked like the front portion had blown away. Somehow she knew it was Logan on top of her lassie and closed her eyes as she swayed back and forth. A scream came from her mouth, and the Laird's arms were around her, holding her taking her sorrow. It wasn't till later that she wondered how an Earth/Justine mutant could do what a Thalian did.

When Marta took a deep breath, Lorenz released her and stepped back. "Do y'all need some help back to the fliv? For now it is best to let the Troopers finish and those from the Byre Berm do what tis necessary."

Marta looked at him and then back at the blackened mass on the ground. Her world had ended. Her wee ones gone, her counselor gone, and the plans for Medicine gone in one violence-filled week. Somehow the next scream from the Sisters under guard penetrated her hearing.

"Lady Marta, tell them what we did was required for Thalia."

She whirled on them and pointed her right index finger. "May the Gar of Thalia throw ye all into the Darkness. Ye are murderers!" She ran for her fliv. She had to be far, far away from this, the final devastation of all that was good in life.

Lorenz watched her, but saw that her movements were sure. If she meant harm to herself, there wasn't much he could do at this point. Physically holding her would violate Thalian protocol, and there was no arrest order for her. He looked briefly at the ten or more Sisters under guard and shook his head. A damn shame they had not died in the fight. Lorenz saw her fliv ascending as he hurried to catch up with his father.

Marta flew the fliv north to the forested region of Don where the largest concentration of Abs was located. That was where she would find her childhood friend Jaylene.

As Lorenz caught up with Llewelyn and Troyner, he heard Troyner say, "She must go to Troy."

Llewellyn turned back to his friend as he heard Marge, from the Medicine Byre Berm, "That canna be. She tis our Maca. Here she stays."

They saw two from Don's Byre Berm running towards them, and Marge stepped forward and held up her hand. "Stay. They are so fused together that both must stay here." She looked over at Llewellyn and Lorenz.

"There tis nay other way. Even now the breeze mingles their ashes together."

Her words were correct. The ashes from the bodies of Logan and Marita had sifted together from the extreme heat and light breeze. There was no separating them. Tears spilled from Troyner's eyes as he watched them gather the ashes.

* * *

Both ceremonies were at the Byre Berm of Medicine. A hologram covered the blackened mass while JayEll spoke the Words of comfort from the Book of Gar.

Malta had whispered to Melanie, "Why are Khali and Diana supporting Kitten, Logan's mither?"

Melanie whispered back to her lassie. "Kitten, Lass of Don, saved Diana's life when the Sisterhood tried to silence her words as the Kenning Woman. Our Chronicles simply call her Di, the Eld Kenning Woman, and Kitten is referred to as the Ab Ki. Khali tis Kitten's sib, but that tis nay in the Chronicles either."

"Oh," Malta gasped and wondered how many other secrets were omitted in the official Chronicles.

All wondered where Marta was. JayEll, however, had seen her at the back dressed in the brown of an Ab and supported by Leftan. He had nodded at them, but did nay speak. They had left as the flames erupted, dissolving the black mass that had been Marita and Logan.

Chapter 40

Camp of the Abs

Jaylene looked up when the orange fliv appeared and plowed into the river bank. She stared in disbelief as Marta stepped out. Marta opened her arms, and Jaylene's long years as the Handmaiden to the Abs recognized sorrow when she saw it. She moved toward her childhood friend with her arms wide open.

Marta did nay care that Jaylene's hair was scruffy and the brown leather apron greasy. She needed the comfort of another Thalian taking her sorrow.

"What tis, what tis?" Jaylene murmured.

Marta looked down at her. "The Sisters of Medicine and Ishner have killed both my wee ones. My life in House tis ended. All blame me for nay stopping the Sisters of Medicine, and, in part, they are right." Her voice broke into a long wail.

Leftan, Martin to the Abs, still wore his Tri blue of Don, but the brown sash of a Martin covering his chest and snapped at his waist, approached. "Do ye need me and the comfort of Gar's Word, Lady of Medicine?"

Marta looked up, her eyes dull, weariness covered her face and bent her body. "Nay now. I must rest. I am nay longer Lady of Medicine, but Ta, an Ab, and I will help here in any way I can." She looked at Jaylene. "Please, let me rest somewhere by myself where I can mourn and where I am able to recover enough to function again."

Leftan watched as Jaylene led her away. Others in the camp shook their heads in disbelief. One woman snorted, "She will leave as soon as she tastes our food and smells our bodies."

That evening Leftan headed for JayEll's home on the west coast of Ishner. He had heard the announcements and realized the Byre Berms of Medicine and Ishner would be busy. JayEll might need his assistance. He left orders with Jaylene to contact him if needed. By now the Abs realized their Handmaiden did use the technology of Thalia when necessary.

The Ab who would be known as Ta collapsed on a blanket-covered straw mat in a rude stick and wooden shelter built in the woods of Don above Rands Ocean. Legend told of Rand of Rurhran that once claimed it in an attempt to claim the continent of Don. The climate here remained cool nay matter the season. Ta awoke twenty-four hours later, shivering and disorientated. She looked down at her orange clothing and shivered. She drew the brown covering up around her and cautiously stepped out of the door.

A young lassie of about twelve was seated cross-legged by the door rose. "Ye are to follow me to the Handmaiden." She trudged off toward the largest building. At least it seemed to be made of decent wood although quite weathered.

Ta licked at her dry lips and followed. She needed a cleansing room and water. Jaylene should ken where they were. She followed the lassie into the building and into the main room where the Handmaiden was sorting through a stack of brown clothing.

"Ah, there ye are." She held up a brown sack dress. "This is for ye to change into if ye really mean to stay here." The Handmaiden then pointed to a small building outside. "That tis what else ye probably need right now. Use it and change into this. Then return here."

The former Lady of Medicine was dumbfounded, but still in a stupor from all that had happened. The ache inside felt like it would cut through her gut and skin. She accepted the dress and hurried to the building. Thankfully it was empty. Three holes were cut into the plank stretching across the back end. A small hole at the top of the door emitted light and air, but the air wasn't sufficient to dissipate the stench from below. The sack dress was rough and seemed to rasp away at her skin, but she felt it was all part of her punishment. Those murderers calling for her to explain all could not be driven from her mind or spirit. She considered throwing the Troy garment down one of the holes, but decided to take it to Jaylene. She wadded it up and ran for the large building. Jaylene was outside talking to the child who had been outside her door.

"Excuse me, Tr, I must speak with Ta. She tis a new recruit, but ye remain here." The Handmaiden nodded at the girl, grasped Ta by the arm, and almost dragged her inside the building and into a small office before explaining to Marta.

"Ye must have noticed, I called ye Ta. That tis your name here and how I will introduce you to the others."

Marta nodded. At least Jaylene had used part of her name. She listened as Jaylene continued.

"It tis good that ye did nay destroy the House garment. I shall keep it for a while. If ye decide to leave us, I'll return it. If ye remain, we can sell it at one of the hiring fairs."

Ta sat huddled in the chair, looking at the wall. It was as though she could focus on nothing until she heard Jaylene shout, "Ta, are ye all right?"

Ta looked up. Her childhood friend was the Handmaiden dressed in a rough, brown sack dress and shoes made of leather from some animal with brown fur.

The Handmaiden handed her a mug. "Here it tis strong pinon tea. I had it made for ye."

Ta gratefully took the cup and drank deeply. Somehow there was a plate in front of her with bread and cheese. "Now eat, and we will talk about what ye will do here."

Ta looked at her and shook her head. "I dinna ken how to live here, but I canna live at House nay more. That life tis o'er."

"Ye can carry this bag and this one." The Handmaiden held up a rough leather pouch made to hang over a shoulder and her medical bag that had been in her fliv.

"How did ye get that?"

The Handmaiden smiled. "I had Leftan contact Troy. They sent a lift with a driver to retrieve the fliv. I insisted that the bag was yere's and must remain with ye."

Ta shook her head. "I am nay longer Medicine."

The Handmaiden snorted. "Aye, but ye still ken Medicine. We need someone to walk the woods or the surrounding community nay matter where we are. That person must gather the healing and medical herbs and plants. Ye ken what they are. Even though we are all Abs and eschew the technology of Thalia, we still need medical care for many things. Ye will supply that. If ye agree, I will bring the rest of the clothes ye need." The Handmaiden looked at her expectantly. "Well, do ye agree, or do ye leave us?"

Ta closed her eyes and nodded her head. "Aye, Jaylene, I agree. Here I remain."

The Handmaiden stood. "Ye must nay use that name again. That person tis as dead as the Lady of Medicine. I am the Handmaiden to the Abs."

Ta nodded. "Very well, but are we still friends?" Desperation was in her voice.

The Handmaiden smiled. "Aye, here we are friends to each other." She went to the door, opened it, and motioned Tr inside.

"This tis Tr. Her mither died in an accident on Rurhran, and her fither cares nay. She tis assigned to guide ye in yere wanderings for plants and herbs. I suggest ye teach her about the plants and herbs and what they do. Life can be short for an Ab. She will take ye where they dispense clothes and then show ye the trails around here. We eat as the sun recedes."

Ta did traipse the trails of the Ab camps located in the back-country of Don, Betron, and Ishner. Tr was her guide and student. Later Tr's lassie would join them. Ta gradually grew older and grey, then white-haired and revered by all.

Chapter 41

Council Of The Realm

It was a somber crowd that gathered at the Council of the Realm's next meeting. It was but five days after the Sisterhood's assault on Medicine and three after service for Marita and Logan. All the House boxes were filled, as were the tiers for less important House members and Tris.

Jolene pounded on the flat surface in front of her. They were at the Guardian Complex of Ayran for the one at Medicine would nay have held all those attending. It also facilitated the handling of the prisoners, and was convenient for those working on the accounts of the stolen credits.

"Welcome to all," Jolene's voice rang out. "Our first order of business is the disposal of all those that committed murder and treason." She pointed to the group of twenty-three women dressed in the brown of Abs and bound by wires. *Tia a shame there tis nay way to end their miserable lives now,* she thought.

"The Council Committee decided that those belonging to the Sisterhood, but were nay near the attack, should nay be charged with insurrection and murder. We have ordered them to wear the colors of their House or be tried. They will be arrested if any are found to be spreading their foul teachings. Does this meet with the approval of the Guardians and Counselors?"

The quick ayes were recorded, and Jolene proceeded to the next item on the agenda. "There ye see those that did attack and murdered fellow Thalians." She pointed to the Sisters with wires on their wrists and under guard of the Troopers. "It tis our duty to pronounce punishment. They all have been stripped and made Abs. I move they be sent to the mines on the asteroids and remain in wires the rest of their lives." Her voice was firm and decisive. "Tis there any discussion or objections?"

"They should nay be sent to the same mine," came Daniel's voice. He was chagrined that the boats used to transport them had come from Ishner.

"Tis nay possible to completely separate them," said Jolene. "Ayran has but ten asteroids being mined. If more are discovered, we would still be short of the number needed to mine them. There would nay be more than two or three at each one. That tis why I recommend they be wired at all times. Any more discussion?"

There was a silence.

"Then we shall vote. Army, how say ye?"

"Aye for sending them to the asteroid mines and wired at all times." The answer was the same from the guardians and counselors of each House. Troyner and his new counselor, Triva were the last in the alphabetic arrangement.

"Take them away and transport them to Ayran's cells till the next space freighter leaves. I ask that the Troopers stand guard at our cells till all the flights are arranged." Jolene had a satisfied look as the imprisoned Sisters were led away. One struggled to break free.

"Where tis Marta, Lady of Medicine? She will speak for us," the Sister wailed and was dragged out by two Troopers.

Jolene looked at the crowd. "The reason we dinna have Marta here for questioning is that she has already removed herself. The only punishment we could have pronounced was to strip her of House status and make her an Ab for a period of five years for teaching or reinforcing a treasonous policy. The latter may have been hard to prove. She who was Lady of Medicine has donned the clothing of an Ab and resides with them."

That brought murmurs from the crowd. Whoever had heard of House willing giving up their status to become a Tri, let alone a despised Ab?

Jolene banged her fist again. "We have another problem that I will need your counsel." She briefly scanned the faces of the guardians and counselors on her right and left. "As ye ken, there tis nay a Maca of Medicine. Since the Lady of Medicine tis nay more, there canna be another birth of a Maca from her." For once, all was silent. "We dinna ken how deep the Sisterhood was into Medicine. Melanie and Malta are working at restoring the medical part. They will let us ken when all tis safe again. I suggest we make Melanie the Guardian and Malta the Counselor of Medicine. When, and if Malta or her brither, Irving, Lad of Ishner and Medicine, produce a wee one, that one shall be called Maca of Medicine. Do any of ye have a better suggestion, or do ye prefer to discuss this arrangement?"

Radan stood. "While Melanie and Malta are far above suspicion, can the rest of us really trust Medicine or Ishner again? These last few days have shown just how much many in Ishner and Medicine hate us."

Melanie stood. "That tis nay fair. My sib put many of the Sisters in positions of power. Marita was busy dismantling that arrangement. Medicin's Tris are loyal to us and to Thalia, as many of the minor House members of Ishner probably are."

"I was in error for letting Ilramina use the boats for Beltayne, but there were loyal Tris of Ishner that used one for going to Don, Rurhran, or Betron. Nay all of Ishner's Tris have been able to reclaim their lifts of flivs. This does nay mean they are Sisters. The fight on Medicine reduces their number considerably. If we dismantle Medicine, what will our space flights or even our populace do without the trained Medicine Thalians?" Daniel's deep rumbling voice grated out.

Pillar hit his speak button. "They attacked Medicine because the population is so low. They kenned that they could control the few that were nay at one of the celebrations. They will nay attack or riot in Ishner as they ken the Tris there hate them and our Troopers would arrive before they had made any advances."

Llewellyn smiled and hit his speak button. "Our Guardian of Army has just given all a lesson in tactics. I suggest we vote on the Guardian of the Realm's question about the Guardian and Counselor of Medicine."

Jolene took a deep breath and began the poll. "Army, how say ye."

"Aye," they both replied as did all the rest, as Radan could think of no other objection.

"Tis carried," said Jolene. "Medicine will have to wait a time for the next Maca." She smiled at Malta. All kenned she had nay planned to join with another. "We shall all have to wait for ye to Walk the Circle."

Pillar stood. "I volunteer." All eyes swiveled to him.

"Pillar, ye are out of order." Jolene glared at him.

Pillar smiled at her and turned to Malta. "I am serious. Ye are the most magnificent lassie in all Thalia. I ask that ye Walk the Circle with me. I pledge to ye my heart and all I possess."

Malta was staring at him with her mouth half-open, her cheeks red. She stood. "Pillar, ye are the most aggravating man I ken. That was to be asked in private when we could…" she stopped, and the crowd cheered.

Pillar was looking at her with surprise in his eyes and his right hand on his heart. "Does that mean ye refuse me?"

"Of course, I'll Walk the Circle with ye. I love ye!" Malta yelled at him.

Now, the crowd was clapping and Pillar bowed to Malta and then to the people in the tiers. Jolene was hammering her fist on the desk. "Enough. We have work to finish. Llewellyn, may I suggest ye find another less disruptive Guardian of Army."

Llewellyn looked shocked. "Oh, nay. Ye all just saw a perfect example of his nay orthodox attacks. Nay are prepared for his tactics, and he wins. He tis the perfect Guardian of Army."

Amusement lit Pillar's eyes, and he bowed his head to the Guardian of Flight and the Warrior's Academy.

"Hmmph," came from Jolene, but she continued. "Now I have a report on the funds stolen from the different Houses over the years. That which was taken during the time of the Justines, Krepyons, and Sisterhood rule tis gone. The Justines had transferred the bulk of it, and the Sisterhood used it to outfit their flivs as fighters when the Maca of Don and his blind-eyed laddie arrived to challenge their rule. Then they used the funds to support Beauty and Belinda and pay those that worked to rescue them." She could hear the murmurs from the crowd.

"Over the years," she continued, "Don, Betron, Troy, Flight, Army, and the Warriors Academy remained free of such thievery. Most of the stolen credits came from Rurhran, Ishner, Ayran, and Medicine. Due to the diligent efforts of JayEll, Lad of Ayran, Jerome, Lad of Don, and JoAnne, Counselor of Ishner, we now ken where and how most of the funds were distributed and what remains." She could see the crowd leaning forward expectantly.

"Since the system was set up under the Justines, most of the funds went directly to Treasury of Thalia. From there, they had forwarded the credits to themselves and to the Kreppies." She used the despised name for the hated overseers. "The funds that went to the Thalian Treasury after the time of the Justines were used by your government to pay for the spaceships, the metals, the fuel cells, the upkeep of the Warriors Academy, payments to the Army for salaries, and equipment, payment to the Warriors who fought against the Draygons, the upkeep of the Guardians of Realm Guardian complexes, and the salaries of those manning the positions around the Guardian of the Realm." She could see disappointment spreading across the crowds faces.

"A certain amount of credits are still available for all the Houses that were systematically raided. Those funds went back to the most important person belonging to the Sisterhood. In other words, in Rurhran, they were returned first to Raven and then to an account that Rocella controlled." Radan started to rise, but Robert put a restraining hand on his arm. "In Ishner, it went to Ilramina. Medicine's credits went to Marianne. Due to the diligent efforts of my younger, JayEll, my lassie, JoAnne, and Jerome, Lad of Don, these credits will be transferred to your holdings tomorrow. Ye will be notified of the amount."

"How and where was my elder spending the credits she had?"

Jolene looked at the angry face of Radan. "The last she was able to take out of the account went to Minnay for that droid they used to attack Daniel. There are still nearly ten million credits left. Ye will need to ask her what she intended to do with the rest."

"All will receive a report of what was discovered. Nay more will be stolen, for those crystals have been removed and will be destroyed. My thanks to the three that were so steadfast in their work." There was a brief round of applause.

Jolene took a deep breath. "Does anyone have any other business? This Council was called to give a report on what was discovered and to settle the issue of Medicine." She waited for a few seconds and continued.

"I have one more item. As ye all ken, I am now over three hundred years of age and have Walked the Circle. I believe it tis time to retire and devote my life to Jada and Ayran. I will need to train at least two more people to create the new crystals. I intend to select two who have the artistic ability and absolutely nay connection to the Sisterhood. I, therefore, am resigning as yere Guardian of the Realm this eve."

For a moment, it was stunned silence. Some of the crowd shouted nay. Jolene pounded her fist. "I have served ye for over seventy years. Tis now time for someone else, and I recommend the one man who has proven his love for Thalia over and over again: Llewellyn, Maca of Don and Guardian of Flight."

"Nay," Llewellyn bellowed before the crowd's shouts became too loud and the anger that grew on Radan's face could erupt in actual words. The crowd stilled as Llewellyn stood.

"All Thalia thanks ye for the guidance and prudence ye have yielded during yere years as Guardian, and I thank ye for this vote of confidence, but I am a Warrior." His deep voice rolled out and over the crowd. "Should the Draygons attack again, and I ken they will as soon as they believe we are complacent and they are strong enough, I will nay sit in that chair." He pointed to where Jolene sat. "I will once again lead our Warriors out to protect Thalia."

"It will be more than a century before they can do that," Jolene snapped.

"Ye may be wrong. We dinna ken what other forces are out there, and sooner or later, the beings from my laddie's planet will appear. They will nay be dangerous at first, but one nay ever kens what they will do if a new warmonger should rule their planet."

Jolene was frowning. "I thought ye were protecting that planet called Earth."

"Oh, I am, but I have nay illusions about their abilities. Sometimes their leaders call for nay but peace and then the killing starts. Other times they threaten war and nay happens for years. The only thing that stops them is the fact that there are so many countries with different rulers, or Macas or Guardians as we would call them, that they are nay united in what they do."

He smiled at Jolene, who shook her head; and then he continued.

"Once again, all Thalia tis grateful to ye and we need another who, like ye, tis a great administrator. I can think of none better than Ribdan, Lad of Rurhran, a man I have worked with for almost one hundred years." He bowed to the man beside him. "Our own Counselor of Flight."

"Aye!" It was Radan standing with a clenched right fist in the air. Robert tugged at his arm, trying to lower it.

"We'll shout later," he muttered.

"Tis a grand introduction. Thank ye, Llewellyn," said Jolene. "Does anyone have another candidate or would like to discuss this nomination?"

Jarvis, her laddie and Maca of Ayran, was serving as Guardian of Ayran. "Llewellyn, our Guardian of Flight, tis correct. Ribdan has performed brilliantly as the Counselor of Flight and the Warriors Academy. I second his nomination."

She almost felt like glaring at her laddie. For years he had neglected Ayran and the Council and now he was negating her wishes. She looked at JayEll, but he remained silent.

Then Pillar, Guardian of Army, rose. "Like Jarvis, and our Guardian of Flight, I have always found Ribdan prepared and always able to address any issue that might arise. I say we vote for him now and he has both of our votes." He nodded at Captain Beni, and Jolene realized that Llewellyn had won.

She smiled at all. "Very well, if there tis nay objection, we shall proceed and record Ayran's vote." Just as Jarvis and Jada had voted "Aye," so did the remaining guardians and counselors.

Jolene stood, and the people stood with roaring and clapping. She pounded at the desk. "If ye will permit me," she was finally able to announce. "Ribdan, will ye please come to the Guardian of the Realm's seat. I will swear ye in, and ye can dismiss all."

Ribdan stood, bowed to the guardians and counselors, and walked towards the seat for the Guardian of the Realm. JayEll bowed and descended the stairs, thanking Gar that he would nay longer need to be Counselor of the Realm. Jolene made room for

Ribdan and continued. "Please bid JayEll farewell as Ribdan will choose a new Counselor of the Realm."

The crowd continued clapping as JayEll bowed when he reached the lower level and moved to Ayran's box to sit next to Lilith, his counselor-for-life. Once he was there. Jolene continued.

"Ribdan, Lad of Rurhran, do ye swear to protect Thalia from all attacks and provide a government of peace and prosperity? If so, answer, 'I do so swear.' "

"Aye, I do so swear."

"Ye are now Guardian of the Realm and this tis your gavel and your chair." Jolene handed him the gavel and pointed to the chair. The crowd stood and cheered.

Ribdan waited until the crowd quieted and bowed first to the crowd, then to Jolene, and then to Llewellyn. "I thank all for this honor and pledge to try and fulfill the demands of Thalia. I can only hope to do as well as Jolene, Lass of Ayran." He again led the crowd in a round of clapping.

Once it quieted, he continued. "Like Jolene, I thank those who have worked so diligently on correcting the credits of Thalia. They will be contacting the Macas and Guardians to arrange for the final disposition. My Counselor of the Realm will be my counselor-for-life, Renie, Lass of Rurhran." Radan and Robert led the cheering for their mother. Renie was in the Rurhran Box and stood to bow to the loaded tiers as Ribdan continued.

"All of Thalia tis still grieving for those lost in this last battle. There tis nay dinner celebration this eve. Jarvis, Maca of Ayran, will alert all the Houses when he and his counselor-to-be will Walk the Circle. Once again, I thank Jolene, Lass of Ayran, for the guidance she has provided all these years." When the roar subsided, he continued.

"Thanks to all, and we bid ye good eve and a safe journey home." He bowed and led the way for the other guardians and counselors to descend.

Chapter 42

Resolutions

True to his word to rectify the stolen credits, Ribdan dispatched Jerome to Ishner first as one of the needier Houses. Medicine had requested a few days to clean out and sanitize all the rooms and medical suits. Medicine also requested Troopers to assist their Enforcers should it become necessary. He let his son, Radan, fret. Rurhran did nay need the credits. He also sent a message through Renie suggesting that Rocella turn over the credits to smooth out any bad feelings.

Jerome arrived early and smiled at Daniel and JoAnne as he hugged both. "Tis a fine morn for finishing this. Then I shall lunch with Ieddie before proceeding to Rurhran."

Daniel grinned and JoAnne raised her eyebrows. "That will put Radan in a foul mood."

Jerome shrugged. "He has plenty of credits, besides, our Guardian of the Realm tis the one who made the appointments."

Even JoAnne smiled at that thought. "He must have his reasons. He kens his son's temperament and feelings toward Don."

Jerome looked at both. "Why does he nay like Don."

"Rocella has convinced him my fither and elder fither stole their kine and sheep when it was Don that was robbed of them during the time of the Justines. They just re-appropriated them," Daniel answered.

Jerome shook his head. "Do the schools nay teach what happened? When ye say kine, ye mean cattle, aye, and how did my elders steal, uh, re-appropriate?"

Daniel's smile barely lifted the corners of his mouth. "Aye, kine are cattle, and my fither refuses to call them anything but cattle. They used their air combos to cross into Rurhran without permission from Rurhran and pick up the kine and sheep. They did nay have permission from the Council of the Realm run by the Sisterhood. Rocella tried using one of Rurhran's air combos to raid the Laird's and Lady's Station of Don to bring the kine back. At least two Sisterhood fighter flivs accompanied her and landed. My fither stampeded the kine straight into all them. Rocella fled in the air combo and left part of her Tris hanging onto the corrals. It was an ignoble defeat for Rurhran."

Jerome was smiling broadly. "I can't imagine anyone attacking my eldest, Lorenz. He was still known as a dangerous man on Earth when he was old." He looked at them. "Which of ye wishes to go with me to the Director of Fisheries Office? I need someone with the right of access to the system there so I can transfer the credits to your main account before removing the crystal."

"Dear Gar, tis that where they were hiding all the credits?" Daniel almost whispered. "Ishmael was nay even suspicious of her. That tis why he put her over the Sisters we had working off their crimes." He hit his com. "Ishmael, I want ye and Ikea at the Director of Fisheries Office now. Jerome and I are headed there."

JoAnne pouted. "Ye are leaving me here?"

"Nay, my love. Ye are invited to attend, and then ye can take the crystal to yere mither."

All were walking into the waterfront office within five minutes and were greeted by Imma. "Good Morrow, my Maca. I did nay expect to see ye so early. Should I bring pina tea?"

"Nay, we will nay be here that long." Daniel nodded at her and led the way into the circular office. Unlike the Maca Tower's

Office, this one did not look out over the waterfront. The screens directly across from the round desk, however, would show the length of the docks if necessary.

Ishmael smiled at the incoming group. "Tis good to see ye." They all exchanged greetings.

Jerome sat in the desk chair and looked up at Daniel. "If ye would initiate the system, please."

Daniel did so, and the wall screen came alive with people busy on the docks loading one of the trollers. Daniel then asked, "Would ye rather JoAnne do the next part?"

Jerome smiled and was busy striking the circles. "Oh, nay, I studied at the Justine Refuge and had Melissa, Priscilla, and even Margareatha as teachers." He brought up the Accounts/Credits and the personal credits one. He studied it for a minute and dove into the person credits and debits. JoAnne frowned. "There will be nay there, but the credits she received for her position."

"There," Jerome stated. Satisfaction was etched in his tone. "Credits transferred for outfitting Beltane boats." He began touching circles, and a huge smile lighted his face and his blue eyes. "There ye are, my Elder. Five million credits transferred to Ishner's credit account."

Daniel took a deep breath. It wasn't as much as he had hoped for, but it would wipe out the debt to Ayran and Rurhran for the orders the Sisters had placed to refurbish the trollers and boats. Even better, the Sisters had utilized but little of the metal or materials. All repairs were now paid for and continuing.

While Jerome was removing the crystal, Daniel turned to Ishmael and Ikea. "Send any request for materials needed for the trollers here to the new director." He smiled at them. "Since Ishmael still has a wee one that needs her fither close by, I am proposing that Ishmael be our new Director of Fisheries."

"Nay," burst from Ishmael's mouth. "I have served as yere Counselor of Ishner till JoAnne could take my place, but now I wish to return to the seas and oceans of Thalia. I belong back on my troller. Melanie and Magda will accompany me as before. It tis nay as if I am gone for years as a spaceman or Warrior. Our time is but a few weeks, and Magda studies on the boat or here in port when we return."

"How will ye do that if Melanie tis serving as Guardian of Medicine?"

Daniel's question brought a frown. "I–I dinna. I will need to discuss that with her." Ishmael replied. He started to turn away and turned back. "Very well, I can serve for a few months while she and our lassie straighten out the wrongs done on Medicine, but then I wish to return to the seas, just as ye wish to return to the Stars." The last was said in a harsh tone.

Daniel smiled. "Since our wee one will be born within eight months, it means that I will remain on Thalia for at least thirty-one more years. I refuse to sympathize with yere plight. Ye have but less than twenty."

Daniel turned to Ikea. "Ishmael has told me how much ye ken in the field of fisheries. Ye are welcome to be here as the second in command or ye will have yere choice of the trollers. In truth, Ishner needs sea Thalians with yere experience."

Ikea straightened. "My Maca, I thank ye. I would enjoy working here and with the ones on the docks, in the processing plants, and with all the captains of the trollers. I grow weary of the long days and nights on the sea."

Ishmael beamed at him. "I will gladly teach ye and introduce ye to all."

Jerome stood and handed the crystal to JoAnne. She practically snatched it from him. "This becomes more and more outrageous," she muttered.

"Oh, just wait till we retrieve the one from Rurhran." Jerome smiled at them. "I bid ye adieu till this afternoon. I'm off to see Ieddie." The others looked a bit blank. Nay kenned the word adieu.

* * *

Radan and Robert were watching in disbelief as Jerome's fingers flew over the circles, and he leaned back and smiled at the two. "There. I have just transferred thirty million credits from Rocella's Sister account to Rurhran's credit account. Now I need a bit of space to open the drawer.

They were all in Rocella's Ops room. She had been banished to the living quarters above. Radan was almost white-faced. "How did she extract so much from Rurhran?"

Jerome stood. He was as tall and blocky as both of the brothers. "This has been going on for two hundred years or more."

"But if I am nay mistaken, neither Ishner nor Medicine suffered such losses. I have nay heard what Troy, Betron, and Ayran lost." Robert's tone was troubled. It was difficult to believe that his elder mither and then Rocella could have extracted such a huge sum.

Jerome shrugged. "From what I was told, Rurhran did nay suffer the same as Don, Troy or Ayran during the Justine War or occupation. Betron's Betta was Guardian of the Realm and did nay allow more than one or two crystals. Medicine was too small to lose much according to what I have learned from the other crystals. Don was nay allowed to acquire any credits at all. As for Troy and Betron, their losses stopped when my elder Andrew removed the crystals at least one hundred years ago."

"I want that crystal," Radan snapped.

"Nay allowed," JoAnne disputed him. "The crystal is to be returned to Ayran per the Council of the Realm."

"Which made that ruling while Jolene was still Guardian of the Realm," Radan refuted. Tis here in Rurhran, and here it stays just like the ones from Don, Betron, and Troy remained in those Houses."

Jerome hesitated. Who had the right here to retain the crystal? Then his mind cleared, and he looked at them. "My land has different rules and laws. I dinna ken all the rules here, but I do have a question. Did Rurhran have to pay Ayran for that crystal?"

All turned to him. "Yes, to procure the crystal, my eldest mither would have had to pay for it, however, I dinna if the Justines made her pay or nay since they were the ones that set this up initially," Robert replied.

"Mayhap, Rocella would ken," suggested Jerome.

"What difference does that make?" Radan verged on shouting.

"If Rurhran had to pay for it, the crystal should belong to Rurhran," Jerome answered.

JoAnne had both hands on her hips as though ready to lash into them all when they heard Robert on his com.

"Rocella, my elder, do ye ken if the Justines made my elder mither pay for the crystal that directed the confiscated funds back into this Sisterhood account?"

"Of course, Mither had to pay for it. The Justines bled every one of their available credits. How do ye think they are still able to pay for any brew or food shipments with our own credits?" She ended the transmission.

Jerome stood and handed the crystal to Radan. "In my world, the buyer owns what she/he has purchased."

Radan grabbed the crystal, a fierce grin on his face. JoAnne was looking at them in disbelief. "I shall bring this before the Council of the Realm." She glared at all and stomped out of the room. She realized it might be futile since Ribdan was now Guardian of the Realm. She had nay intention of ever letting Jerome near the accounts of Ishner again.

Robert smiled at Jerome. "Rurhran thanks ye for yere fairness. Are ye off to Medicine now?"

Jerome put the thin blade back in his case and shoved it into the bag at his waist. "Nay, I have to wait till they alert me that all has been disinfected. They are nay sure which area tis safe and which tis nay."

Radan snorted. "What assurance can they give ye if they are nay there each night to guard everything. Nay believe that Medicine has been truly cleared of the Sisterhood. They will nay doubt revolt again."

Chapter 43

Purifying Medicine

Melanie and Malta were both dressed in the hazsuits Malta had brought from the Warrior's Academy. They had tested the systems for contaminants and found none. They then ran all the hazsuits from Medicine through the system and packed them in secure cabinets and locked the cabinet doors. For now, they were sending any medical emergency to the Medical on that continent or to the Warrior's Academy if a severe injury. So far, there had been nay, a situation they knew would not last.

Next, they pushed the controls to cleanse Marianne's study and lab and hoped the purifying elements would not destroy whatever Marianne had been trying to create. Then they redid Minnay's study area and lab before returning to the Maca's Tower.

The workers from the Maintenance Office had made partial repairs on the door into the hallway from the padports and cleaned the smoke from the walls. Milan was manning the console and guarding the place. He stood and bowed.

"There tis a message from Ribdan, Guardian of the Realm, asking for an estimate of the damage, when we will be open again, and when are ye ready for Jerome?"

"Thank ye, Milan. We'll answer from the office. We should be through before long."

In the office, Melanie hit the circle for Guardian of the Realm, and Renie, Ribdan's counselor and now Counselor of the Realm, smiled at them.

"We are returning the Guardian's call. Tis he available?"

Renie gave a quick smile. "Nay, now he tis in the Ops room going over the accounts again with JayEll and Jerome. I ken why he called ye. I will give yere answers to him."

"We should be open this eve. I'll let all ken as soon as it tis final. As of now, the estimates are nay in. We need a new dome and new glass for our main doors. The damage to the hall from the padport entrance Medicine can repair, but we do need Ayran to produce another metallic glass door for the entrance. Jerome will be welcome when we open in the morning or if he has business elsewhere as soon as he can arrive."

"I shall take care of this. Ye have a good eve." Renie smiled and signed off.

Meagan knocked on the door and stuck her head in. "We have the security cameras ready to go at the two labs ye have cleansed. Do ye think it necessary to install another elsewhere?"

Melanie's laugh was bitter. "Yes, we need three for in the Medical Complex. I want one inside pointed at the entrance, I want one pointed at their controls, and one at the locked cabinets. We need to ken if anyone tries to gain entrance."

She shook her head and continued. "How tis yere wound?"

"Well, thank ye, Guardian. Markle made sure it was well-tended. Fortunately, the burn was nay deep."

Meagan straightened and bowed. "I would like to be able to hire one or two more Enforcers. Tis that possible with the devastation we have suffered?"

Melanie's smile remained bitter. "Since we lost eleven members of Medicine in that 'raid' the Sisters tried, yes, we can afford one more Enforcer. Do ye have someone in mind?"

"Aye, Guardian. Mark tis a bit young, nay more than fifty, but he has had the Warrior's training. Uh, the Lady of Medicine recalled him when the Sisters realized he was on his way to becoming Army."

Melanie shook her head. "Brilliant, I dinna what possessed my sib." She looked at Meagan and realized that Meagan kenned more about Medicine's day-to-day happenings than she did. Her absence while tending Magda and avoiding the Sisters of Medicine had left her a bit ignorant of affairs.

"Meagan, do ye happen to ken a Medical person that I could have tend our Medical facility in case there tis an emergency? Nay of us can stay this eve."

"Aye, that I do. I suggest ye put Meler in there. He tis quite edgy since he was grounded from space for two years after being part of the same flight ye were on, Counselor. He was just released from that restriction. The other would be Mindy, Mark's sib. She could nay abide excluding her brither or fither from her life."

It was Malta's turn to smile. "Thank ye for reminding me of Meler." She stood. "I'll let ye do the contacting, Melanie, and I shall take the nanobots to the Warriors Academy for testing and return them in the morning."

Meagan looked at both. "That can nay be done here?"

"We ran out of time," Malta shrugged. "Plus, we ken the equipment there has nay been contaminated." She hugged Melanie.

"Give Ishmael and my darling younger, Magda, my love. I'll see ye both tomorrow."

Milan's voice came over the office com. "Markle tis on his way into yere office. I could nay stop him."

Meagan stepped out or the way. She kenned her brither, Markle, well. Milan's warning meant he was angered.

Markle gave one bang on the door and opened it. He was scowling at the smiling Melanie. "What do ye mean? Why would ye recall me from Don? I have nay made any errors." He was roaring.

Melanie's smile broadened. "Ye are recalled to become our new Director of Medicine. Ye are the only one I can entrust with that position. Ye ken all of the Medical staff well. The one appointed by my sib was one of those that was burned into death during the raid."

Markle was standing with his mouth and eyes wide open, then he grabbed the chair, and lowered himself. "Are ye sure? Nay male has held that position for at least four hundred years."

Melanie tightened her mouth and nodded. "Aye, we are certain. It needs someone who tis experienced in all facets of Medicine and one that tis old enough to ken the thinking of all the others in positions of power. We must weed out those that would corrupt our young and try to convince them to become Sisters as the only way to reach the important positions in Medicine. I intend to name ye in my cast ere I leave this eve. Ye, of course, may choose yere own assistant."

"Will this put yere life in danger? That would be a tragedy. Medicine has suffered enough."

"We intend to guard her and all that need it, Markle," Meagan growled. "We are hiring a new Enforcer, mayhap two if necessary."

Melanie pressed a circle. "Ye, Markle, now possess the Director of Medicine's home and office. I suggest ye wait to sleep there till Meagan gives the all clear. It needs to be searched and Mini's personal items removed."

"Who will take my place on Don?"

"That will be either Meler or Mindy. Either tis well suited to serve," Melanie answered. "Ye will need to remain at Don this evening. The change takes effect tomorrow." Melanie's voice was brisk. "That tis all for now, as I must finish here and return to my wee one and home."

Chapter 44

A Legacy

Kahli had called the meeting with his fither, Llewellyn, brither, Lorenz, Troyner, and Kitten, his Ab sib and Logan's mither, at Logan's greenhouse. His counselor, Lania, was tending to the mugs and the heated content in each. Their wee one continued to sleep in Lania's sling.

Kitten was there before all, making sure the plants and seedlings were in top shape. The Tri workers had done the main work, but still she fussed over the plants. She kenned what Logan and Marita had planned, but suspected Troyner would object. She smiled at Kahli and Lania as they brewed the drinks and poured them into the mugs before the others arrived.

Lorenz looked puzzled as he and Diana walked into the space. It was soon crowded with Llewellyn and Brenda, and Troyner with Triva. Troyner was in a jubilant mood. He smiled at all and announced, "We will Walk the Circle as there will be a new Laird of Troy." He beamed at all.

After the congratulations and greetings, Kahli pointed to the tray and the steaming mugs. "There tis what Timor, Logan, and Marita were collaborating on to produce as a surprise. They planned to surprise ye at a party they were planning after Beltayne. I felt I must do this to honor them. Please take a taste and give me your opinion, and then I shall explain more."

Troyner was frowning as he reached for a mug. Lorenz had a crooked grin tugging at his mouth. Llewellyn tried to keep his face bland, but suspected what his youngest had been doing. Kahli stood with his arms crossed as the others drank.

Troyner almost bashed the cup down; his jubilation disappeared. "This tis pina pod tea corrupted with another flavor. How dare they steal from me?"

"They were nay stealing," Kahli refuted him. "They were planning to surprise all and ask yere permission to continue the experiment and then open new shops for sipping something other than our brew."

"Or my pina pod tea." Troyner's face was red and his voice loud. "They should have asked permission first." He turned to Llewellyn. "Did they ask yere permission ere they contaminated my tea?"

Llewellyn looked at his friend. "Troyner, they did nay consult me. Why would they? They did nay use another plant from Troy. They used one or more of the coffee plants that Lorenz imported for Kitten to create a small coffee crop for his day-long choice of drink."

Troyner turned on Lorenz. Lorenz smiled at the man, "No, they did not ask me. Why would they? I had told Kitten and then Logan that I didn't care what they did with any excess growth except to ensure that I would always have my coffee. It takes a coffee tree three to five years to grow enough to produce the coffee beans. Then they can produce for a few decades."

"I dinna give a damn about the new plant. This ends and ends now," Troyner shouted and turned to leave.

"Then that ends any legacy that Timor, Marita, and Logan would have left." Kahli's words halted Troyner and he turned.

"What?"

"They all planned to make this part of their life. Timor realized that Marita loved the earth just as much as Logan and kenned it was the only way she could continue with any kind of plants once she was fully involved in Medicine." Kahli waited as he could see Troyner struggling with that concept.

"Why the deception then?" Instead of a shout, Troyner's voice was almost a whisper.

"They dinna ken if they would be successful and if the beans and pods would produce a drink that was different than both and still stimulate an interest in the younger Thalians."

"And when were they going to start this enterprise?" Troyner's voice had become bitter.

Kitten spoke up. "Nay until they had yere permission and that of my eldest fither." She inclined her head toward Llewellyn. "First, they had to make sure the drink was tasty and that there were enough beans and/or pods to make the brew. As of now, there are nay enough plants producing to market anything, but there will be by next year, if this tis allowed to continue."

Troyner looked at Llewellyn. "Ye dinna feel like they were robbing ye or Don?"

Llewellyn smiled. "Nay, had they been successful, we would have many more credits. Remember, they intended to ask our permission before they proceeded."

Troyner pointed at Kitten. "Why would they tell her first?"

Kitten straightened. "I am Director of Fields for Don. I had to ken what they were planting and why. I did nay give them permission to go any farther than they had. As long as it was nay on the market, they had nay injured any."

Troyner's face still looked baffled and angered when Lorenz spoke. "Logan had finally let the rest of Andrew's genes take over. Andrew was great at starting an enterprise and then selling, or rather franchising it to someone else when the credits began rolling into Don's account." He smiled at Troyner. "If y'all kill this now, their legacy dies with them. Let it continue and name it something like TM & L Sips or Bistro, with their head pictures on the front of the building or inside. That way their legacy will live on for years. They would not be forgotten."

Troyner swallowed and looked at Lorenz and then at Llewellyn. "How do ye ken this will succeed?"

"I don't," said Lorenz. "I drink my coffee black, but Kahli thought enough of the brew to call everyone together. The younger people seem to look for something different. It's why Rurhran changes or withdraws one of their brews every fifty or so years and replaces it with something new. They have honed that marketing to an art."

"They are dead." Troyner's voice was bitter. "How can this project move forward?"

"I would make sure the plants grow well and are cultivated as they need to be," Kitten insisted. "It was my Logan's and Marita's dream."

Llewellyn smiled. "And I would put Jerome in charge long enough for it to become a most favorite drink or business for Thalians to enjoy a different kind of brew while resting and visiting."

Troyner swung on Lorenz. "Why nay just name the brew Timor and Marita?"

Lorenz looked at him. "Because this brew is all of them. Their love lives on together; otherwise, all ye have left is pina pod tea."

Troyner nodded. "I will give my permission for the trial. If it really brings in credits, very well, but I want their names remembered." He stalked out without the formal farewells. Triva gave a weak smile and a wave before following Troyner.

Llewellyn looked at Lorenz. "How do ye do plan to commemorate them all besides the name?"

Lorenz smiled, his face changing from hard to soft. "Easy, inside the building under their pictures are their names intertwined in a heart. Kahli can do the design. He needs something to do besides running the school for the enviro person on a spaceship." He nodded at them, and all began the formal farewells.

Kahli and Lania began cleaning the mugs and brew master. Kitten looked at them. "I thank ye both, but I will finish this. I must speak with my eldest fither." They smiled at her and left.

Kitten turned and touched Llewellyn's arm. "Eldest Fither, may I see ye alone? I have a request."

Llewellyn smiled down at her. "Of course." He waved at the departing Kahli, Lania, and their wee one, but Brenda remained.

"Now, what tis yere request?"

"Ye may nay ken, but Andrew, when he had that first heart attack and recovered, had his seed saved at Medicine."

Llewellyn nodded.

Kitten took in a deep breath. "Our laddie tis nay more. I want Andrew's wee one. To have lost them both tis more than I can bear." She clamped her lips together, and her dark eyes pleaded with her Maca and, by marriage, eldest fither.

Llewellyn gave a brief smile. "Ye dinna need my permission for something so personal."

"Eldest Fither, under Thalian law, that seed belongs to Don and to its Maca. Medicine might refuse me if ye dinna give me yere permission on my com. They ken I started life as an Ab." Bitterness was in her voice, for under Thalian law, Llewellyn as Maca could have made her an Ab again once Andrew had died.

"She tis correct," said Brenda.

"Very well, but I suggest, ye let Brenda and me accompany ye to Medicine and formally endorse yere request. Tis that agreeable with ye?"

Kitten threw her arms around her eldest fither and let him lift her high enough to lay her head on his shoulders.

Epilogue

Twelve months had passed since Kitten had requested to carry Andrew's child. Today she held a sleeping, red-fuzzed headed, blue-eyed baby boy, naked except for the blanket of blue that enfolded him. She walked down the blue carpet to the seated Maca of Don and his counselor, Brenda, Maca of Betron. Lorenz, Diana, and Lincoln, Kahli, Lania, and their lassie Leah, were on one side. Daniel and JoAnne holding a black-haired sleeping three-month-old lassie were on the other side.

Kitten's dark, reddish-brown hair was swept back into a bun, and the necklace of silver with the huge blue stone Andrew had made for her hung from her neck. Her dark eyes were alive, and she smiled as she laid the wee one on his Maca's lap.

"I give ye Andrew Junior for yere approval."

Llewellyn smiled at the naked form, picked him up, and stood. "I present Andrew Junior, Lad of Don!" He held the baby aloft before sitting down and smiling at the wee form. He already had the report from Medicine. This laddie had Thalian, Earth, and Justine genes. He would possibly live to be four hundred years. Llewellyn's smile deepened as the wee one briefly opened blue eyes before closing them again. The circle was complete.

First, a big Thank you to Miika Hannia and all the crew at Next Chapter Publishing. Their dedication and assistance has been amazing.

Dear reader,

We hope you enjoyed reading *Thalia - The New Generation.* Please take a moment to leave a review, even if it's a short one. Your opinion is important to us.

Discover more books by Mari Collier at https://www.nextchapter.pub/authors/twisted-tales-and-scifi-westerns-from-twentynine-palms-author-mari-collier

Want to know when one of our books is free or discounted? Join the newsletter at http://eepurl.com/bqqB3H

Best regards,

Mari Collier and the Next Chapter Team

About the Author

I was born and raised on a farm in Iowa. There was no electricity or an indoor bathroom. I will not mention the trials of using that in subzero weather or the hot, humid days of summer. When allergies nearly did me in, Mama took me to Phoenix. I finished school there and married my high school sweetheart. There were two children. Phoenix went into one of its bust economy periods, and we moved to North Bend, WA. My husband started a construction company, and I served as a bookkeeper. When I retired from Nintendo of America, we found refuge in a small community in the high desert of California. I'm an active member of the Twentynine Palms Historical Society, and enjoy family, friends, the local art galleries, and theaters.

My website is http://www.maricollier.com

Facebook:

https://www.facebook.com/Twisted-Tales-From-A-Skewed-Mind-124947397618599/

My handle on Twitter is @child7Mari

Other Works

Chronicles of the Maca:

Earthbound
Gather The Children
Before We Leave
Return of the Maca
Thalia and Earth
Fall and Rise of the Macas

Chronicles of Tonath:

Man, True Man
The Silver and The Green
Marika

Anthologies:

Twisted Tales From The Northwest
Twisted Tales From The Universe
Twisted Tales From The Desert
Twisted Tales From A Skewed Mind

Lightning Source UK Ltd.
Milton Keynes UK
UKHW052130281220
376048UK00008B/433/J

9 781034 141396